Song of the
Curlew

I0586370

Lazaros
Zigomanis

First published by Pinion Press 2019

Copyright © 2019 Lazaros Zigomanis

Republished by ECG Press 2022

ISBN
Paperback: 978-0-6454853-0-1
Ebook: 978-0-6454853-1-8

Cover image: Kev Howlett
Cover design: Blaise van Hecke
Layout and typesetting: Les Zigomanis

ECG Press
www.ecgpress.com

A catalogue record for this book is available from the National Library of Australia

The issues raised in this story are in no way to offend, but to highlight a harsh reality of Australia's past and present, and written in hope of opening discussion and preventing it from further occurrence in the future.

For my parents,
who watched me and supported me as I typed away,
probably never really understanding what I did.

Here it is.

The First Quarter

A New Recruit

B oots. Left first – my kicking foot. Laces tied. Then the right. Socks up, down, up, then back down, bundled around my ankles. Jumper on, but not tucked in. There. Ready.

Our clubrooms were dingy and stunk of liniment that had leeched into the bricks. Outside, training unfolded – the thud of footballs as they were kicked, teammates crying for passes, while others joked and laughed. The camaraderie was tribal, and made me feel I could accomplish anything. It might be some bush league but, at eighteen, I knew – I *hoped* – it could still be a springboard for something better.

I rose from the cold wooden bench and jogged out of the clubrooms, my boots clattering across the concrete apron that led down to our ground. While it was evening, it wasn't quite dark, and still warm for this time of year, although the gentlest breeze suggested night would offer some relief. Two light towers provided a pair of interlinking luminous spheres – one over the forward-pocket, and the other over half-forward. Huddles of players kicked footballs back and forth while our coach, Percy Hunt, watched, hands on hips, his belly bulging in his Ulah Curlews football jersey.

'On with it, Luke!' he told me.

Training was casual – glorified kick-to-kick, followed by loose drills. The young guys ran hard, filled with enthusiasm and eager to secure a spot, while most of the older guys were indifferent. The errant passes and spilled marks were many. The offender usually chuckled, and cantered over to the next group, where other players sucked in deep breaths. Then it happened all over again.

'Let's show some run!' Percy said.

Typical Percy – always trying to get something started as he paced back and forth. And I wanted to encourage the others. When I sprinted out from one group, I marked the ball in front of my face and speared a low pass to our grizzled full-forward, Matt Reynolds. Matt was a veteran of the team – almost forty, he'd played for twenty years, and was one of only two current players to have played in our last premiership. The ball shot through his hands, hit his stomach – as bulbous as the head of any hot air balloon – and ricocheted away. He gasped as he bent low.

'Easy, Luke!' he said. 'Trying to drill a hole through me or something?'

I hid my disappointment, and joined the group he'd come from. They clustered like a herd of sheep wanting to stray. Sean Mercher, my best friend, bounced on the spot at the back, anxious to get into it. He arched his brows at me.

'Waste of a nice pass,' he said.

Sharp, mournful cries echoed across the ground: the curlews – the birds after which we were named – fed in the brush outside the far wing. They usually prowled about on their long legs, their choir so common that most of the time they were background noise, but now – as they scattered in all directions, shrieking – the cacophony of their song stopped training.

'Is that something?' Sean said.

Everybody frowned and squinted. The brush led down a steep embankment to a creek that ran the length of our ground and weaved its way through some of the neighbouring towns. On the other side, clusters of gum trees were silhouettes against a sky that had grown red, the sun just a blot of sombre yellow peeking over a hill.

Somebody hopped the railing – he must've come up the embankment – and approached with an easy-going grace. He was tall and lanky, with wild, frizzy hair, but it wasn't until he hit the edge of the lights that we saw he was Indigenous. The rest of our squad gathered around. The newcomer – mid-twenties maybe, and dressed in shorts and a t-shirt so muddy that he might've been gardening – walked past us and right up to Percy.

Percy was in his forties, stocky, but still kept up with the best of us. Other teams in our league had guys older and rounder, although they were few. Here, in Ulah, we had the tradition that one generation replaced the next, son replacing father, so there was always an influx of youth, as eventual as that could be sometimes. Percy had eight kids, but they were all girls.

'I'd like to play for you guys,' the newcomer said. His big eyes stood out: bright, friendly, but with dark crescents, like he hadn't slept for a week.

'You live here in Ulah?' Percy asked.

'Just moved here. Sorta.'

'Sorta?'

'Got a farm. Sits on the border of Ulah, Warrambatta, and Shandeen Bank.'

Warrambatta and Shandeen Bank were our neighbours, each about as big as Ulah in landmass and population. Of course, geography's funny around here. The land stretches for kilometres but borders are jagged, like the pieces in a jigsaw puzzle. The towns are pinpricks in each piece, the rest empty, except for the animals and the farms and gums.

'Can you play?' Percy looked the newcomer up and down.

'Would I be here if I couldn't?'

Percy smirked. 'Gonna have to be pretty good to play for the Curlews. The season's already started and we're about set,' he said. 'Have a decent-sized squad, too.'

He gestured at the players bunched around them – forty of us, half of those in their thirties and a handful in their forties, the rest in their twenties, and a few like me, Sean, and our two other Indigenous players, Dean Calin and Nigel Vickers, who were eighteen. The newcomer surveyed us, nodded at Dean and Nigel, then turned back to Percy. I couldn't help but feel the newcomer knew the truth about us: you didn't have to be good. Most of the guys played for a laugh. Some couldn't even afford boots or shorts, and Percy would have to loan them equipment from the arsenal of extra stuff he'd collected over the years, and now kept stored in the boot of his car.

'I'm okay,' the newcomer said.

'Just okay?'

The newcomer shrugged.

'Percy Hunt, coach, captain, and centre half-forward.' Percy offered his hand; the newcomer took it and shook it once. Percy grimaced, like the handshake had been too tight.

'Adam Pride.'

'Why don't you join the others? Let's see what you've got.'

'Sure,' Adam said.

'Luke,' Percy pointed me out, 'show him the way.'

'Sure,' I said, and thrust my hand out to Adam. 'Luke Miggs. Centre half-back.'

Like he'd done with Percy, Adam took my hand and shook it once. His hand was huge and cool, but his palm was rough. It wasn't a good feel for a handshake. No wonder Percy had made the face he had.

Adam had those laconic but graceful skills a lot of Indigenous players possess. Every now and again, there was a glimpse of something special – a hard, flat pass, a one-handed mark, and even a snapped goal. Mostly, he fumbled and shanked kicks, which meant he fit right in. Me, Sean, Nigel, Dean, and Harry Ballard – our ruckman, a beanpole almost seven foot tall – nodded at Adam's better efforts.

'Another plodder,' Nigel said.

'If he gets that far,' Dean said.

Occasionally, Adam pulled up and stretched to loosen his muscles. Or he kneeled and kneaded his thighs or calves. He really struggled with flexibility, like he'd spent too long doing nothing and his muscles had locked into place.

I jogged up to him. 'You okay?' I said.

Adam nodded; his long black hair – shooting out, like he'd gotten up and hadn't had time to do anything about it – bounced around his face. 'Yeah, haven't played for a while,' he said. 'I'll get into it.'

The older guys always took longer to loosen up, and were quicker to break down. It's the way it was. It's not something I knew yet, but I worried I'd get there soon enough. Like everybody in Ulah. Blink and you've rusted into place.

Adam saw out the session, although he was flat by the end of it, with nothing left to give. He was about 6'1" or 2", although he seemed taller because he was so lanky. If he didn't get fit fast, he'd break down, and that'd finish his aspirations.

At the end of the night, Percy called us in. We formed a ring around him, although there was a lot of jostling and ribbing between the guys. Not many took Percy's talks seriously, which was a shame, because Percy wanted to be serious. *I* wanted to be serious. But that's the way it went. We were anything but.

'Good session!' Percy said. 'We're looking crisp out there. I know we've been average the last couple of weeks. We won the first two, and have lost the last two. We can change that, though. We can do anything if we really want to.'

This was a typical Percy speech: big on inspiration, low on everything else. The Curlews had often fought on spirit, rather than talent or strategy. It's probably why we so often went so far but fell so short. People didn't even question it anymore. It's who we were.

'Now, we've got you-know-who this week!' Percy said.

Heads dropped and ribbing stopped. *You-know-who* was the Little Reach Scorpions – the scourge of our competition. They were fanatics. At training, they ran drills, had match practice, and put themselves through hell. It's no surprise they honed teams into killer outfits, especially under the reign of their long-time coach, Claude Rankin. Rankin was a tyrant.

'Come on!' Percy said. 'It's not the end of the world! We can make a fight of this!'

'Go away,' Dean said – his slang for, *Get out of here!*

'They always eat us alive,' Nigel said.

'Rankin will eat us alive,' Harry said.

'Rankin?' Adam asked.

'Little Reach's coach,' I said.

'Rankin's the Grim Reaper of football,' Sean said.

'What?' Adam said.

'Footy's life and death for Rankin,' Nigel said.

'Yeah, Little Reach's life, and our death!' Dean said.

'Things can change!' Percy said. 'You go out there thinking like losers, you'll be losers. You make your own reality. That's something I want you to think about. We can change it if we want to change it. Now, hit the showers.'

We meandered off towards the clubrooms like we'd been herded, some of the older guys already lighting up cigarettes and talking about dropping into the pub. Adam headed in the opposite direction, back the way he'd come.

'Hey, Adam!' I called. 'Adam!'

In the centre of the ground, on the edge of the lights, he spun, a wavering shadow.

'You coming?' I asked.

He tapped at his naked left wrist. 'I've gotta get back,' he said. 'Got stuff to do! I'll see ya later.' He walked for a little bit, then broke into a jog, hopped the railing and disappeared down the embankment.

Percy rested one of his big, meaty hands on my shoulder. 'Doubt we'll see him again,' he said.

A fair enough prediction. A lot of people came for one session and never came back.

This time, though, Percy was wrong.

Little Reach

I woke Saturday before the sun was up – normal for me. The anticipation always got me, that today was match day. It was only my second season at this level – and last year, all I'd done was play a handful of games – so the excitement was new, and something I wanted to hold onto. It filled me and energised me, and made Ulah come alive and be something more than this little town – for today, at least.

I stayed in bed until the rest of the world caught up with me, although I could hear Dad shuffling around upstairs. Outside the ravens shrieked that way they do, like somebody kept poking them in the belly and they kept whining to be left alone. The morning seeped through the window, shy at first, but then a golden light that splayed across the walls until they shone. I played the game out in my head, how I would tackle it, what I would do, rehearsing scenarios where I dashed in to the rescue, or repelled attack after attack, although I never was as confident when those things actually happened.

The clock radio's alarm rang, so I shut it off and bounced out of bed. I showered, packed my footy bag, went down into the kitchen and quietly fixed breakfast. Dad was now asleep in his recliner in the lounge room. He would've woken at 3.30 and done his morning chores. On any day but the weekends, I would've helped him.

Dad was a big guy – maybe 6'2" – but he was lean. His joints bulged, and in the last few years he'd lost weight. His skin had the sheen of something the sun had roasted into leather, and I don't remember the last time I'd seen him clean-shaven, although I'm sure he *did* shave.

Behind him on the wall hung a framed picture – the front page of *The Tribune*, the local paper that covered Ulah, Shandeen Bank, and Warrambatta. It was from eighteen years ago, when the Curlews had shocked the Scorpions to win the flag. The picture showed all the players crowded around the premiership trophy, fists pumped triumphantly, smiles huge, along with the headline, 'Against All Odds!'

Sometimes, it was hard to believe that Dad had ever been that young. He was forty-two going on seventy. I'd taken his spot in the Seniors last year when I was seventeen. Maybe things could've been different for him, although I don't know how. He still would've had the farm, all the responsibilities, and his knees had begun to let him down in the last few years; every Sunday he'd wake up stiff, sore, and groaning. But he still put himself through it.

I ate breakfast and made sure my spoon didn't clatter against the bowl, and sat still so that my chair didn't creak. Of course, the whole house creaked. When a good headwind blew, you could hear the place swaying, like it was getting ready to pick itself up out of its foundations and walk to somewhere better.

'Hey, Luke.' Mum came in through the kitchen screen door, letting it clang shut behind her. Unlike Dad, she was still spritely, and you could feel the energy brimming around her. She had a garden out back where she pottered, growing tuberoses. When they bloomed, the smell of them would waft through the kitchen, sickeningly sweet.

'Who you guys got today?' she said.

'Little Reach. At Little Reach.'

That didn't dent Mum. It's not that she didn't know about the game, because she did – she'd gone all the time when Dad had played – but things had changed.

'Tell Dad, huh?' I said.

'I will,' Mum said, washing the plates in the kitchen sink. 'But you know …'

'Yeah,' I said and put my empty bowl in the sink. 'I gotta get going.'

I kissed her on the cheek, got my bag, and headed out. By now, it was blistering. Our summers ran late. All our seasons did. They were six weeks out of sync with the actual dates of seasons.

I walked through our fields, the wheat shimmering, like it was trying to whisper a secret to me. Some days, I'd come in here to enjoy the calm and be away from everybody. Now, I kept walking until I came out onto the dirt road that led back into Ulah, the blue sky unfolding like it would take me to the end of the world. It was a long walk into town – almost an hour – and not a lot of people were out. At our ground some of the other guys were playing a bit of kick-to-kick – probably not the smartest thing to do in the heat, but it burned the nervous energy. I joined in and imagined myself the big shot, like a star warming up an hour before the game in the AFL – the Australian Football League, which was as big as it got.

Percy waddled out from our clubrooms, his eyes flitting from player to player as he performed a stocktake. We were a few players short, although players were known to show up right before the bounce, and sometimes after. Well, usually.

'We ready?' Percy asked.

We broke into groups to convoy to Little Reach. I didn't drive, so I usually caught lifts with Sean. Dean, Nigel, and Harry piled into the backseat of Sean's Ford Escort. Harry was so tall he had to ride with his head stuck out the window.

We screwed around a lot on drives to games – we'd joke, have music blaring, and even shout to teammates in other cars. But drives to Little Reach games were funeral processions. No talking. No joking. No fun at all. The sense of dread was this dark, sinister thing that wanted to smother us, and the game itself became a battle for survival – something we endured to say we came out of it the other end. A lot of teams felt like that about playing Little Reach.

I stared out the window at cows in the paddocks – most of the farms out here were cattle farms, although there was also a handful of wheat farms, like my family's. This whole area used to be frontier territory during colonial Australia. Then gold was discovered – not enough to get anybody rich, but enough to bring people in and strand them when their fortunes ran out. Communities were born, grew into towns – nothing special, really. Except for Little Reach. Little Reach had always been self-important. Haughty. Part of that might have had something to do with the way they grew.

One story goes that when religion came, the people built a church in this place called *Reach*, which is meant to be a translation of some Indigenous name. Most of the towns here – including Ulah – have had their names bastardised that way, until they've become unrecognisable from the source. Anyway, with everybody preoccupied with finding gold, nobody attended services. People joked that the church had *a little reach*, and that's how the town got its name. But that's only one of the stories going around.

I asked Dad once, and he said some people claimed the church had been there first, and that it spat out this town of the damned. Mum had chided him for being silly, and said the truth was much simpler: Little Reach had been this little nothing town, looked down on by the other towns, and they'd worked hard to become the biggest and most productive – first through business, second through football (they'd won three times as many flags as anybody else), and generationally their attitude had developed from that. That story was the boring version. People preferred to talk.

When we arrived, the town stopped. People on the streets glowered at us. I swear this was Rankin's doing – all part of his plan for intimidation; this is how seriously he took things. Dean and Nigel suffered the worst of it. Rankin didn't have any Indigenous players in his team, although that's because nobody Indigenous lived in the town. The people from Little Reach tried to deny it was racial, but some things speak for themselves.

Sean drove us to Little Reach's ground. There was already a turnout for the Teens – every town had three teams: Under 12s, Teens 13–18, and the Seniors. There must've been a thousand people already in attendance, shouting, cheering, parents screaming out encouragement. In Ulah, we drew modest crowds, like everybody, but Little Reach drew every-bloody-one in town.

Adjacent was the church that had been at the heart of Little Reach's foundation – a towering black maw tattooed into space, the stained glass they used for windows like splashes of blood. Once upon a time, the church's spires might've been elegant; now, all but one were broken, ending in jagged stumps. No wonder people said the church had been here before the town – it seemed so old and out of place here, the architecture not something you could pinpoint as Australian or British Colonial.

'I don't know why they don't tear that down and build a new one,' Sean said.

'History,' Dean said.

'History bites,' Nigel said.

A big, battered, blue van with a bull-bar pulled into the car park alongside a crimson Ford Falcon. Our breath caught in our throats – or at least mine did. The van was immediately identifiable: Rankin. You'd think he'd own a nicer car, given how success had afforded him opportunities – over the years he'd become an entrepreneur and begun buying up land. But nope, he drove this piece of crap.

The door opened and Rankin stepped out, although he did it all dramatic-like – first one leg, then the other, and then he rose up out of the cabin. He was a bear, dressed in this big faded denim jacket – his trademark. Once he stopped playing footy, all that bulk would melt into flab. Right now, he was granite. He had a crew cut and sharp grey eyes – metallic eyes, like he was a machine in there – that narrowed down to slits whenever he measured you up.

Fans cheered him. Others came up and patted his back. One of the local constables left a couple of teenagers he'd been lecturing about drinking to shake Rankin's hand. I'd heard stories where the cops had caught him speeding and let him off, or he'd get in some post-match scuffle in the pub with an opposing coach (or player), and the cops would drive the other guy out of town.

But that was Rankin. He was timeless, this legend who'd existed since before I was born. He was playing Seniors when he was thirteen. By the time he was sixteen, he dominated the competition. Rumour has it he knocked back offers from the state competitions, which would've given him the chance to go national. Having seen Rankin play, and having played on him, I know he would've made it. In any league. I would've jumped at the chance.

Rankin had been responsible for turning Little Reach around after a rare drought where they hadn't made the finals – the top five – for three years. In the last ten years, they'd figured in the finals every year, played in eight grand finals, and had won all of them. This year they'd be going for their fifth straight. As usual, it looked like there'd be no stopping them.

We skulked off to our rooms, which weren't much more than a stinking tin garage with rickety benches and cold water plumbing. They were the worst visiting change rooms in the league. Little Reach's rooms had hot showers, massage tables, and lockers. They had a lot of local businesses sponsoring them so they got a luxury setup. Physios and masseuses volunteered their services. And we got this.

I sat on the bench, unzipped my bag, and took out my jumper. The front of the Ulah Curlews' guernsey was white with a black curlew emblazoned across it, looking puffed-up but almost ethereal, like it might know something the rest of us didn't. The jumper had black trim on the collar and sleeves, a black back, and a white number. Mine was 12, which had been Dad's, and also Granddad's.

As I got changed and other players filtered in, Percy gave us another of his famous pep talks. He could turn reading a shopping list into a battle address. He didn't let us down now, telling us Little Reach was just *another* team and nothing would be finer than spoiling their weekend by beating them. What Percy lacked in strategy, he made up for with passion.

'Play the ball,' he said. 'That's the most important thing! Play the ball, keep moving it forward, don't get sucked into these bastards niggling you, and don't let them intimidate you. The only way to beat Little Reach is by playing committed footy.'

A lot of the older players had become desensitised to these gee-ups. The facts were simple: the Scorpions *weren't* just another team. They were bloody awesome. We knew it, they knew it, everybody knew it. We were two wins, two losses; Little Reach had won all their games by an average of twelve goals. Last week they'd won by 121 points against one of last year's finalists.

But there was another reason Percy's address didn't have the required effect: we were short of players. We'd go into every game with a squad of twenty-five or twenty-six that Percy could whittle down to our final team of twenty-two, but now there was eighteen of us. We could still field a side – a forfeit only kicked in if you had less than sixteen players – but eighteen would mean we wouldn't have anybody on the interchange bench.

'We're short,' Harry said.

'Flu's going around,' Percy said, but that was a lie. It was more likely players were worried about playing Little Reach on their own ground.

'We can't beat them with a full team,' Nigel said. 'How're—'

'And we'll never beat them with that attitude!' Percy said. 'If you say we can't beat them with a full team, then what's it matter we're a few players short? And if it doesn't matter, why're we going out there? Why're we here?'

Usually, there'd be a smartarse response to break the tension, something like, *You made us come.* Not now, though.

'I'm tired of being scared of these bastards!' he said. 'I'm tired of this attitude where everybody's indifferent! You know what? Let's take that indifference, and instead of saying it doesn't matter because we're gonna lose anyway, let's say it doesn't matter *because* we have nothing to lose, and nobody – not least of all Little Reach – is gonna stop us, huh?'

The challenge hung there. Percy often went on these benders – too much testosterone pumped into a guy who'd produced eight daughters. We joked about it sometimes: Percy, the suicide bomber without the fuse.

'Well?' he said.

The door opened and Adam came in, dressed exactly as he was when he showed up for training, although his clothes were slightly cleaner now.

'Hey, Coach,' he said, 'I'm here to play.'

More silence. If it were any other game, there might be complaints about Adam slotting into the team after one training session – and a training session he'd struggled to get through. But given the circumstances, nobody said a thing.

Percy sized him up, then got him a jumper with the number 8, shorts, and a pair of socks out of his sports bag.

'Got some boots, too?' Adam asked.

'Some boots?' Percy asked.

'Couldn't find mine. That's why I'm late.'

'Sure. Got some in the car. Get dressed.'

Adam flashed that big grin. 'No worries, Coach.'

A Touch of Magic

Percy stood by the door and patted each of us on the back as we jogged from the rooms. I came last, none of the usual bounce in my step. In his youth, Claude Rankin had been a dynamic midfielder. Now, he'd anchored himself into the centre half-forward position. He was *my* man. And while the years might've slowed him, they hadn't diminished his other talents.

As I ambled by, Percy stopped me and put a hand on my shoulder. 'Don't be intimidated,' he said. 'Rankin's good, but he's not as fast as you, he can't turn on a penny like you. Don't get in a wrestle with him. Run off him. Tire him out. Play off his weaknesses. That'll frustrate him.'

'He'll probably try and hit me,' I said. As good as Rankin was, he had a temper and was known to let a punch or two fly behind play, resulting in a broken jaw or nose for his opponent. He'd put more than a few guys in hospital. Then again, that was describing Little Reach in general.

'Run away from that, too,' Percy said.

Great coaches were full of great advice.

Even more people had gathered to watch, until the ground was packed. When we warmed up, the crowd booed us, and every time we fumbled or messed-up they'd laugh or shout something out. Up the other end, Little Reach split into four groups and ran precision drills. Their urgency snapped through the air as players encouraged one another. In their crimson attire – a golden scorpion splashed down the front of their jumpers – they looked like a professional football team.

Ozzie Rowan, the umpire, called the captains in for the toss. Ozzie – a tiny man with a ridiculous handlebar moustache – was a career umpire of thirty years. He'd not only earned universal respect in the league, but commanded it.

Percy detached from our group, but Rankin was followed by his entire team. They jostled around him, hunting dogs waiting to be set loose. It was exactly the sort of thing we should have been doing, too.

'Should we go?' I asked our guys.

'Go away,' Nigel said.

They didn't get it. Or maybe they did and were scared to. I could lead the charge – and even wandered forward a few steps – but it would look bad if I went and only a few of the guys followed or, worse, *nobody* followed.

While all this was going through my head, Ozzie tossed the coin. Rankin called 'tails' but it came down heads, so Percy jogged towards us and thrust his hand in the air – pointing at the goals where we'd be kicking – like he'd nailed the victory for us in the dying seconds.

'This is our time!' he roared.

It would've been nice to say Percy's zeal was infectious, but most of the guys scuttled away. I hated the sight of it. I took a deep breath, drove down the fear, then bolted across the ground to centre half-back and bounced up and down like I was getting ready for a prize fight.

Rankin swaggered over. Close up, I could truly appreciate what great shape he was in – big and muscly, and toned. That came from how hard the Scorpions trained.

I thrust my shoulder into his chest. At best, I hoped to put him down; at worst, that I'd knock him off his line. Maybe it was a bit of false bravado, but that was better than no bravado, and right now I needed to psyche myself up. But I bounced right off Rankin and almost lost my feet. I steadied myself, now looking like a boxer who'd taken one to the chin.

Rankin jabbed out his hand. 'Good luck, kid,' he said.

I went to shake his hand, but he slapped it away. It wasn't a hard hit; more to show me how easily he could get me. The crowd whooped, like Rankin was a mastermind, outsmarting me that way. I gritted my teeth and told myself I'd use it to spur me on, but even that felt hollow. Rankin outsized me by ten or fifteen centimetres, and twenty kilos in weight. He could probably squash me any time he wanted.

This was only the second time I'd played on Rankin. The first time – last year, in my second game – he kicked four goals, although it could've been ten because he kicked 4.8 on a blustery day. The ball kept coming down, and Rankin kept manhandling me, shoving me out of the way like I was made from paper. We lost that game by ninety-six points.

The opening bounce was palmed perfectly by the Little Reach ruck, Ken Kotz, to his rover, who snapped the ball out of the centre. The kick only went about ten metres, then took a vicious off-break towards my position. I dashed away from Rankin, scooped up the ball, took a bounce through traffic, and kicked it long to a lead towards goal from Percy, who marked it in front of his face. I loitered where I was until Percy kicked truly, then ambled back to centre half-back.

Rankin scowled. 'That's one I owe you,' he said.

I said nothing – no point giving him ammunition.

The first half was tight. We kept within a couple of goals of Little Reach at all times. It felt like our day; the ball bounced our way, miskicks went to teammates, and we were accurate in front of goal. Going into the dying minutes of the second quarter, Little Reach were 12.16.(88) to our 13.2.(80).

Even better, I was having a ripper of a game. Rankin hadn't touched the ball. I'd run off him to create play, I was never exposed when the ball rebounded, and I even had a running shot at goal, although it hit the post. Fortunately, it was our second behind – Matt Reynolds kicked the first.

With a couple of minutes left to play, Percy took himself off for a breather, and Adam came on to replace him. This was a typical Percy move. Often he'd bring new guys on with only a minute or two left so they could get a taste for the game without enough time to have a real impact, positive or negative.

'Got a new blackfella?' Rankin asked, like we'd bought a dog.

'Yeah.'

'They're lazy, you know?'

I said nothing, unsure how to respond.

Rankin's eyes narrowed to those famous slits. I could hear his mind at work. Adam was prey, and Rankin was cataloguing him, working out how he should be neutralised.

'He got a name?' Rankin said.

'Yeah.'

The slits turned on me.

'Yeah, he has,' I said.

When I didn't give him anything more, Rankin smirked. 'Smartarse.'

As the second quarter ticked away, the ball was often locked-up under packs. We'd gotten a taste; we knew we could push Little Reach and win the game, and they didn't like that. It wasn't that they were being beaten around the ground, but that a lot of the stuff they were trying wasn't coming off the way it would usually. We stifled them with a stop-start game, hoping they wouldn't find momentum.

When their full-forward, Murray Verne – a guy who'd led the goal-kicking in our league for seven consecutive years with seven tons – had a shot at goal from ten metres straight in front only to hit the post, more than a few of his teammates dropped their heads. Rankin cursed, berated the day, the ground, his team, our team, his players, our players, and everything else in his line of vision.

I sprinted off him and took the kick-out from Sean at full-back. As I marked, I braced myself for the impact of Rankin cannoning into my back. It didn't happen. He was limping off, like he'd pulled his hamstring.

This was good – they were a man down.

I kicked to Harry, but kept on running, taking the handball back, then bounced once, twice. Adam sprinted from centre half-forward towards the wing. From the boundary Percy screamed, 'Run! Run! No! Kick to Adam!' That's exactly what I did and lobbed the ball in front of him. He marked easily, those long arms extending beyond the spoil of his opponent, who instead rode Adam into the turf to the elation of the crowd.

Ozzie meted out a short fifty-metre penalty for the indiscretion, but as Adam prepared to kick, the bloody siren went. Adam was between half-forward and the wing, about twenty metres from the boundary, and too far out to score.

He put the ball on the ground and pulled up his socks. The crowd hissed. *'Give it up, you mongrel!'* somebody – a woman – shouted. Scorpions fans laughed. Percy, jogging on, waved his hand as if to dismiss her, and got booed for it. I started to lift a finger, but Percy pointed at me: *Don't*. I knew it was inflammatory, but now I'd been admonished, I didn't have the courage – especially with the booing stretching out into one long hiss. Our guys huddled together – all but Adam, who held onto the ball where he'd marked it.

Ozzie ran up. 'Here, give me the ball,' he said.

'I'm having a shot,' Adam said.

Ozzie frowned at him, then at the goals. The distance looked to be one-hundred metres, although later we measured it and it turned out to be only sixty-five. *Only.*

'Come on, give me the ball,' Ozzie said again.

'Give him the ball!' Adam's opponent, Daniel Schwartzer – a real mongrel if ever there was one – said. The Little Reach mechanic, he was best known for his unnecessary repairs, his exorbitant prices, and flirting with other men's partners.

By now, a few players had swarmed Adam's position and the crowd's hooting had become a tumult, like an unrelenting thunderstorm that was going to batter us into submission. We huddled closer – all but Percy, who stepped out towards Ozzie.

'What's the problem?' Percy asked.

'Tell your player to give me the ball,' Ozzie said. 'He wants to have a shot.' Again, he looked towards goal to illustrate the distance.

'Was it a mark?'

'Yeah, so what? Look at the distance, Percy!'

'If it was a mark, he's entitled to a shot.'

'What're you guys doing? Running a circus?'

More individual cries reared up now from the crowd – things like, 'Hand it over, you black dog!' and, 'What've you been sniffing?' These morons probably thought Adam wanting a shot was a tactic to put Little Reach off their game. Had I taken the mark where Adam was and the siren had gone, I'd have kicked the ball to the umpire – like anybody would've. But the way Adam was standing, he was *set*.

'Let him have the shot. Geez, who cares?' It was Rankin, hobbling forward, grimacing, but wanting to show his injury wasn't going to stop him from getting involved. He probably only sided with Adam to be over and done with it all. His real focus would've been to take his players into the rooms and blast them for being in this position on the scoreboard.

The players parted. Schwartzer remained on the mark, puffed, hands on knees. Adam went back, pulled some grass from the ground and threw it into the air to gauge the wind (that got the biggest boo from the Little Reach crowd) before he lined up.

He walked in, holding the ball for a torpedo. When his foot swung through the kick, his leg was perpendicular with his body. That was limber, especially given the way he'd struggled at training. If most others had put that much force behind a kick they would've torn their hamstring from the bone – or their leg from their hip.

The boos of the crowd faded as the ball sailed up and up, and spiralled perfectly through the air. Everybody fell silent as a few of Little Reach's defenders ran back to stop the ball from bouncing through if it fell short.

They needn't have worried, because the ball kept spinning, hitting its zenith some fifty metres from where it was kicked. Gasps ran through the crowd now as the ball came down. It was the most amazing thing I'd ever seen – the black branding on the ball an inky whirlpool as it spun, so bright, so sharp, so fast, like it wanted to cut through the Little Reach arrogance and hostility and carry us in its wake. Finally, it sailed through the goals at mid-post height, and travelled another fifteen metres – about eighty metres in all – before somebody in the crowd caught it, although the velocity of the ball bowled him, and the couple of friends who'd tried to brace him, over.

The goal umpire composed himself to signal the goal. There was a smattering of cheers – the few people who'd come from Ulah to support. Adam grinned at Rankin. It wasn't a triumphant grin, or even an insulting one, as many might've made after such a display. Hell, I would've.

'Thanks, mate,' Adam said with a nod.

Daring to Believe

'It's our day!' Percy hollered, as he paced back and forth. 'You hear me? *Our* day!' His voice bounced off the walls and echoed in every corner. 'We're all over them! *All* over them! Keep getting in there, keep stopping them from getting that run-on! This is *our* day!'

Usually, Percy's half-time addresses were white noise to a lot of the guys – something that was going on while they waited to get back out there. But now a lot of players fixed on him – well, a lot of the younger players. Some – like Sean and Harry – nodded in agreement. Nigel and Dean had their fists clenched. Some of the older players, though – like Matt Reynolds and a couple of the others – had little grins on their faces. I didn't know them well enough to guess whether they found Percy amusing or enjoyed the prospect of a shock win. We'd never been in this position before, especially against a good team, let alone Little Reach. For a moment, we dared to believe.

When we went back out, we charged onto the ground, and sprinted more than jogged through our warm up. By the time we took our positions, there was still no sign of Little Reach. The siren blared to signal that they should be out now. People in the crowd began to murmur. Ozzie looked around impatiently. We all knew what was happening: Rankin was roasting his players for being in this position against us, just lowly hopefuls.

Finally, the door to their clubrooms opened and they ambled out, as if dispirited – perhaps Rankin had taken it too far? He followed them out and limped to the boundary.

'Get a move on!' he shouted.

The Scorpions jogged around the oval once to warm up, then spread into position – Schwartzer had played at centre half-back in the first half, but now he cantered towards me. He rubbed his hands together, and thrust a shoulder into my chest. He wasn't dispirited. He was incensed. They probably all were.

'You old enough to be out here?' Schwartzer asked.

I snorted. 'Nice of you to give away that fifty just before half-time.'

Schwartzer sneered. He was in his mid-thirties and muscled like a pro-wrestler, but I wasn't apprehensive of him the way I was of Rankin. Schwartzer was so big he was usually slow and clumsy.

'Brought Adam within range,' I said.

The anger on Schwartzer's face furrowed so deep it should've left scars. He didn't have to know we had no idea Adam would kick the goal either. I bet Rankin had berated him at half-time. Rankin was like that. He made examples of players.

'Screw you,' Schwartzer said.

'Snappy comeback.'

We played on inspiration through the third quarter, buoyed by Adam's huge goal and often looking to him to produce some other miraculous feat. But there was nothing. He couldn't work his way into the game, and several times pulled up short, as he'd done at training earlier in the week, doubled over and panting. The crowd laughed at him and mocked him and he fumbled even worse, until Percy took him off. He walked to the bench but didn't sit, instead pacing as he clapped and shouted encouragement.

Late in the term we hit the lead for the first time in the game, thanks to Percy. He took Matt from full-forward and plopped himself in the goal square. Percy was a terror on the lead; while he wasn't quick, he used his body to keep his opponent out of the contest, and he marked and kicked four goals in quick succession.

At the final break, Percy exhorted us to keep doing everything we were doing, to fight it out. Everybody nodded and cheered and patted each other on the back.

'One more quarter!' he said as we huddled around him. 'One more quarter! You know what I want from you?'

All eyes fixed on his.

'Nothing more than what you've been giving me!' Percy said. 'Than you've been giving each other! Than you've been giving the team! One more quarter!'

'One more quarter!' Adam said.

'One more quarter!' Percy said.

'One more quarter!' we echoed.

Going into that last quarter, we were two points up and the possibility of victory sank into our heads. This was Little Reach! Little Reach losing in general was rare. Us beating them was unique. But that expectation of victory swelled until it left no room for composure, and we started making unforced errors – we fumbled, handballs and kicks missed their targets, and we kept choosing the wrong options.

Little Reach must've smelled our nervousness, because things finally clicked for them. Schwartzer nailed a mark right in front of me and goaled to put the Scorpions up by four points. The ball came back down and was locked in near the goal-line, where Sean won a free for being tackled high. I led and called for the ball but the kick slewed off the side of Sean's boot and fell into Schwartzer's arms. Schwartzer then kicked a difficult goal from the boundary – Little Reach were ten points up. The crowd cheered. I wanted to will us back into it, and hated that it was my opponent who'd kicked those two goals. When Schwartzer ran back up to me, he thudded his shoulder into my chest. I shoved him back, but might as well have hit a wall.

From that point on, Little Reach repeatedly won the ball forward, and we couldn't withstand the barrage. In the next twenty minutes they piled on goal after goal after goal – nine of them rattled off as if it was a training drill and we were stationery obstacles to be navigated. Their fans began their chant, the slow, grating cry of 'Scor-pee-ons!'

When the siren went, the Little Reach crowd roared and Rankin hobbled out onto the ground, clapping his hands over his heads. 'What they deserved, boys!' he said. 'This is the season we go undefeated!'

The Scorpions had had several seasons under Rankin where they'd lost only the one game. The undefeated season was a big thing for Rankin – something he'd been chasing as long as he'd been coach. I couldn't imagine being that dominant you could have that as a goal.

We slumped towards our rooms. We'd lost to Little Reach before, but never like this. We'd dared to believe we could win it – dared it until we almost held it in our hands. And then we'd found the burden of it all too heavy.

The final score was Little Reach 27.20.(182) to our 19.6.(120).

'Heads up!' Percy said, back in the rooms.

'We got pulverised,' Matt said.

'We did,' Percy said, 'but we pushed these bastards for three quarters.'

'Go away! Three quarters—' Dean said.

'Yes! Three quarters! Maybe I'd be a lot more negative if they came out and smashed us in the end—'

'They did,' Nigel said.

'We choked,' I said.

'That's right!' Percy said. 'We choked! And that's something we can work on because we pushed them! If nothing else, we can take that out of the game.' Percy scoured the room. 'It comes down to whether you want to be glass half-empty or glass half-full?'

'I wanna be glass too-big,' Nigel said.

That brought a laugh that dissolved the disappointment. Nigel was always good for that.

'As for this …?' Percy said, holding up a worn but shimmering gold card – a drinks card for our pub awarded to our best-on-ground. 'He shut down Rankin, and he kept Schwartzer clueless.'

'Schwartzer was born clueless,' Nigel said, for more laughs.

'Luke!'

He held it out towards me. Sometimes, he gave it out as encouragement – that's how I'd won it my first and only other time, in my third game last year.

'Schwartzer kick-started their goal spree,' I said.

'Luke, we've just had this conversation as a team,' Percy said. 'Half-empty or half-full?' He thrust the card into my hand.

I looked at it. It wasn't much but, shiny and wrinkled in my dirty palm, it made me think of what could be.

The Ulah'lah

Our local, the Ulah Pub, sat in the centre of town, this big old wooden thing with a pointed roof and rusty weather vane that whirled and squealed in the wind. The building might've been a cathedral originally, but had been converted into a pub, restaurant, and hotel, replete with tables and chairs outside overlooking the street, and a beer garden shielded from the sun by big bright umbrellas.

To everybody from Ulah, the pub was affectionately known as the Ulah'lah. I don't know how the nickname had come about; that's what it had been for as long as I can remember – ever since Mum used to send me to fetch Dad when he played for the Curlews and would enjoy a few too many beers post-match.

My drinks card entitled me to six free beers – not that I got them all. As soon as we arrived, Sean snatched the card out of my hand and cashed it. I got one beer out of it. Another went to Sean, one to Adam – as the newest player on our team – and the remaining three to whoever got in first.

Adam and I settled at a table in the corner, and I revelled in being here – with my teammates, having a cold beer, while we wound down the night. I gulped from my glass, felt the coldness of the beer slide down my throat. I'd watched Dad and his teammates do this, share this union – they trained together, fought together, and then they cooled down together. It was a rite of passage. I took another drink. With a couple more beers, I'd be relaxed, and that would help soothe the disappointment of the loss. But Adam's face screwed up as he sipped.

'Beer okay?' I said.

'I don't drink a lot,' he said.

He did that night, although he didn't have much choice. Everybody drank lots those nights. And as we drank more and felt looser and happier – guys playing games of pool, or singing to songs from the jukebox – it became like a party. Not just for us either, but for anybody else who'd come to the Ulah'lah. Percy even got up on a table and recounted highlights from the game, including how I'd done well on Rankin, before closing with the enormity behind Adam's goal. People who hadn't seen it scoffed that it could be true, although the players – and few fans who'd made the trek to Little Reach – assured them it was. The only detail Percy *did* embellish was to suggest the boots he'd loaned Adam had helped Adam with the distance.

'A touch of Percy magic,' Percy said, to laughs that filled the Ulah'lah.

The best thing about those nights – for the unattached, at least – was getting attention from single women. Players were local celebrities, not that it meant much most of the time. With how much we drank, we didn't have a lot of luck. But it was nice to feel wanted and special before the drudgery of life and jobs took that all away again.

One girl I noticed – as always – was the bartender, Amanda, who was Percy's eldest. I'd had my eye on her since primary school. Call it a crush. While Percy was big-boned and big-bodied, Amanda was slender – she had an athlete's build (her mum had represented the state in karate), with these gentle features and almond-shaped eyes that were faery, like she'd sprung out of the bush itself. Her blonde hair was tied back, like she wanted to take the glamour out of it, but she still glowed, although maybe that was me making so much of her. It didn't feel like she belonged here, in such a small town.

At one point during the night she brought over beers for Adam and me. I sat up straight, ran a hand through my hair, and told myself over and over to behave as sober as I could. The last thing that would impress Amanda was showing how much the beer was getting to me – and it *was* getting to me. I hadn't been doing this so long I could absorb it, like some of our veterans.

'Here you go, guys,' Amanda said.

When she leant over the table to put a beer in front of Adam, her blouse flapped open to reveal the strap of her lacy red bra curled around her shoulder. I squirmed and stared longer than I should have. I couldn't help it. I pulled my gaze away as she put a beer in front of me. She smiled. Warmth flushed around my neck and my hands grew clammy. I'm sure she hadn't caught me. But I felt guilty all the same.

'Thought you were being left unattended,' she said.

'Thanks, Amanda.' I wanted to sound cool, but 'thanks' was lost in a splutter, like I'd cleared my throat, and all I got out of her name was 'Manda'. I coughed, and said, 'Hey, Amanda, this is the guy that kicked *that* goal, Adam Pride. Adam – Amanda.'

'Pleased to meet you,' Amanda said.

'Likewise,' Adam said.

He shook her hand and Amanda had the same reaction I did when she felt the roughness on his palm. She flipped Adam's hand over.

'Oh, what's that?' she asked.

There was a scar on his palm about the size of a golf ball, a mini crater, like a meteorite had crashed there.

'Accident,' he said, flipping his hand to show the scar continued on the other side, although it was smaller and bulbous on the top of his hand.

'Oh.' Amanda cringed. 'How'd that happen?'

'Blade of a pick went through my hand.' Adam grinned. 'That's what happens when you have your hand in the right place at the right time.'

'Don't you mean the *wrong* place at the *wrong* time?'

'Same difference, isn't it? Looks bad, but I don't feel it anymore.'

'Surprised it didn't leave any permanent damage.'

'Nah, went dead the moment it happened. Didn't know nothing after that.'

'Excuse me,' Amanda said, as she was called back to the bar to serve some of our thirstier teammates. She joked with the guys as she poured them beers. They laughed and lowered their heads, like schoolkids with crushes – even the older ones, who'd been doing this sort of thing for years. She had a disarming quality. Even when she'd asked Adam about his hand, she'd done it in a way that hadn't seemed intrusive.

'You like her, huh?' Adam asked.

'What?'

'Why don'tcha go talk to her?'

'Not right now.'

'When?'

'In a bit.'

I fuelled my nerve with beer, beer, and more beer. So I'm hopeless, but I'm not the first guy to find courage at the bottom of a glass. The one thing I did count in my favour was she had brought over beers for us – unless she was being courteous to the new guy. I couldn't tell. I never can with those things.

'You should go,' Adam said again.

'What?'

Adam tried to push me off my chair. 'Go talk to her.'

'I'm building up to it.'

'You wait long enough, you lose your chance, and then it's gone forever.' Adam shoved me so my chair rocked and I wobbled up into a standing position. He put his feet up on my chair so I couldn't sit back down. 'Go!'

I made my way to the bar while Amanda deflected the advances of Sean. Sean and I had come up together into the team, although I was a boar, while he was stylish – he had the talent to make something of himself, talent I envied. He also usually had more luck with the ladies, showing that same grace he did on the field. But even he'd never had any luck with Amanda. Nobody did.

'Hey, Luke,' Sean said – *slurred*. Then he turned to Amanda, who was drinking a raspberry and lemonade. 'Luke killed them today. Totally killed them, and that prick Rankin.'

'So Dad told everybody before,' Amanda said.

'Oh yeah. I was wondering why that sounded familiar.'

Amanda smiled at me. 'That's great, though.'

I blushed.

'Still, you two shouldn't drink so much. It can't be good for your playing.'

'You're right. You're right!' Sean said. He downed what was left of his beer – half a glass – in one gulp. 'I'm gonna stop! Tomorrow! But for now …?'

'You're hopeless,' Amanda said. 'What about you, Luke?'

'I'm okay,' I said, covering the top of my glass. I wasn't, really. I had only a third of the glass left but I wanted to impress her with my abstinence, although abstinence in my state was like putting a Band-Aid on an amputated limb.

'What about Adam?' Amanda asked as she poured Sean a beer. 'He looks kinda lonely.'

Adam watched me from the corner. He'd drank as much as anybody, but it hadn't affected him, other than for a strange, wistful look on his face.

'Pour him one,' Sean said. 'And me. You know, to keep him company.'

Amanda poured two beers. Sean grabbed them from her and stumbled across to Adam. Adam took the beer, and toasted Sean. Sean spilled half his glass when he thrust it for the toast, then fell into a chair opposite Adam.

Amanda poured another glass and pushed it across the bar towards me. 'Go on,' she said. 'You want another one.'

'Thanks.' I grinned. Then I remembered Sean hadn't paid. He was good at taking off when money was needed. I fumbled in my pocket. 'Let me get that …'

'Don't worry about it,' Amanda said. 'On the house, from me, for your game today.'

'Thanks.' Here was my biggest problem. I didn't know whether she was flirting or being generous.

'Seriously, though,' Amanda said, 'you shouldn't drink so much if you're looking at a career.'

I liked the way she said it – it wasn't know-it-all, the way that might drive you mad and get you to do the opposite out of spite. It was nice.

'Yeah, I know,' I said. 'Just sometimes I think it's too late.'

'At eighteen?'

'Out here, though. In the middle of nowhere.'

'At *eighteen*?'

'I'm nineteen this year.'

'Your birthday's in December, isn't it?'

'You know my birthday?' I was flattered.

'You guys were in here drinking the day you turned eighteen – I remember because I'd just started working here. So you don't turn nineteen for over six months.'

'Still …' Her remembering didn't seem so flattering anymore.

'It's never too late, is it?'

'You really believe that?'

'I think everybody gets a second chance in life.'

'What's that mean?'

'You haven't even had your first chance yet, Luke. So, yeah, I believe it's never too late. Especially if this is what you want to do – it is, isn't it? Play football?'

'Yeah. I guess.'

'What're you going to do to make that a reality?'

'What do you mean what I'm going to do? I'm going to play.'

'That it?'

'What else is there?' I said.

'Just asking.'

'What about you?'

'I want to get out of here,' Amanda said.

'Out of Ulah?'

Amanda nodded.

'Doing what?'

'I've been taking an online course in writing.'

'Writing? When?'

'Last couple of years I was doing high school.'

'You kept that quiet.'

Amanda shrugged. 'I want to get into journalism. I've even asked Scott Harrow at *The Tribune* if I can write for them on the side.'

'That's amazing,' I said. 'I never knew any of that.'

'I only really talk to Dad about it. Not much point airing your dreams around here.'

'So where do you want to go?'

'Melbourne, maybe. Eventually. Try to write for one of the big papers.'

I felt a pang of loss, even though Amanda and I were only friends. Good luck to her, but so much for my crush. That she wanted to take on the world showed me why she did stand out around here – because she wanted to be bigger than this place, wanted something more, and you could feel that aspiration brimming from her. There was nothing wrong with Ulah if you were happy with small-town living. But there was also nothing wrong with reaching for something greater, too.

We talked until closing and time *flew*. It could've been because I was drinking, and drinking always blurs time. But the truth was that when you get in those moments you enjoy, you can never hold onto them. They slip right through your hands, until all you're left with is the memory.

There were only a handful of guys still around, still playing pool. These were the experienced hands who'd gone through this routine for years – like Percy and Matt Reynolds. Others, like Sean, slumped with heads on their hands on tables, sleeping and oblivious to the world.

Adam was still sitting with him, still drinking, his face impassive. As I went to wake up Sean – who didn't want to wake up – I looked at Adam and said, 'You gonna walk home at this time? You can stay at my place, if you like.'

'Nah, it's sweet,' Adam said. 'Like the night air. Walk will do me good.' His voice didn't slur, his eyes weren't glassy; the alcohol hadn't touched him at all.

Adam helped me pick up Sean, one of us to either side of him to get him walking. He was still asleep, but was in that automatic mode where his legs ticked over, even if his mind didn't.

We walked to the door with the rest of our teammates. I threw a hand up at Amanda, who was wiping down the bar. 'See ya, Amanda.'

'See ya, Luke,' she said. 'See ya, guys.'

That was something – I'd gotten a personalised farewell.

Outside, it was cool, although I could still taste the day's heat in the air and feel it on my skin. We exchanged goodbyes and back-slapping about the game, culminating with a typical Percy closer.

'Great effort today, guys. Let's build on it,' he said. 'You gonna be okay to get home, Adam? If you want, you can stay over. I'll drive you back tomorrow morning – afternoon, more likely.'

'I'm okay, thanks, Coach,' Adam said, his voice clear in the night.

'Ya sure?'

'Yeah, thanks, anyway.'

'Okay. See ya all at training,' Percy said.

With that, everybody – except myself; Sean, who was waking up now; and Adam – split.

'Pub closed?' Sean asked, looking around. 'I wanted another drink.'

'Yeah, that's definitely what you need,' I said. 'Hey, Adam, we'll walk you a bit of the way.'

'It's okay,' Adam said.

'Just to walk off the beer a bit.'

'Sure.'

A Little Walk in the Night

' The way you talked about Rankin,' Adam said as we headed towards our ground, 'I thought he was going to be a monster.'

Sean chuckled around a yawn, then stretched. He blinked, getting his bearings – the Ulah'lah was central to Ulah, and at the highest point of town. Then everything sat on gentle slopes. Our ground was down the road – one of the few flat spots around here. The clubrooms were this small brick splat on the concrete apron, in front of it a solitary bench empty and forlorn, the light towers off, and the football oval this wide expanse of green ringed by a metal railing. It looked so peaceful.

'Wasn't Rankin's best showing today,' Sean said, and then straightened up, so a swagger came into his step. 'Good. Stuff him, the prick.'

'Hey, he got them to let me have my kick.'

'Yeah, that was a surprise.'

'Not bad when you hear that stuff coming over the fence.'

'Yeah,' I said, embarrassed that we'd done nothing. It had all become so commonplace over the years, those sort of comments. It used to happen when I watched Dad playing. People would laugh. Then the laughs stopped, or people would frown at the offender. But that was about it. Nobody liked it, but nobody did anything about it – especially not in Little Reach. 'I'm sorry about that,' I said.

'That's life, isn't it?' Adam said.

'It shouldn't be.'

'It's okay.'

'It still shouldn't be.'

Adam didn't say anything more. The anger boiled up in me, that he had to wear it like that.

'Rankin's a prick,' I said. 'Him and his generals.'

'His generals?' Adam asked.

'They're like his assistant coaches. That's what they call them. Generals. They help him run the team. There's Schwartzer—'

'Murray Verne,' Sean said.

'—and their centreman Terry Bell. That's all of them, isn't it?'

'Yeah,' Sean said, 'not counting *whatshisname* – Dungbar?'

'*Dunbar*,' I said. 'Ken? No, Kevin.'

'Yeah, that's it – Kevin Dunbar. The one who *offed* himself.'

'He killed himself?' Adam said.

'Yeah. About five years ago.'

Neither Sean nor me knew Dunbar. He'd been before our time as players. Apparently, he'd been another prodigious talent, and while he'd gotten offers from the Big League, he'd stayed with Rankin to help resurrect Little Reach. I didn't understand that. Country football was something, and apparently Dunbar had gotten a few sponsorships to hang around, but the AFL? That's as big as you could get. Maybe that was a sign of what football meant to Little Reach.

'How come?' Adam said.

'Think things got on top of him,' I said. 'Stories came out that he owed the bank, was going to lose his house – typical stuff around here.'

'Around everywhere,' Sean said.

'Yeah,' Adam said.

When we got to our oval, Sean sprinted twenty metres ahead of us, calling, *'Lead! Lead!'* Then he dove, crashing into the grass. But like I said, Sean was stylish, and he rolled back to his feet, and threw his arms triumphantly up into the air, calling, 'Sean Mercher!' His voice echoed through the night.

That got Adam and me started with him, and we played shadow football, feigning passes to leads, marks, and sidestepping opponents who weren't there. When we got to the other side, we keeled over the boundary railing trying to catch our breath. My throat burned and I could taste the beer gurgling in my stomach, wanting to come back up.

'I need to get fit again,' Adam said.

'Probably help if we didn't drink so much,' I said.

Sean burped in agreement.

'On that note,' Adam said, 'I better head off.'

'You've still got a way to go,' I said. Adam had said he had a farm on the border of Ulah, Warrambatta, and Shandeen Bank, which meant he had a hike of a couple of kilometres.

'And *you* want to keep walking with me?' Adam laughed. 'You'll get lost out there in the night. Thanks, anyway.'

He was right. After the creek, it was open country – lots of hills, spotted every now and then with gums. By daylight, it was no problem; stick in one direction and you'd hit a town or a road sooner or later. Or a farm. But now, drunk, in the dark, dragging Sean behind me? No way.

'Okay, we'll catch ya,' I said.

'Thanks, guys.' Adam hopped over the railing. 'I'll see you at training.'

'See you, Adam!' Sean called after him. 'Luke, I'm never drinking again.'

'Yeah, right.'

'I'm not! Serious!'

Adam headed down the embankment and into the shadows of the creek. From where we were, we couldn't see anything. I gulped, sure Adam had disappeared. Or fallen. I don't know why. I grew worried he wasn't going to emerge from the creek. He'd be stuck down there, trapped and helpless, and we'd go home oblivious.

'Wait here,' I said.

'Where're you going?'

'Want to make sure Adam's all right.'

Before he could argue, I jumped the railing and trotted down the embankment, holding my hands out for balance. I'd forgotten how steep it was – almost a straight drop, although there were little ledges you could use as footholds. I poked my feet tentatively trying to feel my way, but then something snagged my ankle and I plunged forward, like I was flying. When we were kids, we used to slide down this slope on torn walls of cardboard boxes. Now, that seemed crazy.

I hit the springy grass that coated the embankment, bounced, rolled and rolled, then thudded into the bank of the creek, which was nothing but a trickle after summer. Winter would fill it so that crossing was only possible by selecting a path across the boulders in the creek bed. If we had a *really* good winter, then forget it; the whole thing submerged, and you had to try the nearest bridge.

I expected to see Adam, but I'd forgotten something else about the creek – it was bloody pitch black down here. When we trained, enough of a glow from the oval's floodlights spilled across so you could pick your way through, but now I couldn't see my hand in front of my face.

'Luke!' It was Sean.

Getting up, I performed a checklist: no cuts that I could feel, no sprains, and definitely – and most importantly – no breaks. On the crest of the opposite embankment, Adam rose up, a silhouette against the starlit sky.

'Luke!' Sean called again.

'Yeah, coming!' I shouted back.

I headed up the embankment.

The Turning Point

When I got home, I tried to be quiet, I really did. But my key missed the front door lock for about thirty seconds; in easing the door closed, I thumped it; and then I stumbled down the hall. It didn't matter. Somebody was up. I could make out the TV, low, almost inaudible. Its screen flickered through the archway leading into the lounge – it had to be Dad watching. Usually, he was in bed by eight or nine, although sometimes after a couple hours napping he'd get up for the late news. But it was beyond late news time now.

I stopped at the archway and, trying to be casual, leaned against the jamb. The flickering light of the TV bounced off the shapes in the lounge until they were shifting shadows. Dad was in his recliner. A cigarette dangled from his mouth. He didn't smoke. He used to. But Mum put a stop to that a couple of years ago when his blood pressure tests came back scary bad. Now, he'd suck on unlit cigarettes for the taste of tobacco.

'Dad,' I said.

He didn't look up from the TV. I couldn't see what was on, but by the sound of it, it was some infomercial. That was Dad, also; sometimes he'd wake, and either he'd potter around in his shed, doing things he complained he couldn't leave until the morning, or he'd put the TV on with the intention of sitting there for a couple minutes, only to become transfixed.

'You're up late,' I said.

'So are you.'

'Yeah.' I tried a shrug, and almost slid off the jamb.

Dad looked at me. I couldn't see his eyes, but I could feel them.

'How'd you go?' he said.

'Got smashed by ten goals.'

'Oh.'

'We led going into the last.'

'So what happened?'

'Don't think we knew how to see it out.'

Dad tilted his head. The TV's light revealed his pursed lips. He made a *hmmph* sound and went back to his infomercial. That was it. That was always it. Beyond asking the result, Dad didn't want details. I could've volunteered that Percy judged me our best player, but felt embarrassed. Maybe if I'd said it straight away. I pushed off from the jamb, grabbed a drink of water from the kitchen, then went to bed.

The next morning, I woke with a dryness in my throat, a furriness on my tongue, and my head feeling clogged – one of the costs of drinking the evening away. When I got up, I felt unsteady, and it wasn't until after my shower, breakfast, and brushing my teeth, that I felt normal – well, at least a little bit.

I wandered out of the house and sat on the top step to the verandah. The wheat swayed and rustled, perhaps relishing the peacefulness. And it was. I could've been the only person in Ulah – in the world – it was that quiet, but that only made me feel alone and unfulfilled. Perhaps this was going to be my life.

I got up, walked through the wheat and took the road into Ulah. Sean – despite his vow to never drink again – and some of the others had gotten together for lunch at the outdoor tables of the Ulah'lah. I joined them for a couple of beers, drinking the first against my better judgement, and the second with a newfound thirst. This was all part of what had become my routine. On Monday, it was help Dad with the chores, then drop into the

Ulah'lah again. This time we sat inside, where I kept stealing glances at Amanda, looking good in a denim skirt and peach blouse. She smiled at me a couple of times, but I think she was only being polite. I had another couple, then went home and flopped out in front of the TV for an hour or two before hitting the sack.

Then Tuesday evening at training, everything changed.

We milled around on the ground, chatting, evening settling on us with a soft orange glow that spoke more of summer. The curlews on that far wing of the ground wailed as they had last week and there, like last week, was Adam, coming up from the creek. He hopped the railing and jogged towards us. He was dressed the same. It wasn't really odd given most of us wore the same clothes for training, but usually it was sports stuff. Adam's clothes weren't, except for the boots Percy loaned him.

'Hey, guys,' he said, and flashed that big grin of his.

Percy emerged from the clubrooms and we formed our ring around him. We waited for the usual Percy bluster, and he opened his mouth like he was going to go for it, but he stopped, walked back and forth, folded his hands behind his back and nodded once.

'I know this is a game to most of you,' he said, his voice low, so we had to lean in to hear. 'And that's fine. It *is* a game. But for a bit there Saturday, we pushed Little Reach. I know some might say it was luck or whatever; so be it. It might've been. But I enjoyed it. I enjoyed going toe-to-toe and matching it with them.'

'Until they smashed us,' Matt said.

'We should've beaten them!' Adam said.

'You're dreaming,' Matt said. 'Not like you did anything anyway, that one fluky goal aside.' He glared at Percy. 'Just accept what it is.'

'Why?' Percy said.

'Because it's what it's always been.'

'How can you say that? You played in our last flag eighteen years ago. It wasn't like that then.'

Matt lowered his head.

'This is my eighth year as coach – we've scraped into the finals a few times, but usually we're an average team, and I don't think we need to be. I look around and I see plenty of talent. But we don't get the best out of ourselves.' He took a deep breath. 'Look, I want to get into it with all of you – I want to get *serious*. On Saturday, I saw the potential of what we could be. Let's build on that. It'll be hard work—'

Some of the players groaned – Matt the loudest.

'It'll be hard work,' Percy said again, 'but there'll be rewards. If you don't want to, I understand. But I can't keep doing it this way. And I won't. I'm sorry, that's like extortion. But I've done this a while, and for what? To pass time? I want more than that. And I feel deeply about this. So, who's with me?'

Players looked at one another. Some bowed their heads. Matt sniggered. Percy slumped – whatever bravado had fuelled this suggestion now ebbed away. He took another deep breath – before, it was for fortitude; now, it was like he was going to sigh and throw it all in. I opened my mouth.

'I'm in!' Adam said.

Percy's head lifted.

'You barely count!' Matt said. 'You've only been here one game.'

And whatever fuse Adam had tried to light fizzled out. Heads went down again. Percy looked around expectantly. Matt towered behind him belligerently – Matt had been captain-coach once, before Percy, his tenure renowned for a string of low finishes and legendary post-match drinking sessions.

'I'm in, too,' I said.

'You are?' Percy said.

'And me!' Sean said.

'Me, too!' Nigel said.

Other players joined in, although Matt and some of the others stood their ground, like they were squaring for a fight. Mostly it was the older players. The problem is these guys represented the seniority in the team, and some of them had held down positions for years, so their voices carried more weight.

'Don't forget me!'

This came from little Ronnie Waite – Ronnie was forty-something (nobody really knew his age; it seemed he'd been around forever) and was the only other current player to have played in our last premiership. He was tiny, with a weathered face that had seen too much hardship, and frizzy blond hair that made his head look like a dandelion. His vote broke the tension, and then he clapped his hands, as if to signal the end of the stand-off.

'Let's get to it!' he said.

He jogged from our ring and scooped up one of the errant footballs.

Training turned into a comedy shtick as we struggled to get organised and fouled drills we'd never done before. We improved as the night wore on, but it was still a rabble. Matt and some of the others complained, using it as evidence that this wasn't the way it was meant to be.

During one drill, Adam shot a pass at me low and hard. It hit my hands and I was already preparing to kick the ball to the next person in the chain, but I was planning and acting before I'd finished taking the ball cleanly, so it bounced from my fingertips and trickled away. I had to stop, run back, and pick it up. Matt groaned and rolled his eyes.

'Keep at it!' Adam said, as he ran past me.

I held up my hand to acknowledge my error. 'My bad!' I said, and kicked the ball to Sean.

And like that, something changed – taking that accountability showed everybody that screwing up wasn't something to be condemned for, or feel bad about, and that we could improve if we kept pushing.

On Thursday night, we were better. Sorta. At least the effort was there, and training was loud with lots of encouragement and applause for efforts. The session took on an entirely new feeling. Then Amanda and some of her friends came to watch, standing under one of the light towers.

'What're you doing here?' I said as I ran back to fetch an errant kick.

Amanda held up a pen and a notebook. 'Got the cadetship with *The Tribune*!' she said. 'They've asked me to cover your matches!'

'That's fantastic! Congratulations!' I said. 'Guess you're following your dream.'

Amanda smiled.

The presence of Amanda and her friends pushed us to another level – nobody wanted to look bad in front of them. But Matt and some of the other guys quickly ran out of puff – or interest – and bent over, hands on thighs, and sucked in deep breaths. A few of them even fell to the ground and lay there. A couple lit up cigarettes.

On Friday, traditionally a quiet night because of the match the next day, I bumped into Percy at the Ulah'lah. We took a seat at the bar and, as Amanda poured us beers, Percy told me that a number of guys had pulled out of the squad.

'Couldn't take the new drills,' he said. 'They said if it was going to be like that, they couldn't be bothered. Matt led the charge.'

Percy reeled off other names. Matt was the best of them, but there were others almost as good, so it was disappointing they didn't want to get more out of their talent. Then there were lots of fringe players who only came when there was a spot to fill or to have a kick.

'That's eleven players,' I said, counting the names.

'Uh-huh.'

'Because they're afraid of training hard?'

'Luke, you're young. These guys run farms, they work, some have wives and kids. They play footy as a laugh. Same with some of the younger ones. They play to run around a bit, have a few beers afterward, and flirt with the girls who watch. If footy becomes more work than work, then what're they in it for?'

'Little Reach isn't any different.'

'I guess it's in the attitude.'

'I'm sure we'll be able to cover the guys we've lost,' I said, sipping from my beer.

'Ronnie's still in and that's good, because he's a clever little forward, and he gives us some experience – he's going to be vice-captain. I want you to be deputy vice-captain.'

'Me? I've played only nine games, Percy!'

'I want somebody newer in there, and I think you can set a good example. Honestly, Luke, you're probably not going to be required to do much other than what you've been doing, and I think some of the other young players will look up to you.'

It seemed a choice made out of desperation. Still, it was a flattering offer, and Percy's logic was sound. And what would I have to do? Percy and Ronnie would handle all the real stuff. All I needed was to go out there and play my best.

'Well, sure, I guess,' I said.

'Great. Because we're really going to rely on you young guys coming through.'

'With the harder training, there's bound to be improvement.'

'Yeah.' But Percy had that look in his eyes of somebody who'd staked his last hundred dollars on lotto tickets. He took a long drink. 'I've always wanted to do this.'

'What?'

'Get into it.'

I frowned, unsure what he was saying.

'Luke, I'm forty-three. You know how many premierships we've won in my time as a player?'

'One?'

'Yeah. Eighteen years ago. *Eighteen*. Going on nineteen. Against Little Reach, too. And I didn't play. The missus was giving birth to our first *that* day.' Percy's eyes rolled in the direction of Amanda. 'But we were a good squad that year. I thought there'd be other opportunities. It's amazing the way time chews you up and spits you out. Next thing you know, half your life's gone by. Worse, you wonder why you haven't tried harder to get the things you want, instead of settling for the things you have.'

There wasn't much I could say to that.

'I'm not gonna play forever. None of us will. But I want to have one last real tilt at it. It's what I've wanted to do since I became coach. But I've never had the confidence – not with the way guys like Matt and the others treated it all as a bit of a laugh. Screw it. Now's the time. Before it's too late. We've never been good enough, so I figure the only way that we can get good enough is to get serious.'

'If you're going to be serious, Dad,' Amanda said, from where she wiped down the bar, 'should you really be drinking until midnight?'

'Fair go, Amanda!' Percy said. 'We're not professionals. And we're playing at home tomorrow, so it's not like we've got a drive in front of us.' His eyes widened. 'Hey, if we lose, don't write we lost because we were sitting in here drinking.'

'It hadn't even occurred to me,' Amanda said, 'until now.' She counted how many of our teammates were also here tonight, pointing her finger at each one. 'You've got half the team in here.'

'*I* don't have them in here; they came here of their own accord. It's not like there's an option. Anyway, nobody drinks that much the night before a match.'

That was true enough. Percy and I had only drunk six beers in a three hour span. Then I decided to be true to myself. I finished my beer and got off my stool.

'Okay, I'm heading off,' I said.

'Already?' Percy said.

'Setting an example, Coach,' I said and headed for the door. 'You don't think the Little Reach players are out drinking tonight, do you?'

'Nah!' somebody to my left called out. It was Nigel, who sat with Sean and several other players. 'They're probably out sacrificing goats so the devil will grant them success!'

That brought a laugh and even got me smiling. I held up my hand in farewell. 'See ya, tomorrow,' I said, then threw a casual wave in Amanda's direction. 'See ya, Amanda.'

'See ya, Luke.'

Another personalised farewell. And now I was deputy vice-captain. They were little accomplishments – things that most other people probably wouldn't have considered twice. Still, as I left the Ulah'lah, I grew sure they were the beginning of something bigger.

The Second Quarter

The Dingoes

Although all the towns out here were small, Warrambatta was *tiny*. Nestled in amongst the hills and surrounded by farms, Warrambatta's central feature was their big eight-pump service station – and it was still *service*, somebody running out to tend to any cars or trailers that might pull through. But that was Warrambatta: the hub between where you'd come from and where you were going, the nexus between the past and the future.

It was little surprise that their football team, the Warrambatta Dingoes – so named because dingoes wandered the hills around Warrambatta, as well as made the occasional foray into a farm – were perennial cellar-dwellers. They didn't have many people to draw from. Everywhere else, there was always somebody new coming up.

In Warrambatta, you kept seeing the same team five years straight – they even had the oldest player, a fifty-seven-year-old farmer, Roy Jenkins, who'd been playing forty years, and played with his kids, and now played with one of his grandkids.

With personnel like that at their disposal, it was little wonder Warrambatta had won the second-most wooden spoons in our league (twelve) and only the one premiership. This year, sitting 1–4, they looked destined to notch-up spoon thirteen.

It was just as well they were our opponent, because I'll tell you one thing about our new training regime: it hurt. And I wasn't the worst-off. As one of the younger guys, I was in better condition than most. Before the match, we lounged in the clubrooms and stretched and massaged one another, trying to find relief for sore muscles. A handful of other guys we'd expected to play were no-shows. I hoped our new attitude paid off quick because if any more players dropped out, we wouldn't have a team.

Adam arrived late again. He was already dressed in his jumper, the boots Percy had loaned him, and white shorts – white shorts being the shorts we wore when we played away. This was a home game, which meant we wore black shorts. Percy had to fetch him some. Adam didn't seem embarrassed by his limited wardrobe. He even carried the rest of his clothes – the same ones he wore to training – in a plastic shopping bag. But this wasn't unusual around here either. People weren't necessarily poor, but football gear was considered a luxury.

'I hardly have to tell anybody here that we've had a bit of a changing of the guard,' Percy said.

No, he didn't – gone were Matt and the other regulars; now a lot of young faces looked back up at Percy, beaming, hopeful, and nervous. Some of these guys had sat on the fringes of the team for years. But the one thing they had in common was how invested they were in everything Percy had to say.

'Ronnie's our new vice-captain,' Percy said, 'and Luke our deputy vice-captain.'

Players clapped, and thumped Ronnie or me on our backs. Ronnie, who'd been bouncing a cigarette on the back of his hand, put it away quick, and nodded in acknowledgement with a sly grin. I blushed and lowered my head. Sean plonked himself down by me, threw an arm around my shoulders and shook me.

'Now I know you're all sore from training,' Percy went on. 'You're probably wondering what you've let yourself in for and if it's all going to be worth it.'

A few of the guys murmured, some others chuckled. But there was relief, too – that Percy acknowledged it showed we were in this together, and he was aware of what we were going through.

'We're going to see the dividends,' he went on. 'It'll come. Don't worry. But as far as today goes, we can't let them get on top of us, or we'll be scrapping the whole game trying to get back into it. Get on top and they'll give it up, like they always do. We have to hit them hard and fast.'

Percy was right. For about a total of ten minutes, the game looked dangerous as the Dingoes kicked the first four goals – with no thanks to myself or Sean, our opponents getting two apiece. My guy got the jump on me with the two leads he made, and by the time my whining muscles answered, he'd marked. The same happened with Sean.

But it wasn't long before our bodies warmed up, and we started to apply the pressure. Our movement of the ball was also crisper than usual. Not a lot, of course – it's not like a couple of training sessions were going to transform us immediately, but players were developing an expectation of where their teammates should be running. Because we had a younger team across the park, there was a lot more energy, too. Warrambatta kicked only one more point for the first half, while we kicked 3.3 in the first quarter, and 5.0 in the second, to take the score to us 8.4.(52) to the Dingoes 4.1.(25).

What helped was the home crowd – don't let anybody ever tell you different about how important they are. Every time we neared the ball, made a play, or had a shot, the crowd cheered us, while every time the Dingoes had the ball the silence was so thick it amplified every individual disparaging remark. And when a crowd of several hundred laugh at that comment, it stings. About the only people not cheering were Matt and some of the others players who'd dropped out. They stood in one pocket, drank beer, smoked cigarettes, and scowled.

Early in the third quarter, Sean went down like he'd done a knee or something. But it was only a cramp – probably a result of the heat and how much he'd drank the night before. He tried staying on, but the next time he ran for the ball down he went again. It looked like it was going to be one of those really bad days where the cramps hit over and over.

Percy dragged Sean and had Adam come on in his spot. I ran up to him as he assumed his position at full-back. He bounced on the spot and rubbed his hands together.

'Can't say I've played full-back before,' he said.

'Don't be nervous,' I said. 'I'm here.'

'Thanks.'

Playing full-back wasn't easy, and I wanted to take care of him, even though I was really finding my way myself. Being a defender not only meant watching your opponent, but looking out for your teammates – especially if they were new to the team.

At the next bounce, Warrambatta got the clearance and their centreman kicked the ball long over my head. I ran back, but Adam was already sprinting off the goal-line. His opponent blinked, like he couldn't believe how fast Adam had set off.

The ball took a weird bounce in front of Adam, but he snaked it in with one hand, sidestepped two opponents, and handballed to me. I handballed back to Adam as he ran past and zipped through the centre, weaving around opponents like they were witches hats. He kicked a long, flat pass to Percy, leading out from centre half-forward. Percy marked and Adam still came. Percy almost seemed mesmerised into handballing the ball back to him, and Adam kicked long and true for a goal to the roars of the crowd.

I jogged up to Adam as he cantered back towards his position and low-fived him. 'Well done,' I said.

'Thanks.'

'Maybe you should be taking care of me.'

'You're doing fine.'

That bit of play set the tone as, for the next five minutes, Adam ran off his opponent, wreaked havoc, and created goals for our forwards. Percy then swung Nigel to full-back, and moved Adam into the centre. The Warrambatta coach swung a hard-tag onto him, a lumpy redhead who stood shoulder-to-shoulder with Adam and grabbed the hem of his jumper.

The umpire bounced the ball and Adam moved before anybody else did, read the play even before Harry got his hand to it and tapped it down. Adam snared the ball on fingertips, twirled between two Dingoes, and stabbed a pass to Ronnie leading out of the pocket. Ronnie marked it, played on, and snapped a goal.

Adam astonished everybody for the next ten minutes with plays like that. Wherever the ball was, there was Adam; whenever he was swallowed within a pack of players, he would emerge unscathed, like he was dancing out of an avalanche. Then he would lope clear with those big, long strides of his and shoot the ball onto the chests of our forwards so hard and flat it knocked them over. Or else he would kick beautiful long goals as he streamed from packs, leaving opponents grabbing at thin air.

Hometown crowds cheer, they scream, but they don't applaud, not like fans at a tennis match clap for long rallies. But as Adam was an unknown quantity to them, that's what they did: they applauded. Even Matt and his cronies were wide-eyed and open-mouthed.

Adam did nothing else after that fifteen-minute period. Five minutes into the last quarter, Percy moved him from the centre to half-forward, but all he could manage was to spill an easy mark. Percy moved him to the forward pocket, where he took one mark in front only ten metres out and sprayed the kick. It didn't matter. By then we led by forty-two points – and would win by fifty-three.

When the final siren sounded, our supporters roared – a blanket of adulation that fell over the ground. Usually, fans kept wins in context. We'd only beaten the Warrambatta Dingoes, and we did that all the time, even by margins as big as this one.

But maybe now they saw something more.

Mixed Signals

Our fans filled the Ulah'lah – dangerously overfilled it, until they seemed melted together, other than for an array of bobbing heads. As we entered, they roared until we could feel the Ulah'lah shake, and somehow – I have no idea *how* (although later, somebody told me some people spilled into the beer garden, and back out onto the street) – they parted to let us through. Then they patted our backs and tousled our heads, and gestured at the bar, where a long line of beers waited. Then the chanting started again: *'Ulah Curlews! Ulah Curlews! Ulah Curlews!'* You couldn't hear anything else. Sean tried to shout something in my ear, but it was drowned out. The chanting kept going until Percy scrambled up onto a table and held his arms out for silence. Light glimmered off something in his hand – the drinks card.

'Well, well, well!' he said. 'Not a bad effort!'

A cheer rose up and somebody shouted, 'We shit it in!' Then more cheers, until Percy gestured – like the conductor of an orchestra – for some quiet. Almost begrudgingly, the noise ebbed away, until only the general hubbub of conversation and beer being drunk remained.

'We're going to do our best to make this a season to remember!' Percy said, and held his hand up immediately, to stop the cheers before they rose up into a crescendo. 'We're all committed to it!'

In the corner, I saw Matt and some of the others sneer.

'And today was a start!' Percy went on. 'One win, but one to build on! As for this …' He flicked the drinks card in his hand, so it shot out between his thumb and forefinger. 'It's so hard to judge in a game where everybody contributed so positively, but for somebody who offered us highlights of magic and in only his second game, Adam Pride!'

The applause was punctuated by shouts such as, 'On ya, Adam!' and 'Well done, Adam!' from people who didn't know him, but it showed how impressive he was that he got that reaction. He smiled but kept his head low, like he was embarrassed, and weaved his way through the crowd to collect the drinks card, while fans pounded him on the back or thrust out their hands for handshakes. He took the card from Percy, waved it once in acknowledgement, only to have Sean flit past and snatch it from him.

'I'll get those!' he said.

The immediate aftermath was a blur – lots of beer, lots of laughter, lots of spontaneous chants of *'Ulah Curlews!'* I'd never seen anything like it in my short time playing, and couldn't remember anything like it when Dad would come here after games. Then again, maybe it had happened and I'd been too young, or hadn't noticed because the adulation hadn't been aimed at me. But I sat back and basked in it. We never knew what we'd get in any season, but now it felt like we'd learnt to fly.

It was an hour before the crowd began to thin, and another hour before the Ulah'lah reverted to what it would usually be on a Saturday if there'd been no football on: busy, people now out for a meal, or to share a couple of beers and watch the AFL match on TV, or bet on some of the horse and greyhound races. The celebration of our victory was an undercurrent, swallowed into the route of a typical Saturday night in Ulah. As Sean grabbed a tray full of beers, Adam, myself, Percy, Dean, and Harry, sat in a booth, and were finally able to reflect on the game.

'When you get a bit of endurance behind you,' Percy was saying, shaking his head in astonishment, 'man, you're gonna be something.'

'Yeah, I haven't played for a while,' Adam said. 'Tank sorta ran empty there.'

Percy leaned back and folded his hands behind his head. 'See, this is a result of the new training regime.'

'Get your hand off it, Percy,' Sean said as he came back with the beers and slid them onto the table. Then he slumped into the seat next to me. 'We've had two sessions, and most of us felt dead out there!'

'Hey, hey, hey,' Percy said, grabbing a beer, 'it's physical memory. It doesn't matter how many sessions we've had. The training's reminded your bodies what you're capable of.'

'If we played this well feeling only this bad,' Dean said, 'imagine how good we'll be if we get plastered before a game!'

'Hey, hey, hey,' Percy said, 'I'll have none of that.'

'Just gammin', Perce.'

Percy lifted his glass. We all toasted. Light sparkled off the glasses and blazed through the beer golden and bright. Then we settled back and drank. We could've been just like anybody else in here – friends enjoying a social beer – but it now felt like we were something more, something knitted together for a common purpose. Or maybe that was me being romantic.

'So, where'd you live before you came down here, Adam?' Percy asked.

'Western Australia. Opportunities looked good down here so we moved.'

'*We?*' I asked.

'My wife and my son.'

Harry looked up – although twenty-two, Harry already had a wife and two sons. 'You've got a kid?' he asked.

'Yeah,' Adam said.

'How old?' Harry said.

'Four.'

'I've got two boys,' Harry said. 'Four and two. They come down and watch every game. You should bring your family down some time.'

'Wife's not much for the game,' Adam said.

'I'll tell you,' Percy said, 'I've seen good players in my time but that out there today, that was … *freakish*.'

'Ball fell my way,' Adam said.

'Fell your way!' Percy said. 'This was everything: you winning the ball, you escaping opposition, you tackling, kicking—'

'Guess it was one of those things,' Adam said, shifting restlessly. He rubbed at the crater scar on his palm with his thumb. 'But it's a team thing.' He held up his glass for another toast. 'Don't let anybody ever tell you different.'

'To the team,' Percy said, and we toasted again.

While the rest of the guys drank themselves towards oblivion, I tried for moderation. The decision to do so had teased at my mind, growing until it threatened to become a resolution – mostly because of what Amanda had said. What was I doing to make my dream a reality? This was it. I wouldn't drink in the week leading up to a game, and take it easy in these post-match sessions.

Nearing midnight, most of the guys played pool. Percy drew on his authority to name Adam his partner, probably thinking his abilities would translate to another sport. Unfortunately for Percy, Adam was hopeless. I watched for a while and even played a couple of games, partnering Sean to amass a winning streak of one game. After that, I retreated to the bar. Amanda, writing in a notepad, smiled at me. I grew suddenly self-conscious. Did I look okay? Was I going to slur? What if I didn't know what to say? The sad thing is I'm sure these doubts would've hit me even if I hadn't been drinking.

'How many?' Amanda said as she rested her notepad and pen on the bar, and started preparing glasses. This is how predictable we were. Another resolution popped into my head: for every beer I drank, I'd drink a glass of water. It was stupid, but since I'd been drinking it seemed the most logical and magnanimous concession possible.

'A round of beers,' I said, 'and a glass of water.'

'Who's the water for?' Amanda asked, as she poured it.

'Me.'

'You haven't been drinking as much.'

'Trying to cut down,' I said.

'Congratulations on becoming deputy vice-captain, by the way.'

'Thanks.'

As Amanda poured the beers, my eyes fell on her notepad. Amanda's handwriting was a loose scrawl, and one big word caught my attention: 'Curlews'. I twirled the notepad on the bar – carefully, I thought, so Amanda wouldn't notice – and began to read. I *shouldn't* have, because it might've been something private, like a diary, but I did all the same – one of those decisions you make without really thinking about it.

Curlews reap benefits of training?

A new-look Curlews side, missing a number of stalwarts, smashed the Warrambatta Dingoes in a lopsided affair. After the Dingoes got the jump with four early goals, the Curlews wrestled back control, then dominated the game.

It was a disciplined performance from the Curlews, who this week launched a new training regimen to maximise their performance.

'Hey!'

Amanda snatched the notepad back and scowled at me, although mixed in with the anger was hurt. This was her first draft report of the match she'd been asked to write for *The Tribune*.

'Everything okay?' Percy said from where he was lining up his shot on the pool table. Now all eyes were on us.

'Everything's fine,' Amanda said in this flat voice.

She stuffed the notepad under the bar and poured the beers. It should've been left at that, and the other guys went back to their game, but Percy was unblinking, and I felt my heart thump harder than it did when I'd been given the job of minding Rankin. It wasn't that I didn't want to get him off-side – and I didn't – but that I didn't want to disappoint him.

I could've tried to bluff my way through it, but that would've been wrong, and if Amanda wanted to push it, wanted to tell Percy that I'd taken something that didn't belong to me, then I deserved whatever I had coming.

'Amanda?' Percy said.

'Everything's fine, Dad.'

Percy stared at her a moment before returning to pool. Amanda was still filling glasses, then plonked them on the bar so they splattered. I wanted to apologise, but didn't know how, so I picked up the first set of beers and delivered them, then the next set, and the next set – eleven in all, the last, with my glass of water, sitting on the bar waiting for me.

'I'm sorry,' I said finally. 'I was curious.'

'It's okay.' Amanda made change for the money I gave her. 'I overreacted. Everybody will be reading it on Monday. I shouldn't be so self-conscious.'

'I shouldn't have been touching it, no matter what. I'm sorry. Really.'

'It's okay. It's just that I'm ... *worried*.'

I frowned. 'About?'

'What if it's not any good? What if Scott at *The Tribune* tells me he doesn't like it? Or he publishes it and then everybody else laughs at it?'

'I'm sure it's fine. The bit I read sounded great.'

'You would say that.'

'Yeah. Maybe.'

'Haha – very funny. You want to read the rest of it?'

'What?' I sat down on one of the stools at the bar. 'Are you serious?'

'Yeah.' Amanda paused, maybe to convince herself it was what she really wanted. 'It'd be good to get somebody's opinion.'

'Sure.'

She retrieved the notepad – now a bit crumpled – and put it in front of me, smoothing out the pages. 'Tell me if you have trouble with any of my … writing. It can get messy,' she said, but I could swear she was going to say, '*Tell me if you have trouble with any of my words*'.

My jaw clenched. So I was a small-town bumpkin, but so was she. I wasn't stupid. None of us were. Okay, a lot of guys around here only had a primary school level of reading – I'd bummed through school, and missed more and more towards the end as I helped Dad on the farm – but there was more to the world than book smarts.

I almost wanted to find an error, but the first draft was great. She touched on a number of things that went deeper than the game, such as potential and preparation. She wrote that a contributor to Little Reach's success was their preparation, and if we could lift ourselves we'd be able to emulate what we'd shown against Warrambatta on a regular basis.

'It's really good,' I said when I was done, putting down the notepad.

'You're not just saying that? I want you to be honest.'

'No, I mean it,' I said. 'It's spot on. I'm surprised you didn't mention Adam.'

'I was getting around to him. I've still got a bit to go. Thanks, Luke.'

'My pleasure. If you ever want to run anything else by me, just ask. I'm happy, you know, to read anything, or if you wanted to, well, chat—'

'Thanks.'

Her tone was sharp. She grabbed a dish-towel and scrubbed the bar, like she was trying to rub the varnish off it, but I recognised she was making herself busy. I didn't get it. We'd just been okay. I even thought maybe we'd connected again, if not even a bit more than our last conversation, and I'd shown some of my commitment by laying off the drinking. But now she was skittish.

The obvious thing for me to do would've been to excuse myself and re-join the others around the pool table, but I couldn't. Not now. I'd wonder. And I'd worry it to death. That was just me.

I took a drink, tried to catch Amanda's gaze. She made sure I didn't, stacking glasses that were fine where they were. So be it. It was time for the all-or-nothing approach.

'Everything all right?' I asked.

'Everything's okay.'

'Something's happened.'

Amanda stopped cleaning up. 'I've got to tell you something and I don't want you to take this the wrong way.'

'Go on.'

'You're nice, Luke ...' She trailed off.

'I'll try not to take that the wrong way.'

Amanda chuckled. 'No ... I enjoyed talking with you the other week, and I like you – I really do, I like you a lot – and I know you like me, but right now I'm not really looking for a relationship.'

'Okay,' I said.

I rose from my stool and picked up my glass. I wanted to be anywhere but there. And drunk, too – screw my newfound vow to take it easy – so I didn't have to deal with the rejection. All the euphoria from our victory soured into this thin, sickly feeling in the pit of my stomach.

'I still want to be friends, but I'm saying, right now, I've got a lot of stuff going on, so I'm not looking for anything more.'

'It's okay,' I told her. Okay like being hit by a car. 'I'll let you get back to it.'

'You don't …'

You don't have to. A pity offer. But of course I had to. And even she must've realised it. I couldn't keep staying here now that this chasm had opened up between us. We were in the same pub, but we might as well have been standing in different towns.

I went back to the others, their laughter too loud, the light from the bar too bright, the smell of beer too thick. That was a pre-emptive shoot-down. I hadn't even tried to pick her up – well, not really. I'd offered to read her stuff, but that wasn't a pick-up. That was being nice. I lifted my glass to scull it. It would offer some consolation.

I had the glass of water in hand. The beer stood forlorn on the bar. I didn't want to get it. It was too humiliating on so many levels – that I'd forgotten it, and that I'd have to re-approach Amanda after storming off. Nor could I send somebody to get it for me – that would make the misery of my non-existent love-life public.

Amanda glanced at me, but I looked away and downed the water in one gulp. It washed away the taste of beer in my mouth, and I felt the water run cold down my chest and steel my resolve. This was not the place for me. I feigned the biggest yawn I could.

'I might get going,' I said.

'Already?' Sean said.

'Tired.'

I said my goodbyes, and slipped out without looking back.

The Hard Yards

I t started literally with the fluttering corner of a newspaper page.
When *The Tribune* was delivered to the newsagent in neat, orderly stacks, not many people thought any more of it than they would any other week – and it's not like anything different happens around here. *The Tribune* usually is a bunch of feel-good stories about what businesses are doing, how people are going, articles recycled from the newspapers that cover the other towns, and – of course – there's the sport. There's really not a lot else. About five years ago, a small fire broke out in the Ulah'lah's kitchen, and it was news for weeks.

Now, Monday morning, Adrian Granger was doddering past the newsagent, the way he always did on his way to work at the butcher. He usually went straight there. But the corner of the top newspaper fluttered right onto the final scores of our game. Adrian was seventy, and held a club record of 537 games for the Curlews. He didn't retire until he was fifty. He'd followed every game the Curlews had played since. Now he picked up the paper and read it on the way to work, then left it out on the counter. From there, Adeline Tierney – who ran a florist – picked it up and idled through it while she waited for her order of sausages. Wayne Phelps, the local accountant, read it peering over her shoulder, but then grabbed his own copy on the way to work.

While *The Tribune* was well-read, it was also quickly discarded or disassembled to use in the bottom of bird cages. Now, it was everywhere, and everybody was flipping straight to the article about us. I finally saw it when Mum brought the newspaper home with her shopping, and splatted it – already opened – on the kitchen table as I ate my breakfast of Corn Flakes.

'Deputy vice-captain, huh?' she said.

'That's in there?'

'Uh-huh. Congratulations.' Mum kissed the top of my head. 'Why didn't you tell us?'

I shrugged.

'Everybody's reading about the game. Everybody's got their face buried in a newspaper.'

And on and on she went, although I didn't pay any attention, as the title – in this black, bold text – and by-line leaped out at me:

Curlews Soar!
Amanda Hunt

The article expanded on what I'd read in the Ulah'lah, and even challenged whether we were lucky against the Dingoes because they weren't very good, or the beginning of our training regimen was taking us to a new level. It was a real double-handed compliment that had me gritting my teeth. The draft I'd read hadn't been anything but positive. Not so here. Then it went on to talk about Adam and his on-field wizardry, the changeover in personnel and appointments (like my deputy vice-captaincy), and how other players – and I was first amongst a list of other names (all of them young players, like Sean, our star centreman Sam Corchoran, Harry, Nigel, and Dean) – should use his example to realise their own potential.

Tuesday evening at training, there wasn't a lot of talk. Some of the players glared at Percy – Amanda was his daughter, after all, so here he was trying to nurture us to something greater, while his daughter questioned how legitimate we were. But by some indignant, unspoken agreement, we powered through training, and that session became the base on which we built. We didn't run ourselves into the ground like Little Reach did – not that that would've worked since we didn't have years of this sort of preparation to build on – but we ran drills that honed skills, sharpened tactics, and improved on-field structures. It was hard work, but the guys enjoyed it because it made us feel better about ourselves and about our game, and also refuted Amanda's question of whether we were for real.

But I pushed myself further.

The beer I left on the bar was my last for the season. Amanda wanting to be *friends* gave me no reason to go to the Ulah'lah – well, at least not the way I used to. I still did after matches, but I stuck to the water, and never hung around long enough for my resolve to be tested. The guys were surprised by my commitment; even Amanda was, because she'd look at me like she was trying to work out what I was doing. Or maybe she was trying to work out whether I was upset at her or something. I didn't know myself, to be honest.

Mum and Dad also queried me. Dad always had a bottle of beer over dinner and, as soon as I got old enough, he'd pour me a glass. Then it became habit – almost a form of bonding, while everything else (like sitting down and having a normal conversation) disappeared. We'd sit at the kitchen table, Mum would serve dinner, and Dad would pour the beers. It was the way we kept our relationship alive now. One night, I put my hand on top of my glass as he went to fill it.

'What's wrong?' he asked.

'Nothing.'

'You're not having a beer?'

Mum put a pan full of chops on the kitchen table and rested her palm on my forehead. 'Luke, you okay?'

'Mum!' I pushed her wrist away.

'Luke!' Dad said.

'I'm ... off drinking.'

'You're off drinking?'

'I'm off drinking.'

'Why?' Mum said, sitting down. She frowned. 'Do you think you have a problem?'

'I don't have a problem! I want to take footy seriously.'

'You want to take footy seriously?'

'I want to take footy seriously.'

This was the typical echo conversation we had when they couldn't accept something I was telling them. They exchanged a look. I couldn't believe I had to justify myself. Dad still had the bottle of beer ready to pour. He filled his own glass, put the bottle down, and took a chop. And that was it. We ate. In silence.

Since I wasn't going to the Ulah'lah, I had a lot more spare time. At first, I sat in front of the TV, but Mum kept nagging me, asking if I was okay, so then I retreated to my bedroom. I had a whole stack of novels from school I'd never read, and got stuck into those – stuff by Stephen King, then Lee Child, and then even some classic stuff, by Jules Verne and Charles Dickens and Jane Austen. I'd never been much of a reader, but had never really given it a chance. Now, I let myself go and escaped into some fictional world. Once I got into the stories and started to enjoy them, I wondered why it had taken me so long.

One evening, I was lying on my bed reading Stephen King's *Pet Sematary*, when I chanced a look out the window – not much light was left in the day, the sky nothing but a gradient of glowing embers as dark, bulbous clouds gathered. I lay my book face down on my bed, went downstairs, out onto the back doorstep, and stretched. It was going to rain. I knew that. And now it felt like a challenge to take on the weather before it did break.

So I began to jog.

I went through the wheat, shimmying and whistling around me, stalks slapping me like they were encouraging me to get on with it. My breath was loud in my ears – too loud, like I was trapped somewhere dark and had only my fear for company. I doubled my speed and broke out onto the dirt road that lead into the fiery sunset that tapered through Ulah.

A couple of times I stopped, panting, my throat burning, and my ears cold, and I'd walk until I'd caught enough of my breath that I could break back into a canter. By the time I jogged into Ulah – night closing in on me, the sky nothing now but rolling clouds – sweat dripped from me, and my t-shirt and shorts were soaked. Unknowingly – or at least not consciously – I'd made the Ulah'lah my destination, and doubled over outside the front door as the Ulah'lah's cook, Willie McKenna, emptied some scraps into a bin.

Willie was another former premiership player. Forty, his hair had already thinned to a sunburned scalp, he had this big hook nose with a bump in the bridge, and he was a weed who bent whichever way momentum took him, although that could've also been on account of how much he drank. A promising footballer in his twenties, the game had gotten away from him because he enjoyed the post-match festivities too much. He'd found a purpose at the Ulah'lah, though: he was a brilliant chef – well, some of the time. Now I blanched at the sight of him – his clothes hanging from him, and a cigarette dangling from his mouth. He might've been a scarecrow warning me not to go in.

'What's up with you?' he said. 'Death chasing you?'

'Nah …' I knew he was trying to be funny – he had probably already had a few, but I shuddered, then forced myself to straighten. 'Just taking a jog.'

'Don't overdo it.'

Willie dropped his cigarette, squelched it out with his foot, and opened the door. The typical noise of the Ulah'lah – the chatting, the games of pool, the television – clamoured out at me, and I felt desperately like having a beer, although a water would've been better. A water would be perfect. The door closed behind Willie, silencing the noise. I took a step toward opening it, even reached out, but then stopped. What I really wanted was to be out of the dark, to not be alone. It was Willie. *Death chasing you?* I shuddered again. It was a stupid quip, but it got inside me.

I jogged back down the street from the Ulah'lah – it wasn't even a jog, but a quick walk, as my thighs and calves tightened and pain sheared all the way from my hips up into my back. I'd definitely overdone it, and knew I should walk back home, but each step I took thudded heavier into the road, each stride gained speed, until I was sprinting not only from Ulah'lah, but from Willie and his comment, like a spectre hovered over my shoulder, ready to catch me should I slow down. Then I was bolting as the clouds burst and rain tumbled down, Ulah a blur around me, and there was nothing now – no pain, no tiredness, and the apprehension that Willie had kicked off burned like a fuel that powered me.

About a quarter of the way down the dirt road, I fell to my hands and knees into a muddy puddle and dry-retched. I had nothing left to give. But I felt good. My mind was clear, and all my muscles were loose. I walked a quarter of the way home until I'd stopped puffing, then jogged the rest of the way, although I did pause for a couple more breathers.

I fell into a simple pattern from then on: read when I was free, do my chores around the farm, and train. Every weekday, morning and night I'd jog, until that route into Ulah and back became too easy. Then I extended my range, doing laps of blocks in Ulah while I was there. I also exercised – push-ups and sit-ups – as well as repetitions of weights, increasing them weekly by ten. Then there was the everyday stuff. One afternoon I came home to find Dad unloading fertiliser from his truck. Without being asked (which, I have to admit, was a rarity) I joined him, taking sack after sack into the garage, until I was lapping him.

Dad paused, put his hands on his hips, and panted. 'Easy,' he said.

But I kept going, until my shoulders grew sore, my arms trembled, and my back cramped. Dad watched me, halfway between the truck and the shed, shaking his head. Most other times, he would've hollered for my help and now he was there, disapproving. *Parents.* Never satisfied. But I finished the job. From then, I was always by his side, unprompted, whenever hard work needed to be done.

It wasn't long before all this activity showed in my performances. I ran harder and for longer in games; I was stronger when I bustled opponents or when I had to break tackles or split packs. Then catch-cries exploded from the crowd: *'Go, Luke!'* or *'On ya, Miggsy!'* or cheers when I took a mark and countered an opposition attack. My confidence grew, and I backed myself more and more, charging out of defence to counter-attack, or barking orders at teammates to cover opposition.

I'd always been a battler with a bit of talent, but now teammates saw if they improved their off-field application, they'd reap on-field benefits. It started an epidemic that ran through the team. And as we got better, things happened for us. It was like those three quarters we'd played Little Reach where the ball bounced our way. You'd think that kind of luck can't hold, that it *won't* hold, but it did. We couldn't do a thing wrong.

Still, it was nothing compared to Adam.

Each week, the bursts of time he dominated in a game increased until he was owning whole games. But it was more than that. He'd snap goals from impossible angles, kick them from unbelievable distances; he'd take one-handed marks, or screamers where he stood on an opponent's shoulders; whenever the ball fell anywhere near him, it'd be in his hands a moment later, and if he wasn't shuffling and sidestepping through and around opponents, he'd drill the ball to teammates, never missing a target.

The crowds grew to watch him. After matches, the Ulah'lah was flooded – people would not only be shoulder-to-shoulder until they couldn't move, but also shoulder-to-shoulder in the beer garden and out on the street, recounting feats they'd witnessed that very afternoon. The Ulah'lah actually had to put on more staff to deal with them all.

It wasn't contained to Ulah, either, as our neighbours in Warrambatta and Shandeen Bank also came down. It wasn't like they had much else to watch, as the Warrambatta Dingoes and the Shandeen Bank Bunyips were both struggling. So they came to see Adam, until the most amazing thing happened. The Dingoes and Bunyips started winning. Some said they lifted to win their supporters back. Others said we'd inspired them. The whole municipality was changing.

As far as our attendances went, it didn't matter, because people kept coming. They came from Yerombi and Grasstree, from Harwood and Verdune, and even from as far as Mollongong and Piper's Hill. The funny thing was that they didn't come to see Adam perform, but to *fail*. Before the game, strangers scoffed, saying nobody could be as good as they'd heard. After the game, every one of them went home in awe.

That we kept winning also increased the crowds. Given we hadn't won a flag in eighteen years, all but the diehards had become apathetic. Now, people who'd stopped coming, or had never come, were there because we were a chance, and they dragged others with them. Not only that, we even had a little cheer squad. The members had flags and floggers that they waved every time we kicked a goal.

Winning did something for everybody. Ulah had never been anything – just another heap out here amongst the heaps, living in the shadow of the Little Reach aristocracy. Nobody ever questioned it; why would we? But winning made everybody feel like we could do anything, and the prospect of knocking off Little Reach made everybody feel like kings.

That possibility entered our minds after our Round 11 pulverisation of the Harwood Platypuses by sixty-two points. After the match, we sat in the change rooms, heads down, tired, muddy, and quiet. Despite the victory, there still existed that tinge of disbelief. Was this real? Were we lucky? Perhaps flu or gastro or something had run through Harwood, because they'd played like deadbeats. But then I lifted my head. Adam grinned at me. Then Sean looked at me. Other heads came up as each player realised this was the reward for all our hard work, it was like a series of bells that chorused into a single triumphant peal, and it spoke a simple truth: we'd disassembled them. What else were we capable of?

In five weeks, we had our return game against Little Reach. Could we beat them?

Over the next three weeks, we beat the Gully Dragons by thirty-five points, the Piper's Hill Wombats by twenty-six points, and the Yerombi Kangaroos by fifty-three points. With each victory, our confidence and self-belief grew, as did the reality that Little Reach loomed closer and closer. We all relished the possibility of knocking them off, but were also worried they'd shatter our brave new world.

In Round 15 we played the Mollongong Maulers, who'd been in last year's grand final, although Little Reach had thrashed them by thirteen goals. Still, Mollongong were considered the second-best team in the competition. If Little Reach was the powerhouse, Mollongong were the perennial runners-ups. Our match against them was meant to test how good we'd become.

Steady rain that wiped out days at a time had started about three weeks earlier – about a fortnight ahead of schedule for around here. Saturday was cold and the rain relentless, the sort of rain that you get out here that has no respect for people or civilisation, and reminds you that at any moment we could have a flash flood that could wash us all away.

Still, people were everywhere; they stood huddled in coats and under umbrellas; behind them others had arranged stuff to stand on, like crates or pallets. And behind them, people had parked their cars and trucks to stand on their hoods, while others stood on the roofs. It was the biggest crowd I'd seen. There had to be three or four thousand. Sean suggested it was as high as six, but his estimating was worse than mine.

The game was scrappy. We slipped in the wet, fumbled the slimy ball, and were unable to kick it with precision once it grew waterlogged. It became a match where we relied on frenetic pressure, where we kept coming and coming and coming at Mollongong until they made mistakes or coughed up the ball. Skill was impossible. Not for Adam, though. He played like it was dry. The wet, the mud, the rain, it might as well not have existed.

Mum started taking me to games when I was a baby to watch Dad. I'd never seen the Curlews win a flag, but I'd seen them win finals, and I'd seen them achieve amazing underdog wins. Yet, in all that time, the crowd had never been as rapturous as they were when the final siren sounded to signal we'd beaten Mollongong by thirty-five points.

The crowd bounced up and down, arms thrust in the air, cheering, chanting, *'Ulah Curlews! Ulah Curlews!'* The whole town might've been here. The rain hiccoughed, and then quit, like even it had given up in the face of everybody's zeal.

From the time we'd lost to Little Reach in Round 5, we had gone undefeated and jumped to second on the ladder. Mollongong hung in at third, and Warrambatta and Shandeen Bank had slotted into fourth and fifth.

Even though it seemed we were on our way, I couldn't help feeling that it could all come crashing down around us at any moment.

The Day After

Sunday morning, I woke before first light, my room still dark. The only sound was the wind whispering through the wheat outside. I closed my eyes and expected I'd drift off again, but now I didn't feel any tiredness and my mind was clear. It was like everything had been wiped clean, and now I lay here, disembodied, until a worm of unease burrowed in, a sense that something was missing.

I flipped onto my side and thought about what I might've forgotten – my bag at the club, a chore Mum or Dad might've wanted me to do, a door unlocked. As I went on, the list grew more and more outrageous. Outside, the ravens ushered in the morning while I considered other possibilities – maybe I'd done something silly during the game, or at the Ulah'lah afterward, and was feeling remorseful. Nope. Nothing. Finally, as morning bleared murkily through the window, I dragged myself out of bed, determined to get on with the day.

I got dressed and brushed my teeth, unable to shake that feeling. It nagged at me, a sore that wouldn't let me ignore it. Then I went down into the kitchen and fixed myself some cereal. As I ate, Mum came in and put the kettle on. Although she was behind me, I could feel her eyes on me.

'What?' I said.

'The juggernaut rolls on.'

'The juggernaut?'

'That's what everybody's calling the Curlews.'

'Who's everybody?'

'Everybody would be *everybody*, Luke. They're talking about our winning streak and how we smashed Mollongong yesterday.'

'We hardly smashed them, Mum.'

'We usually don't beat Mollongong.'

I shovelled some cereal into my mouth, and mumbled indifference.

'People are saying we could challenge this year,' Mum said.

I didn't know what to say, afraid that if I agreed I might curse it.

'Little Reach this week,' Mum said.

'Yep.'

I finished my cereal and took my empty bowl to the kitchen sink.

'Me and Dad might come watch that one.'

'Really?'

'Don't sound so surprised.'

I stiffened. 'It's just that you and Dad don't come much to matches.'

'It's not easy for your dad.'

'It's just a game.' Once the words tumbled out of my mouth, I knew they were a lie.

'Nobody wants to face growing old, Luke. Even before your dad stopped playing, he was having troubles with his knees, with his back, with his right hip. You saw that, him hobbling around. He had things hurting you didn't even know about. But he pushed himself because of the way it made him feel when he was out there. It's not pleasant facing your own mortality. Especially around here.'

'What do you mean "around here"?'

'If it's not the footy and competitiveness of the game, and the cheers of the crowd, what else is there? Well, at least as far as your dad's concerned.'

I didn't know what to say – she was right. I wanted to make a career of footy, but was it just because I loved playing? Or because I felt Ulah didn't have anything else to offer me?

I must've looked sickly or something, because Mum put a hand out and rubbed me on the arm.

'So, think we're a chance?' she said.

'What?'

'Against Little Reach?'

'I hope.'

'Well, hopefully you have a little more say in it than that.'

'Thanks, Mum.' I kissed her on the cheek and left the house.

Although it'd been flash flood weather yesterday, and it was overcast this morning – clouds that would've looked like a storm to an outsider – there was a balminess in the air that suggested, by noon, it would be blue skies and pushing into the twenties.

I put on a pair of sandals, then searched for Dad – I wasn't sure why. Maybe, after what Mum had told me, it was to connect. But part of me also didn't want to find him, because I wouldn't know how to get into it with him. Since people were talking about our premiership chances this season, maybe we could talk about our last premiership. Back then, the Curlews had been a dour outfit that had ground out wins. Our team today was something else. Certainly not dour, or battlers, or underdogs. That's what Ulah teams usually were. But, with a mixture of relief and disappointment, I didn't find Dad.

I'd never been a walker for fun, but now every Sunday morning I lapped Ulah. It took a couple of hours and loosened muscles that were tight or sore from the game the day before.

Today's walk took a lot longer, though.

Once I'd left the farm, was through the wheat, and onto the long, dirt road that led into town, a ball of dust appeared in the distance – a car. Yep, sure enough, a ute sped by, then skidded to a halt. I jagged my head back. The ute reversed to catch up with me.

'Hey, Luke!'

It was Mick Jacobs, a grizzly old fart with curly hair and a bushranger's beard who'd played footy with Dad – and had played in the last premiership – but had retired ten years ago after injuring his knee and becoming a borderline alcoholic. The knee he recovered from; the drinking took his legs out from under him – another of a series of guys who enjoyed the revelry too much around here.

'Great game yesterday!'

'Thanks, Mick.' I didn't know if that comment was aimed at me or the team.

'What d'ya think about next week?'

'Here's hoping.'

'Hoping? Ha! You'll smash the bastards.'

'We'll do our best.'

'You'll smash the bastards, I tell ya! You'll smash 'em!'

It was the first of a number of encounters: David Ash, the apprentice butcher, was hosing down the outside of his shop. He waved a hand at me, and then shouted how he hoped we'd 'butcher' (trying to be funny, obviously, ol' Dave) Little Reach; Paul Brackie, one of the local constables, stopped me to dissect the game, and discuss ways to beat Little Reach; when I went into the General Store to buy a copy of *The Tribune*, Margie England prattled about Claude Rankin and how his Scorpions were 'gonna get their comeuppance next week'. Wherever I went, people wanted to talk about how we'd crush Little Reach.

It started getting too much, all this hype about the game, and it made me nervous. I didn't want to get this far ahead of myself. I knew it was rude, but I opened my copy of *The Tribune*, and skimmed through it as I walked so I wouldn't make eye contact with anybody. I also wanted to find Amanda's match report on the game. Andy Newman had covered the games in Sunday's copy of *The Tribune* for over thirty-five years, but his reports had grown increasingly generic, saying things like, *It was a tight tussle in this quarter*, or, *The domination was evident for all to see*. Lots of people began to suspect that Andy never watched a full game, and he extrapolated his commentary from the quarter-by-quarter scores.

Amanda did go to the games, and she cited specific passages of play, talked about strategies, and highlighted players. That she had direct access to the coach and whatever he had to say rounded out her reports. She'd gone from pieces one-fifth of the page in the Monday edition to half-page articles, to taking Andy's spot in the Sunday paper with stories three-quarters of the page. Although she'd questioned our legitimacy initially, she'd gone on to talk about how our continuing improvement and consistency was a testament to our newfound dedication and professionalism. She regularly talked about Adam and his brilliance, but also me as a leader in the new era of the team. The praise should've felt good, but it fell into that chasm that now existed between us.

Now, as I opened *The Tribune* to the sports, I stopped. The headline that dominated the page in big black letters was:

March to the Flag?
Amanda Hunt

Underneath it was a picture of me, muddy, face contorted into a grimace as I took a mark in a pack.

The article – a full-page article now – detailed how we comprehensively outplayed Mollongong from the outset, despite the terrible conditions, and we now shaped as a genuine premiership contender. Our biggest test would come this week, against Little Reach, which would show how far we'd come, and also highlight what else we might need to work on.

That's when it finally clicked to me what was bothering me, although it had been hitting me in the face the whole morning: from the day we'd beaten Harwood – a month ago – we knew the test would be playing Little Reach again. But there'd always been another game – Gully, Piper's Hill, Yerombi, and Mollongong. Now there was nothing but us and Little Reach.

It was time to find out how genuine we were. If Little Reach had a specialty, it was pulverising contenders. No, wait. They pulverised *everybody*. But when they identified a threat – especially an improving team – it became a vendetta for Little Reach to obliterate them.

What if we weren't up to it?

Of course, we were on a curve; we were always improving, but I worried that if Little Reach shattered our confidence, we wouldn't be able to put it back together again. Our team was younger now. A lot of the guys hadn't been around long enough to learn to deal with setbacks, me included.

'Luke!'

It was Sean, with Dean and Nigel, sitting at one of the Ulah'lah's outdoor tables, empty plates in front of them, so they'd probably had an early lunch. Each had a beer. Six other empty glasses were stacked in two teetering columns of three in the middle of the table. I crossed the road and joined them, wondering if they had the same fears. Probably not. They rode our success without contemplating a wipe-out – I bet most people did.

'You want a beer?' Sean asked.

The smell of it coming from them and their glasses made me gag – it's one of those smells that's not pleasant when you're not drinking yourself. I tried not to show my distaste, and even felt a bit annoyed at being so full of myself.

'No,' I said.

'Sure?'

'Uh-huh.'

'This day's been so sweet,' Dean said.

'Why?'

'Beers,' Nigel said, toasting his beer, 'on the house.'

'Robby Allen wanted my autograph,' Dean said. Robby was the captain of the Under 12s.

Sean leaned across the table. 'We're like celebrities around here,' he said. 'Bet this is what it's like for the Scorpions, for Rankin, that bastard.'

'Don't get carried away,' I said. 'We haven't done anything yet.'

'What d'ya mean we haven't done anything?' Sean said. 'We're second. And look at the team we've got. Have you ever seen anybody better than Adam?'

Nigel snorted into his glass. 'He's unnatural.'

'Unnatural?' I said.

'You know what I mean,' Nigel said. 'Guy's staunch.'

'There's you, too,' Sean said.

'Me?'

'Come on, Luke, you know how good you're getting. We're all getting better. People are saying we're the best Curlews team since our premiership team, if not better.'

'But they got the job done,' I said. 'We've still got to get past Little Reach.'

'Reach-smeech,' Nigel said.

'Little Smeech,' Dean said.

'Just saying,' I said, but the problem here wasn't what I was saying, but they'd had a few and were in the slipstream of beer-talk and all the enthusiasm that generated. Like everybody boasting to me before about how we'd smash Little Reach, it made me nervous. 'I'm gonna get going.'

'You just got here,' Sean said.

'Gonna help my dad.'

I got up from my chair as the door to the Ulah'lah opened and Amanda emerged with a tray of beers. She must've anticipated the improvement in the weather, as she was wearing a pair of cut-offs, a singlet, and over that a shirt tied at the midriff. Our eyes met, and it looked like she was going to say hello or smile or something.

'I'll see you guys, huh,' I said, crossing the road.

Amanda was another issue entirely. I hadn't spoken to her since the pre-emptive rundown. Of course, after I'd given up drinking, that meant I didn't hang around the Ulah'lah much (and when I did, I never bought beer), and if I wasn't around the Ulah'lah, there wasn't much opportunity to talk to her. We also had that chasm between us now, although I probably widened it more in my head than it actually was.

By the time I got home, I wanted to do some weights, but I didn't get a chance. The weights were in the shed, and Dad was in there stacking a shipment of timber he'd bought ages ago. He'd wanted to put up a new fence as the old one was wobbling, especially when it poured, but he only ever found time to move and re-stack the timber from one side of the shed to the other.

I thought about what Mum had told me and tried to find the words. Memories flew through my mind – when, as a kid, I used to go watch Dad play, and after the match he'd stay out on the ground in his kit and have a kick of the football with me until it got too dark to see. Then he'd go to the Ulah'lah, and I'd go home and dream about when I'd be old enough to play. When I did start playing for the Under 12s, we didn't kick around the ball as much – I was growing independent, and he seemed happier to hang with the team. Still, as I got older, Mum would send me to grab Dad from the Ulah'lah. He'd invite me to sit with him and some of the other players, and I'd listen to them as they'd discuss the game. Sometimes they'd ask my opinion, and Dad would sneak me a sip of his beer. But those things happened less and less as I grew into my teens and hung around with my own friends. Looking back (and taking into account what Mum had said) I see now Dad was struggling with injuries and pain, and realising it was all coming to an end for him, so maybe it all wasn't as enjoyable as it should've been – another reason we drifted apart.

Dad finally noticed me standing there in the doorway, my shadow long and thin over the floor of the shed. His chest heaved as he nodded to me – that was all, a nod to acknowledge me. I forced my mouth open, and wanted to ask some question that could lead into the sort of conversations we used to have, but nothing came, and the next time Dad picked up a piece of timber, I grabbed it by the end to help him. He smiled at me this tight, pained smile, and then I had nothing to say.

For the next couple of hours, Dad and I stacked the timber, finding some partnership in this menial, if not meaningless labour. Maybe I was trying to find something that wasn't there, that couldn't be there again. We might've grown in different directions. It happens, and isn't anybody's fault.

About mid-afternoon, we were done, both of us covered in sweat, facing one another in the shed; Dad a prematurely antiquated version of me, me maybe what Dad must've once been, full of hopes and dreams and a whole lifetime to try and accomplish them.

Little Reach next week, huh? Dad might've asked.

Yep.

You might be a chance. From what I've heard, you guys have improved. And that Adam, the things I've heard about him; is he as good as they say?

Probably better, Dad.

Hear you're becoming quite the player yourself.

I don't know — I guess.

You guess? You should hear the way people talk.

Really?

Yup. You should be proud. I am.

Mum says you might come watch?

Of course we will.

That should've been how the conversation went, but there was only one word spoken.

'Thanks,' Dad said.

He left the shed and I went into the house and showered.

The Scorpions

The siren – long and sharp and relentless – punctured my thoughts, and I lowered my gaze to see the football ground unfold before me. Rankin jostled my arm and tugged at the hem of my jumper. The rest of Little Reach's forward line was exactly that – a line that extended straight behind me: one of their half-forwards, Jason Mason, stood five metres behind us; their next half-forward, Shane Rudd, behind him; and on it went, up to Murray Verne and Sean, at the top of the goal-square. We could've been playing leapfrog. Once the ball was bounced, they'd most likely spread and try to disorganise us. You had to give it to Rankin: he was a tactician.

The biggest surprise was Daniel Schwartzer, who'd been assigned the unenviable task of tagging Adam. Schwartzer was an average player who could bob up and do something useful now and again, but was otherwise better known as an enforcer because of his size. It was surprising that, in Rankin's totalitarian regime, Schwartzer hadn't been replaced by somebody younger and better – better Scorpions *had* been replaced over the years. But here he was, bumping shoulders with Adam. Schwartzer would most likely blanket Adam, and not worry about trying to get the ball himself. Little Reach had hamstrung themselves a player in their midfield, but I guess it would be worth it if they could keep Adam quiet.

The crowd – bigger than it had been for Mollongong, bigger than I had ever seen it – hushed. Now it got into my head: this was not only our biggest test (and far and away the biggest test of my young career), but I was being watched by more people than I'd ever played in front of. All of Ulah had to be here, and many of Little Reach's fans had trucked over to lend their presence. I wanted to be at my best, even closed my eyes and tried to will it on myself, but now the doubts began to creep in, cracks in my façade that the quiet magnified.

The siren blared again, this time to signal the commencement of the match, but the roar of the crowd swallowed it up until that was all you could hear. The umpire – Ozzie Rowan again, who got a lot of Little Reach's games (probably because he was confident enough to handle them) – lifted the ball into the air, positioned it between both his hands, then bounced it.

Rankin exploded from the mark; his right elbow slingshot into my midriff. The breath burst from my lungs. Rankin fired towards Adam and crashed into his back. Adam crumpled shapelessly, like Rankin had knocked the very skeleton from his body. The Little Reach contingent of the crowd popped. Before I had a chance to react, pain shattered my own back and everything went dark as my shoulder thudded into the ground. I rolled onto my belly, like I was preparing to do push-ups. The jeering crowd reoriented me. Adam lay on his back, arms outstretched. Rankin lauded over him like a boxer celebrating a knockout.

'Stay down, you dog,' Rankin said.

Rankin spun, and spiked the heel of his boot into the palm of Adam's right hand – I have no idea how a bone didn't break. Adam's face contorted, but he made no sound. I would've squealed. Then Rankin was gone and Adam glared at me, clenched a fist, then staggered up to his feet like he was rising up from his grave.

I came up even slower, swaying, knees feeling like they might buckle. Everything seesawed; my back felt broken in two, and I struggled to catch my breath. Jason Mason shoved me as he strolled past. He must've been the one who ran into me, like Rankin had done with Adam.

'Hey, champ,' Mason said.

The crowd still hooted. It wasn't just Adam and me struggling: Sean at full-back, Nigel in the centre, Dean on the wing, and Percy at centre half-forward – they all teetered. They must've all been flattened like Adam and I were.

Punctuating the booing was a roar – the Little Reach faithful cheered as the Scorpions kicked a goal. From the bounce, Ken Kotz had palmed the ball to Terry Bell who'd streamed from the centre, downfield, and into an open goal. With me, Adam, and Sean floored and the other defenders running around aimlessly trying to cover everybody, he'd had no opposition.

The crowd's animosity shook the ground until I thought it might shear in two and swallow us all up. This was going to get violent. Something would spark. It wasn't going to take much, especially given what had happened. The Little Reach fans would get cocky, somebody would take offence, and there'd be a fight. Or, as Little Reach got on top, our supporters would erupt.

As Little Reach got on top.

Funny the way that assumption jumped into my head. Just like that. We'd beaten everybody up until this game, but Little Reach was the benchmark. They were showing us what it took to be winners, and some of our guys didn't like it.

Rankin ran up to me and prodded his shoulder into my chest. I fell back. Time slowed for an instant. I'd put so much work into improving my game and taken such pride in how far I'd come. That Little Reach could come to Ulah and treat us like this, that Rankin – who'd orchestrated the barbarity – could have the audacity to put me down again, incensed me.

My butt hit the ground, but I shot back to my feet. I clawed the scruff of Rankin's jumper and swung him. He became weightless in my hands. I swung him again, not seeing, not knowing, just acting, then let him go. He flew through the air and hit the ground, rolling. The crowd's booing transformed into elation. Somebody shouted, *'On ya, Miggsy!'* Then somebody had me around the neck – big muscly arms that reeked of antiperspirant. I flailed to get away from the smell as much as anything else. The headlock broke; Sean had sprinted in to wrestle off my assailant – Schwartzer.

Ozzie scuttled up to me like an errant crab. 'Free against you, Luke, to Claude!' he said. 'Unduly rough play! Fifty metre penalty against Sean for remonstrating. Claude!' Then he whizzed up to the goal square, to set Rankin's free-kick.

Rankin pulled himself up and followed Ozzie. Schwartzer disentangled himself from Sean and ruffled my hair. This prompted a number of Little Reach players to follow his lead, or to bump me. Sean and I shoved them away. Some of our teammates scurried in and wrestled opposition, although it was more like they wanted to be seen doing something rather than out of any real belligerence or defence. The Little Reach fans taunted me. Somebody mocked the earlier cry, *'On ya, Miggsy!'* Then somebody else screamed, *'You're a dud, Miggsy!'* Laughter followed. And then, swallowing it, our fans booed Little Reach.

Percy ran up to me, patted me on the belly. 'You okay?'

I nodded, not trusting myself to speak.

'Stand tall,' he said. 'Remember, other players are looking to you as an example.' Then he ran back to his position.

Rankin kicked the goal and jogged back to me as I scanned the crowd. The first people I saw were Matt and his friends, red-faced and leaning over the railing to rave at the closest Scorpions. The rest of our supporters hadn't stopped booing, and you could pick out snippets of individual catchcries. People insulted Rankin, derided Little Reach, and then a woman's voice, clear and almost singing, shouted, *'C'mon, Luke!'* The blonde hair was like the sparkle of gold amongst the faces – Amanda. I didn't have long to think about it, though: Rankin bumped into me – not too hard, just to let me know he was back. He gloated, this big ruddy face, those narrow eyes slits that might've been depthless.

'There was the one I owed you,' he said.

I stretched my arms. My back, chest, and right shoulder were all sore, but they hardly registered. My anger overrode everything. We had to refocus. Some of our guys had heads bowed, like they'd decided this was going to be too hard, and the price to be competitive too much to pay. Others smouldered; you could see it in the stiffness of their gait; the way they tilted their heads and stretched their necks, like they were preparing for a fight.

Nobody was here for football.

And, like that, we were broken.

I want to say Little Reach kept up the dirtiness, but they didn't. Oh, they played physical – bumped us where possible, slung us with tackles, collided with us in contests, but it was all fair from that point. They let their football – which was fast, crisp, and precise – do the talking.

Our players were no longer a team, but individuals in the same jumper. A few tried to take it back up to Little Reach. Even little Ronnie bumped Schwartzer only to bounce right off him. A few times I tried to hit Rankin hard in contests, but twice gave away frees that resulted in goals. Both times I vowed not to do it again, but that anger still raged inside me and I couldn't get my mind back on the game, couldn't get it back on Rankin as my opponent.

Little Reach steadily built their lead, and with each goal they swarmed the goal-kicker and celebrated so outrageously and so long that in the centre of the ground Ozzie had to wait until they'd gotten back into position before he could bounce the ball. Our fans booed them, but the more they booed, the bigger the celebrations became, until the fans – that little contingent of Matt and his friends all relentlessly hurling insults aside – shut up because they couldn't bear it anymore. Just like that, the crowd went out of it. The expectation burst. That belligerent optimism we'd been hearing all week vanished. The silence became condemning. This is how easy it was to be cast back into obscurity. And that's when the Little Reach faithful let us know it. They hooted us and mocked us and singled us out for condemnation every time we messed up. Then their chant began, that slow, mournful *'Scor-pee-ons!'*

If not for Adam, Little Reach's lead would've been greater than the fifty-five points it was with only minutes remaining in the second quarter. As usual, he was everywhere. The only problem was that none of us were coming along for the ride. Adam would steal the ball from packs and fire it out, only for somebody to fumble it; he'd take a mark in defence and kick long, only for somebody to drop it; he'd tackle opponent after opponent, until their sheer weight of numbers won the ball away and he was left spent, on his knees. The only time he succeeded was when he did it himself, pirouetting from congestion, running clear and kicking long or, sometimes, truly at goal. More often than not, he was gang-tackled and ridden into the ground. Then other Scorpions would pile on top of him, or some of them would dive in knees-first. They were making Adam earn his possessions. But when the bodies cleared, Adam would get up, sore, exhausted, and battered, but still unbeaten.

Close to half-time, Terry Bell kicked a ripper torpedo from Little Reach's centre half-back position. Rankin and I misjudged it as the ball spiralled over our heads. Sean and Murray Verne attacked the ball. Sean soccered it on the half-volley, but it went straight to Jason Mason. Mason sidestepped one player, dummied another, then snapped the ball through. The celebrations came again, only this time Mason gave our fans the finger.

The Little Reach fans roared. The sound was amazing. There had to be at least a thousand of them who'd made the trip up for the game, but it sounded like so much more. And it showed the way they thought – even though their team was smashing us, here is where they took the most joy, in this single, puerile gesture. Most of them also stuck their finger up at us. Only Matt dared retaliate; he jumped the railing and sprinted for Mason, but Paul Brackie and another constable immediately wrestled him down, then dragged him off to the laughs of not only the Little Reach faithful, but the Scorpions players.

'You're pretenders, Curlews!' somebody called out. I don't know if it was one of Little Reach's fans or one of ours. Given there was no response, I guess everybody was in agreement. Ozzie bounced the ball and again the Scorpions won it away, Schwartzer – no less – snapping it out of the pack high into the air. Rankin and I ran for it but the siren sounded. I marked the ball as Rankin slowed down. He rubbed the back of my head.

'At least you know what it feels like now,' he said.

The Scorpions converged on the middle of the ground, gathering around Rankin, and then they moved off in a tight huddle with military precision to the applause of their fans. Percy waved his finger in a circle like he was trying to gesture us in, but the only one who went to him was Adam, and then me belatedly, while everybody else drifted off the ground, defeated.

Just Not Football

We dribbled into our change rooms. Some of the guys slumped onto benches, heads in their hands; others lay down on the benches, their arms dangling; a few sat on the floor, with their backs to the wall. Only Percy remained standing, although he paced back and forth, back and forth, back and forth, like each time he was trying to summon the words to encourage us, or to rationalise what had happened, to assure us that it wasn't as bad as it seemed. Finally, he stopped by the lockers. Now the silence wasn't just silence. It was a prison. To have come this far, and to be shown up like this – our failure trapped us in a reality that we couldn't escape. And another half remained to be played.

Percy punched the door of a locker. He scraped his knuckles and dented the locker door, and the crash of the impact startled everybody, although gazes that came up went straight back down. Nobody wanted to face Percy either – not because we were afraid, but because we'd disappointed him.

'Right!' he said, striding up to us. 'Who wants to go down like this?'

Nobody said a thing.

'Well?'

'What're you talking about?' Dean said.

'They came to bully us. That's exactly what they've done!'

'Game's over, Perce,' Nigel said.

'You know what? I don't care. I *really* don't.'

'Deadly,' Nigel said, which was his way of saying, *Cool.* 'I don't think we do either.'

'What do you mean you don't?' Percy said. 'How can you say that? What's the point of going back out there?' He tugged on Nigel's collar. 'Or wearing this? What's the point of it all?'

'What do you want us to say, Perce?' Nigel said. 'What do you want any of us to say? They're too good.'

I'm sure everybody had been thinking it – the margin didn't lie. But now that somebody had said it, it became an unavoidable truth.

The anger seethed inside me – not that we were getting pulverised. I could live with that if we'd tried. But somewhere, we'd forgotten to do that – at least the way we'd been trying in the last couple of months.

'So, we can't win?' Percy said. 'Is that it?'

'No,' I said.

'See?' Nigel said.

'No.' I looked up, breath short and sharp. 'I mean … I hate this. I hate that they've come here and done this to us. That we've stopped playing our game. They're killing us because we're not doing what brought us here.'

'That's right!' Percy said. 'They came, they rattled our cages, and we couldn't cope. The first couple of minutes aside, they've played football, and we've heard footsteps. Is this the way we're gonna go down?'

'It's ten goals, Perce!' Sean said.

'I don't care! How many times do you want me to say it? *I don't care about losing this game.* I want to take these bastards on. We lose, we lose. But at least we do it standing. If we let them do this to us, if we let them beat us this way, that's it – they'll always hold it over us. And we'll never get any better than we are. They'll show us up to be pretenders. Is that what we want?'

Even Nigel didn't quip.

'I want to be better than that,' Percy said.

The challenge hung in the air. It was an impossibility. Teams didn't come back from ten goals down – well, not against Little Reach. But I could see some of the players wanted to believe. They didn't want to go down like this either, bullied into submission.

'Come on, guys!' Adam said. 'It's like Percy said – we don't have to win! We just have to try. Let's take the fight to them!'

'That's right!' Percy said. 'Let's take the fight to them by playing the game we've developed. Let's show Little Reach they might've surprised us, they might've shaken us up, but now we're drawing a line, which they're no longer crossing! Let's bloody their nose and show them where we've come from, and how good we can be!'

'Let's do this, guys!' Adam said.

'Yeah!' I jumped to my feet.

Others followed: Ronnie, Harry, Sam Corcoran – who was usually as stoic a guy as you could know – then Sean, Nigel, Dean. Heads lifted. Players glowered at one another. They revved one another up. They roared and shrieked and howled.

We sprinted from the rooms before the siren had gone, and jogged around the ground to warm up. Our fans were quiet – at least those who'd stayed; a few spots looked sparse, so people had gone home early. No such luck with the Little Reach faithful. They hooted us and booed us then chanted, *Curlews suck!* Clap-clap-clap. *Curlews suck!* Clap-clap-clap.

'Listen to that,' Percy said. 'You listen to that and you remember the best way to shut them up is to show them we're not going to be bowed.'

The siren went and Little Reach cantered out of their rooms – some of their guys even strolled out, like they were heading out for a social kick. A few of them joked and laughed. Rankin scowled at them and they shut up, but I got the feeling they'd cashed their lead in as a victory. They had every right to, but the sight of them so relaxed made me angrier.

When we lined up back in position, I ran my hands through the grass, then planted my feet. Rankin bumped my shoulder on the way past and I shoved him. He frowned at me, and I glared at him – there must've been something unsettling about it because he turned away quick, and Rankin usually didn't turn away from anything.

Ozzie bounced the ball so it sailed straight and high into the air. Kotz soared – knee first – into Harry's chest and tapped the ball in Schwartzer's direction. Terry Bell burst in from the wing. Schwartzer's hands cupped for the ball. Adam's hand snaked out. Bell, low, pitched his shoulder. Adam rode Bell's bump, poised and balanced as ever. Schwartzer and two of the other Little Reach players – Andrew Close and Barry Deck – swallowed Adam up but then, as if time stopped for everybody but Adam, Adam sidestepped. The three would-be tacklers collided into one another. Adam banana kicked a low pass to Ronnie. Ronnie – being scragged by his opponent – thrust his open hands at the ball and palmed it, like a volleyball tap. Running past, Adam caught the ball, steadied as the crowd hushed, and kicked. The ball never got higher than a couple of metres off the ground, a blur as it spun. When it went through for a goal, our fans roared as we reminded them what we were capable of, and in hearing their response they reminded us what we were striving for.

'It's just a goal!' Rankin shouted as everybody jogged back into position. He clapped his hands together. 'Let's get it back!'

Harry won the next tap-out, which went straight to Adam. He tried to snap it out of a pack, but Bell smothered it. Sam recovered the ball, but was tackled by Kotz. The ball flew into the hands of Close, who kicked long towards us.

I didn't premeditate what happened next. If I'd tried, I probably would've screwed it up. I leaped, flying through the air until my knees poised on Rankin's shoulders and hands reached for the ball. The crowd screamed. Not cheered. But *screamed*. Everything began to slow down. The one thought that shot through my mind was I was so high up, I didn't know how I was going to come down.

The ball stuck to my hands. I landed on my feet and rolled to absorb the impact. The fans applauded now. Not a single Little Reach fan shouted out anything – they had no right to, but I thought they might anyway.

I sprang to my feet and watched the play unfold in front of me, players streaming in all directions. I kicked the ball long to Sam, running towards half-forward. He marked, handballed to Adam. Adam dummied around one opponent, spun, straightened up and kicked another long, long goal.

The crowd roared again, but now it wasn't exultation but a belief that lifted us. Our players stood taller. A swagger returned to our step. Whatever enthusiasm Percy had ignited could've easily fizzled out if we didn't back it up with some results, but here they were. Around us, Little Reach players looked at one another, or to Rankin. Their lead was still huge, but this wasn't the way it was meant to be: we might've only gotten two goals, but in their view there shouldn't be any resistance left whatsoever.

It began with Adam winning the ball in the middle. Then others got on top: Harry in the ruck, Dean and Sam in the middle, Percy and Ronnie up-forward. The few times Little Reach launched counter-attacks, Sean and me thumped the ball away or took intercepting marks. Everybody began winning their positions. Confidence refilled us, connected us, drove us.

It also set the tone for Adam's feats. If he'd been good in the first half, he was awesome in the second. He won the ball, snatching it out from before the eyes of his opponents; he evaded tackles while opponents' fingers brushed at the back of his jumper; he sprinted away from hapless pursuers; he nailed teammates with pinpoint passes; and he kicked goals that you knew were goals the minute the ball left his boot.

Little Reach floundered. Their players argued about who their opponents were, or where they should be. Others fumbled. A handful even came in late with head-high spoils. Their history, their reputation, the way they'd bullied us in the opening minutes, didn't matter. Who they were disappeared. Now, they were like Mollongong, or Baden Creek, or whoever – just another footy team, and that's exactly how we treated them.

We whittled away their lead in that third quarter from sixty-one points to twenty-eight. I must've taken ten marks to repel every counter-attack they launched. What I missed, Sean mopped up. But it was Adam who was unstoppable. He had a hand in everything.

At the three-quarter-time break, Rankin sat his players down on the wing and hollered at them. He paced back and forth, his face red, veins pulsing in his temple and neck. I couldn't make out what he was saying, but I could guess. In comparison, Percy huddled us in a ring around him, and his voice was quiet, so we had to lean in to hear him.

'You know what this game's become about?' he said. '*Not* the win. It's about the *next* goal. That's it. We get the *next* goal. Then once we get that, you know what comes next?'

'The next goal!' Nigel said.

'Right! You keep focused on that next goal, no matter what!'

The siren went and we sprinted back into position. The Little Reach players came slow, bodies tense, jaws set, eyes blazing, automatons who'd been set to destroy. Rankin planted his hand in my chest and thrust. I fell back a step and pushed him back. He sneered at me and grabbed my collar and yanked me to him. Other players ran in from both sides and for about the next thirty seconds, we wrestled one another. The siren sounded, and other players ran in and tried to drag their teammates clear.

'Get back into position!' Percy shouted.

But on and on it went: things would begin to settle, and then another skirmish would break out. The crowd jeered. I ran in to break up a wrestle between Sean and Murray Verne. Rankin grabbed me by the back collar and wrenched me to the ground.

I bounced straight up but Percy intercepted me and pushed me away. Then Ozzie bolted in and blew his whistle.

'Free kick!' he said. 'Against you, Claude, for instigating. To you, Luke!' He tossed the ball to me.

'Run!' Percy said, sprinting towards the wing. 'Luke! Luke!'

I kicked the ball out in front of him, teammates breaking to flank him. The melee evaporated as Scorpions had to chase their opponents. Percy handballed the ball to Nigel, who handballed it to Dean, who handballed it to Sam. He kicked it long to Ronnie, who marked, all alone in our forward line. Ronnie spun and snapped the ball through, and then did something he'd never done in his whole career: he danced, knees wobbling, both index fingers jabbing the air.

The goal focused us – here was the job we had to do. But we should've guessed what was coming: Nigel went down first, a late spoil from Verne became a roundhouse – and that was one of their more subtle attempts. Verne was reported, but that didn't do Nigel any good as he was helped from the ground.

Next, Little Reach's full-back, Todd Bakker, cannoned knees-first into Ronnie's back as Ronnie went for a chest mark. Ronnie's face spiked into the grass, and it was minutes before he got back up. He went off, but had to come back on when we ran out of able-bodied players.

I was next: Schwartzer kneed me in the bridge of my nose as I dived on the ball to lock up play. An awful crack echoed in my head, although there was no pain. Something wet coated my face. Sean told me I was bleeding. I put a hand to my nose, and there it was: blood all over my fingers. Percy urged me to the boundary and I staggered off, where somebody threw me a towel to stem the flow. Despite my complaints, I was kept off as a precaution against concussion.

Several other guys went down one way or another – Harry, Dean, Sam, our wingman Ben Jones, and our other half-forward Michael McMasters. In total, eight guys from Little Reach were reported.

'Hurt them on the scoreboard!' Percy said.

He ran around calming players, repeating this over and over. But as his charges fell around him, he began to throw his weight around, bumping into Scorpions, and slinging them when tackling them. He became a force that even most of the Scorpions didn't want to confront – *most*. After Percy sprayed a shot at goal and kicked it out of bounds, Schwartzer ran up to him, grabbed his collar, shook him and laughed at him. Then Percy punched him – a hook that shot up from his hip. Schwartzer went limp where he stood, then fell. Percy shook his hand. It was the hand he'd used to punch the locker – if he hadn't damaged it then, it definitely looked like he had now, with his ring finger jutting out at a weird angle.

A melee erupted, with Scorpions running in to grapple Percy, then our guys charging in to help. It was mostly wrestling, and it was amazing it didn't get any uglier – maybe thanks to Ozzie. Since Percy had kicked the ball out on the full, Ozzie insisted the Scorpions take the free kick. But since the wrestling continued, he declared the time had elapsed for the free kick, and he ordered the boundary umpire to throw the ball back in. The melee continued to spill across the ground – except for Ronnie, who ducked out, picked up the throw in, ran in and kicked the goal. Then he did his little dance as Rankin complained about the ball being thrown in when nobody else was ready. Ozzie penalised Rankin for complaining with a free kick in the centre. That finally broke up the fracas and shut up any arguments, players hurrying back to position, but the Scorpions were rattled now – everything seemed to be going against them.

We came at them, although slower, almost begrudgingly, while they'd given up all pretence of playing football. With just under ten minutes to go, we'd reduced their lead to eight points. Ronnie, now at centre half-forward in Percy's absence, marked when Adam cleared it from the centre with a snap, played on, dodged two opponents, and drilled a goal. Again, he danced as teammates converged on him.

Somebody ran on the field – a drunken Little Reach fan who scampered up to Adam. Adam thrust out a hand to keep him at bay. The drunk tried to grab Adam's hand, but Adam sidestepped him. The drunk face-planted the grass, tried to get back up, then stumbled again. Then Constable Brackie was there, seizing him by the arms and dragging him off.

'*Watch what you're doing, you black bastard!*' somebody shouted.

Then the Little Reach faithful booed, a single uninterrupted note, like Adam was the one in the wrong. Ronnie ran up to Adam and patted him on the back and offered him some words of encouragement. Adam nodded, then loped back to the centre. He rubbed his hands as the abuse continued – abuse that grew vitriolic as Ronnie, jogging back into position himself, surreptitiously gave them the finger, holding it low, next to his stomach. Ozzie exchanged a look with Adam. Adam nodded. Ozzie lifted the ball.

The next bounce brought all eyes back to the football. Adam snapped another clearance. Ronnie marked on his chest, but his opponent came in late, and in the act of trying to spoil the ball whacked Ronnie in the head. Ronnie fell to his knees, one hand clutched to his face – if he hadn't been injured before, surely he was now. Adam ran towards him, possibly to check on him, but then Ronnie sat up and handballed. Adam never broke his stride. He took the ball and kicked long and true for another goal, then cantered past the pocket of Little Reach fans, holding out his hands like an airplane. They hated that and hissed and screeched, but they hated more that they were down.

We were four points up.

Then the adulation of our fans smothered them. There could've been tens of thousands of people there. The areas that had been sparse now bloomed again. Somebody took up the chant: '*Ulah Curlews! Ulah Curlews!*' Then everybody was chanting – even us seated on the bench. It was like a tribal drumbeat that pumped through every body and every heart.

Kotz thumped the next bounce all the way to centre half-back. Rankin scooped up the ball. His opponent now was Sam, who had to pinch-hit in my absence. He slung himself at Rankin, locked onto his hips and dragged Rankin down to his knees. Rankin fired out the handball – although it looked more like a throw – to Bell, who speared a pass to Verne. Sean spoiled Verne's attempt to mark, but the ball rolled to Mason, who picked it up and snapped a goal.

The chant died. I don't know that the response of the Little Reach faithful was so much a cheer, but a chorus of people all screaming their individual derision – a cacophony of hate and anger that was frightening in its hostility. They couldn't even celebrate properly, and instead reduced it to something personal and violent.

Percy sprang to his feet. 'There's time! There's time!' he called.

The ball remained locked in the middle of the ground for the next several minutes as Little Reach players dived on it time and time again. Then Kotz managed another thump. Bell kicked the ball off the ground. It flew over Rankin's and Sam's heads and towards Murray and Sean. Murray gathered up the ball and tried to sidestep Sean, who tackled him to his knees. The ball trickled loose. It should've been a free, and our fans chorused, 'Ball!' but instead, the umpires let the play go on. Mason picked it up and was tackled. Another chant of, 'Ball!' The ball spilled to Shane Rudd, who tried to snap. Sam smothered and Sean ran in to pick it up. Rankin cannoned into him, and the ball bounced away. Schwartzer – stumbling around, his head bandaged up – was lucky enough for it to fall into his hands. He snapped a goal, then ran towards the boundary, arms thrown up. He slid on his knees – the way a soccer player might after he's kicked a goal. His teammates swamped him. You could feel the hope deflate. We had nothing left.

Little Reach kicked three more quick goals after that: another to Mason, where he roved a contest between Rankin and Sam; one to Verne, who marked on the lead; and the final one to Rankin from a mark, the deficit now blowing out to twenty-six points.

When the final siren went, one of our fans jumped the railing – none other than Matt. I have no idea how he was free – maybe when they'd grabbed him earlier, they'd only given a warning. But now he raced for Rankin. Other fans jumped or darted under the railing and followed him. Some of the Scorpions gathered around Rankin, while others dashed for the rooms. Wrestling broke out. Then punches. Then the cops came to try to pull everybody apart. Other cops formed an escort around Rankin – I didn't even recognise half of them; somebody must've called them in from other towns because things had started to look so ugly.

We gathered around our bench; Percy, his face mottled, moved to and fro amongst us, patting players on the back with his good hand, and checking how each of us were. Every now and again, he glanced at the cops trying to push their way through angry fans so they could get Rankin off the ground. Then Percy looked at me.

'How's it feeling?' he asked.

The bridge of my nose throbbed, and my face was all sticky from the blood.

'It probably looks worse than it is,' I said.

'It looks pretty shocking.'

'It's not that bad.'

'Adam, you okay?'

'Fine, Coach.'

'Animals.' Percy shook his head. 'I guess it comes from Rankin but it's feral. It's not football.' He clapped his good hand on Adam's shoulder. 'I'm sorry.'

'Not your bad, Coach,' Adam said.

Our fans fell away from the cops and threw trash at Rankin – everything from food wrappers, to cigarettes, to half-filled beer cans. Rankin didn't blink. He held his head high, a grin on his face that might've been carved into stone.

'You think this was a bloodbath?' he said. 'You better hope you don't play us again!'

His grin broadened and he threw one fist up triumphantly. Then he looked over at us, thrusting his fist back into the air. His lips twitched, and then became a thin straight line as his eyes widened. He was one of those guys who always had a method to his madness, so the reaction was a surprise. Maybe the sight of me and my bloodied face made him realise how brutal Little Reach had been.

But I doubted it.

The Message in the Mirror

As far as medical practices go, all we had was a clinic that had two general practitioners, one physiotherapist, and a dentist. The clinic was open regular work hours Monday to Friday, and until lunch on weekends. If there was an individual emergency, you could try your luck calling one of the two doctors. But if something big happened, then you had to drive out to Mollongong, which had a little hospital that serviced everybody out here.

That's where we went after our game. We washed up as best as we could, and then Percy wordlessly handed Adam the drinks card. Nobody queried it. Adam deserved it. But I don't think anybody was thinking footy right about now.

Percy called ahead to Mollongong Hospital to tell them we were coming, threw Sean the keys to the decrepit minibus we sometimes used to truck out to games, and off we went. While all the able-bodied players – about half the team – retreated to the Ulah'lah, Sean drove a sore and sorry lot out to Mollongong.

It was quiet in Emergency – it's not like disasters regularly hit small towns. A couple of nurses performed triage, and then prioritised us for the doctors to see. Nigel was first. They asked him some basic questions – his name, his address, that sort of thing – and while he got his name right, he was fuzzy on everything else. They diagnosed him with concussion, decided to keep him overnight for observation, and cautioned he probably shouldn't play for the next fortnight. I was next. I passed the concussion test, but a crookedness in the bridge of my nose suggested a small break. The doctor had me lie on a cot and tried to shove the break back into place. I thought it was stupid – this wasn't what you'd consider surgical, the way he planted his feet in the floor, told me to hold still, and prodded his thumbs into the bridge of my nose. Then this grinding pain flared, followed by a *click*. And that was it. He had a nurse sit down with me, and she lay plaster strips across my face – across my forehead, down my nose, and out over my upper lip – until she'd made me a mask to hold the bridge of my nose in place.

'It's a small break,' the doctor said. 'Hardly noticeable. And I think I fixed the worst of it. Wear that mask a week and you'll be fine.'

By now, Percy's right hand had swelled up around the knuckles, and the skin had gone purple. X-rays revealed three cracked knuckles. The nurse taped up his index and middle finger, and his ring and little finger, then bandaged his hand.

'Try and keep your fingers straight,' the doctor told him. 'That'll allow the knuckles to heal properly.'

'Can I play with it taped up?' Percy said.

'Sure – in about six weeks. Not before.'

Sam, Dean, Ben Jones, and Michael McMasters all had bruising to their faces. Ronnie – astonishingly, given he'd been whacked in the face twice – had nothing more than a blood lip. Out he went to sneak a cigarette. The others were prodded and sent for x-rays to check for things like fractured cheekbones or fractured eye sockets but, fortunately, no greater damage was found.

It was after eleven when we stumbled out of the hospital and bundled back into the minibus. We drove in silence, tired and dealing with not only the loss, but also the humiliation of the way they'd treated us. I kept waiting for Percy to say something, but he didn't. He stared out the window at the passing gums like he was trying to work out where we went from here.

I got up and took the seat next to him. 'It hurt?' I said.

He held up his bandaged hand. 'Yeah. You?'

I touched the mask on my face. It scratched against my cheeks, but there was no pain in my nose. 'No, not really,' I said.

Percy went back to looking out the window and I leaned back in the seat. He sighed.

'It's a game,' he said.

'What?'

'In the end, it's a game, but it comes down to …' Percy held up his bandaged hand.

'That's Little Reach.'

'That's Little Reach, but I'm not any better. I punched Schwartzer. Just out and out punched him.'

'I don't think anybody's going to hold it against you.'

'No, I guess not. But it's still not right. And makes you wonder if it's worth it.'

'What about what you said at half-time?'

'I know.'

Sean parked the minibus outside our clubrooms, and we walked up the road to the Ulah'lah. It seemed forlorn in the dark, the lights dim, only a handful of cars parked in the lot – although that wasn't much an indication of anything. Almost everybody walked there. But it was midnight, so most people probably would've gone back home and been snuggled in their beds. It sounded good. That's what I needed to do, and I considered not making an appearance, then decided I would for unity – I'd sit down with the guys for their first beer, and then I'd go home.

Dean grabbed the door and ushered Percy in, then me, and then everybody came behind us. Percy slowed once we got into the main bar. I bumped into his back, and Sean did the same behind me. I stepped around Percy, and the other guys drifted to either side to flank us.

The Ulah'lah was full: not only Adam and our other teammates bunched around the pool table, but people crowded at every table, some with kids sleeping against their arms or in their laps, or clustered into booths. As one, everybody rose. Others came out of side rooms, including Constable Brackie, leading Matt. Matt clapped, and others followed, until the applause was overflowing. At the bar, Amanda poured a line of beers. Unsurprisingly, Sean got to them and began handing them out. He picked up a glass of water amongst the line and frowned at it. Then he thrust it at me.

'Yours, I believe,' he said.

The applause died down and Matt grabbed a beer. He held it up to toast Percy. Percy gaped at him, then held up his own glass – then everybody did, and for several moments all you could hear was the television. Percy clinked his glass against Matt's. Everybody toasted whoever was closest – a symphony of clashing glasses.

'We lost,' Matt said, 'but they didn't beat us.'

A chorus of *'Yeah!'* filled the Ulah'lah, and then the individual cries came – that Little Reach were cheats, that they were scum, that next opportunity we had we'd pulverise them, and that if they tried the same stuff that it wouldn't end well. The boasts were probably bravado, but Matt was right. We'd lost, but we hadn't been beaten.

Adam stepped forward from the pool table, waving the drinks card in the air. 'There's this, too!' he said.

'I gave that to you,' Percy said. 'You were clearly the best—'

'It's a team game, Coach.' Adam grinned. 'And there's somebody who doesn't get enough credit for keeping the team together – especially when everything seems to be coming apart.' He thrust the card at Percy.

Percy's mouth dropped open. The guys around him slapped him on the back, while others cheered and applauded. Still Percy didn't move. He gaped at the drinks card, then looked up at Adam.

'It's not like I did much,' he said.

'You rallied us at half-time when we were coming apart. You spearheaded our comeback. And, if nothing else, to the coach who ran around warning us to stick to football and not to resort to violence, only to then knock out Danny Schwartzer!'

Danny. Schwartzer hadn't been called that for years. It made him sound like some punk kid, although – age aside – that wasn't far from the truth.

'I'm not proud of that,' Percy said.

'And that's what makes you different to them.'

People cheered, and then laughed when Sean snatched the drinks card from Adam's hand and said, 'I'll take care of that!'

From there, the mood picked up until people were joking and drinking, and a few times the chant of *'Ulah Curlews!'* broke out spontaneously. At first, I thought it felt the way it did after a win. But that wasn't quite right. I sat in the corner and tried to puzzle it out as I nursed my glass of water while Sean and Harry played Adam and Percy – Percy using his bandaged hand as a bridge – in pool. No, what was different was that a win hadn't created this good feeling. This was us – not just the players, but everybody – coming together.

And it had all started that night Adam showed up.

Almost as if he'd heard my thoughts, he looked up from the shot he was about to take and grinned this big grin that was all teeth and sparkled in his eyes. I held up my hand to acknowledge him. He nodded, then went on to play his next shot. I smiled and felt good, the bitterness of the afternoon's game frittering away. This was as real as it got – not fuelled by beer or victory but simply by togetherness. I closed my eyes and enjoyed it, felt that vibe fill me. But it wasn't long before my head dipped and I sat up straight, realising I was nodding off.

'Hey, I'm going,' I said.

'Already?' Percy asked.

I pointed at my face-mask. 'Think I should rest. I'll see you at training.'

I didn't look at Amanda as I got up. I didn't mean to snub her; I *never* meant to snub her, but as this went on it became harder to acknowledge her, especially here where she'd shot me down.

I lumbered out of the pub and had only gotten a little way down the road when the door to the Ulah'lah opened and closed behind me. I didn't look back, thinking it was somebody else leaving for the night, but then her voice shouted out to me.

'Luke?'

Now I didn't know what to do. Did I stop? Did I slow down? Did I walk quicker? I'd built this up too much. I should stop – that was the normal thing to do. Instead, I shoved my hands in my pockets and walked quicker, my breath puffing and misting like the steam on an old locomotive.

'Luke!'

I could hear her running to catch up, and I couldn't pretend I hadn't heard her, so I stopped and pulled my collar up. She ran her hands up and down her arms – she was in this sleeveless blouse, which was okay in the warmth of the Ulah'lah, but out here at this time? I took off my jacket and held it out for her, and she donned it like a cape.

'Thanks.'

I grunted noncommittally.

'Awesome mark you took today,' she said.

'Thanks.'

'One of the best I've seen.'

I should've been flattered, but our chasm swallowed up the compliment.

'A lot of the oldies are saying it's the best they've seen.'

'That's something.'

'Yeah.'

Amanda swivelled on the spot. I clenched my jaw.

'You haven't been around a lot lately,' she said. 'And this is probably the best time for it – when you're winning, although it's a shame about today ...'

Her voice trailed away, like she wanted me to pick up the conversation, but she was going to have no such luck. I wasn't being resentful. I just didn't know what to say. Where did we take this? My feelings had obviously been clear, and that hadn't worked out for me. It didn't leave a lot of room.

'Is it because of what I said a while ago?' Amanda asked.

'I've stopped drinking – during the season anyway.'

'I've noticed.' Amanda nodded. 'I'm proud of you for that.'

'Proud?'

'Come on, I'll walk you home. I want to talk to you.'

'Home? Home's like an hour away.'

'I'll walk you a bit then.'

'What about the bar?'

'I'm not the only bartender, Luke. Come on.'

She threaded her arm around mine. I liked how warm she felt against me – the cold was seeping in, too, now that she had my jacket. I wanted to huddle closer, maybe put my arm around her. It felt right. But I'd already been shot down for considering being forward, and this wasn't considering it but making a move, so instead I kept my hands buried in my pockets.

'Listen,' Amanda said as we walked, 'I want to explain *why* I said to you what I did.'

'You don't have to.'

'Yeah, but I *want* to. I feel I owe it you. I was too abrupt, and I didn't mean it to be like that. I've wanted to talk to you about it since, thinking about what I'd say, how I'd explain it, but I built it up in my head until I made it near-impossible. Do you know what that's like?'

'Um, yeah.'

'So, I apologise in advance if I get the words out wrong. Try and take this the way I *mean* it, and not the way it might come out, okay?'

'Sure.'

Amanda took a deep breath. 'I want to get out of here.'

'I know.'

'All right. Good. The thing is I don't want to get involved with somebody who's going to anchor me here. That might sound cruel, but there's a cycle here. Kids grow up, replace their fathers in the team, go to the Ulah'lah, get married, buy a farm or work in town or whatever, have kids, and then it starts all over again. Then, after a while, people get that *look* about them.'

'That *look*?'

'Yeah. They don't know they've got it, but you see it, like somewhere deep inside they know they're going through the motions, and this is it for them. Their whole life's scheduled, day by day, week by week, month by month, year by year. The only time they really come *alive* is when they're doing something they really want to do. Around here, most of the time that's footy. And there's nothing wrong with any of this, okay? I don't mean to be putting people down. Some people are happy to work, have families, and have a laugh on the weekend. For some that's enough. I see that with my dad. He's happy to juggle work and family and footy – and he's great at all of them. He's so nurturing and supportive and there's nothing he loves more than coming home at the end of the day and being with us. And I love that about him. But there are others who don't know how to find that in themselves, and they struggle – they drink or stay in the Ulah'lah all day gambling. I see them, Luke. *I see them.* And I think the truth for me is I won't be able to find that contentedness here like my dad has. I need to find that somewhere else. I want to get out of here and, you know, chase my dreams.'

'And you're telling me this because …?'

'I thought maybe you realised a bit of that feeling, too … the way you stopped drinking. Everybody sees you, jogging, exercising. Everybody talks about you.'

'What?'

'Not in a bad way. Some people are in awe of you.'

'Really?'

'Like Matt Reynolds. He's in the Ulah'lah a lot now between jobs – he talks about seeing you jogging.' Amanda laughed. 'He smacked one of his friends who made fun of you running all the time. Matt said you should be respected for pushing yourself that way.'

'*Matt?*'

'You saw Matt tonight. He acts tough, but he's not – well, not when it comes to footy and that. But it's not just him. I hear a lot working there at the Ulah'lah. Lots of people talk about how driven you are. Everybody thinks you've become the best and most important player in the team. Behind Adam, of course.'

'Of course.' Still, flattering nonetheless.

'So … you understand what I'm saying, right?'

'Yeah. But you want to be a writer. There's an avenue for you. Somebody in my position, I'd have to get drafted. Tell me, how many players are drafted from some country league into the AFL? I can't think of one. Then there's Adam. Who's going to notice me playing alongside him?'

'People might come to see Adam, but the rest of you are also on display. It's probably the best way *to* get noticed.'

'Still, I don't see any talent scouts. And, honestly, I haven't even thought about what comes next. I want to play, to be the best I can be.'

'This is why I'm talking to you. I'm heading into the city at the end of the year. I'm going to take everything I've written, my résumé, put it all in a folder and shop myself around. All or nothing. I want you to come. You can try and get onto the list of a club in the VFL, or something like that. Then people might notice you, right?'

It made sense. All the states had lower leagues. In the case of the VFL, the Victorian Football League, the AFL clubs used it as a second-tier competition. The AFL clubs either sent players back to their reserves clubs in the VFL, or to affiliate clubs. Those VFL lists also comprised guys who played only VFL. A handful who displayed consistently good form made the AFL clubs sit up and take notice. It seemed such an obvious solution – or at least an alternative: if I wasn't going to be discoveed out here, then I should move to somewhere I *could* be discovered.

'Think about it, huh?' Amanda said.

We reached the edge of Ulah, where the town ceded to the long dirt roads that spider-webbed out to the various farms. Only you couldn't see anything else at this time: it was black out there, except for the pinpoints of the street lights, the distance between each growing progressively longer before they disappeared into nothing.

'I don't get it,' I said. 'You're saying this to me now, but you wouldn't have a couple of months ago, would've you?' *When you shot me down.* 'Because back then, I was another anchor, wasn't I? And now you're thinking I'm not.'

'Luke, I've always liked you – I told you I really liked you. You're not full of the bluster like everybody else, charging in, singing *rah-rah-rah* – even when you were drinking.' Amanda laughed. 'You're not full of sleazy pick-up lines or drunken charm or the belief that everybody should be a groupie to you because you play for the team. You've always been a bit quiet. Polite. Respectful. Well, most of the time. And I've missed our chats. I pretty much noticed that from the moment you stopped coming to the bar.'

I shivered and my teeth chattered, but I didn't feel the cold.

'I'm sorry – not really for what I said, but because of how I handled it, and how I underestimated you. I thought … well, you know now.' Amanda swayed on the spot. 'So, think about it, huh? And …' She took a black felt pen out of her back pocket and held it up. I stooped and she wrote something on my forehead. 'This isn't hurting, is it?' she asked.

'No.'

When she finished writing, she capped the pen and put it back in her pocket.

'I gotta get back,' she said. She rose up on her toes again and kissed me, lightly, on the lips. 'I'll see you later.' She took a step away.

'Amanda?'

'What?' she asked.

'I … What …?'

She kissed me again, her lips full against mine – soft and wet, as her body melted into me. Again, I felt her warmth against me – but all of her. I slid my arms into my jacket and around her waist, feeling the arch of her back and the curve of her hips. A thousand things went through my head then. What did I taste like? Was my breath bad? How good was my kissing? But then she pulled away, although her hands clasped behind my neck, and she smiled at me.

'Get it now?' she asked.

'I guess.'

'You guess?'

I shrugged.

'You're hopeless!' Amanda pulled off my jacket and tossed it to me. 'I gotta get back. I'll *see* ya tomorrow.'

She jogged off, back up the street, until she faded into the night. Then I was alone, my jacket slung over my forearm, and what popped into my head wasn't the magic of what had happened, or how unreal it all seemed, but whether the concussion test back at the hospital had been right. I might still be there, in some bed next to Nigel's, imagining all this. But as my shivering grew worse, I could only think that, no, I was out here and it had happened. I put on my jacket and went to untie my face-mask to see what she'd written, then stopped. The nurse had put the mask on a couple of hours ago. What if I took it off and my nose popped out of place? Not that that was likely. Still, I decided to leave it – at least for now.

By the time I got home, the cold had made my ears ache, my nose throb, and my fingers stiff. It took almost half a minute before I could get the key in the front door lock and let myself into the house. The warmth and security of home embraced me. Light flickered from the dining room: Dad, up late again. I considered going straight to bed, but I couldn't go Phantom of the Opera on him or Mum. They were going to see me sooner or later.

I headed down the hallway, leaned on the archway adjoining the lounge. Dad was in his recliner, eyes fixed on the television.

You'd think the moon landing was on or something, the way he was mesmerised. But by the sound of the television, it was an infomercial.

And between us, silence.

'Hey, Dad.'

Dad kept his attention fixed on the television, making me feel self-conscious, leaning there in this face-mask Amanda had left a message on – a message I was anxious to read. But this was more important. I wanted Dad to see how I'd been injured. I wanted him to see me.

'I'm going to bed, Dad. Night.'

'That was some footy today.'

'You came?'

'Mum told you we would.'

'I …Well, I guess I didn't know if you had.'

'Yeah.' Dad nodded his head once in a gesture that was meant to encompass me and my face-mask. 'Little Reach. They'll stop at nothing.'

'Yeah.'

'You okay?'

'Yeah.'

'Good.'

Back to silence, other than for the infomercial imploring viewers that they wanted more value.

'Night, Dad.'

'Luke?'

'Yeah?'

'Great mark, too.'

'Thanks.'

'Night.'

I bounded upstairs, darted into the bathroom, switched on the light, and stared into the mirror.

Writing on a rough, curved surface like the face-mask mustn't have been easy, as Amanda's handwriting was almost hieroglyphic.

Reading it backwards in the mirror didn't help either, so it took almost a minute's deciphering before I could make out three words:

Take a chance

The Third Quarter

The Freakishness
of Adam Pride

S unday I woke battered and sore – not only my nose, but also
my back where I'd been hit. I eased myself out of bed, then
showered, standing under the hot water until it soothed all the
aches and pains. Once I was done, I checked myself in the mirror:
bruises marked my back and right shoulder, and crescents ringed
my eyes. My nose was okay, though – a little swollen, but not
enough to be noticeable. And it was straight. That was something.
Last thing I wanted – especially at eighteen – was a bruiser's nose,
all fat and misshapen. I put my mask on and got dressed.

Down in the kitchen, I fixed myself some cereal and mulled
over the game, thinking about things we could've – and *should've* –
done better. It all came down to those opening few minutes. They'd
shaken us, then outplayed us while we feared further attacks. In
the second half, we'd shown we could take it to them, although
I guessed a lot of them had mentally switched off, thinking the
game already won.

The screen door clattered open and shut and Mum bustled in,
wearing her felt gardening gloves. She put her hands on her hips as
she looked at me. I wasn't sure how to respond, so I kept eating my

cereal, although my face-mask now felt like a sign that screamed, *Look at me!*

Mum shook her head. 'Those thugs,' she said. 'Your father nearly ran onto the ground, you know? I had to hold him back. He did give Rankin a serve. Later, when Rankin tried to sneak—'

'Rankin? Sneak?'

'Yes. Tried to creep out, like he wouldn't be noticed. They all did. I don't know if they were scared or embarrassed – probably a bit of both. Your father got in Rankin's face, calling him all sorts of names. Constable Brackie had to restrain him. We nearly had a fight then and there. Especially with the mob that had gathered.'

'Dad?' I blinked.

'It was something to see.'

'I spoke to him last night – he didn't tell me any of this.'

'He was quite embarrassed when he'd cooled down. Made a spectacle of himself.' Mum took off her gardening gloves, laid them on the kitchen counter, and filled the kettle. 'Some of the people there – like Matt Reynolds and Mick Jacobs – tried to get him out to the Ulah'lah for a beer. They'd all played and drank together. I thought they might have a few, then drive out to Little Reach. Lucky your father turned them down. Instead, he went and fiddled around in the shed for a couple of hours to cool down.'

I felt a sudden closeness to Dad that I hadn't for years. I just wished I didn't have to hear this second-hand, although there wasn't much choice. He had his walls, I had mine, and the funny thing is nothing had really happened to erect them – nothing other than both of us growing older.

'So, does it hurt?' Mum said.

'My nose?'

Mum nodded.

'It's sore.'

'Is it bad?' Mum grabbed the edge of the mask and peeled it back.

'Mum!' I sat back and readjusted the mask. 'Doctor said that it wasn't that bad.'

'Well, that's something. What's that up there – on the top?' Mum peered closer. '"Take a chance",' she read. 'What's that mean? You didn't write that – that's not your writing.'

'Amanda wrote it.'

'Amanda? Percy's Amanda?'

I nodded.

'Something going on between you two?' Mum smiled. 'Well, well. So what's she telling you?'

'Mum! Please.'

'Mum please, what?' Mum asked.

'Amanda wants me to be more proactive,' I said, not sure what to say. It was too early to be talking about plans, or anything like that. I was still trying to deal with it all myself.

Mum must've worked that out, too, because she nodded. 'Speaking of Amanda,' she said, 'you should check out *The Tribune* today. I didn't want to bring it home. I thought it might set off your father. But definitely have a look.'

'Why? What's on it?'

'Wait until you see it.'

I raced through the rest of the cereal and rinsed my bowl in the sink. Then I excused myself and headed outside. It was grey, dark clouds jostling to keep the sky out. A heady breeze swayed the wheat until it looked like rows of people with their heads bent low. It felt like mourning – a sadness for what had happened yesterday, although I'd no sooner had the thought than it was gone.

The walk into town was slower than my usual walk, and I found lots of new aches throughout my body – creaks that needed oiling. I'd never felt this before and put it down to the physicality of the game, something that my body would get used to, and would force it to toughen up … until it couldn't anymore. Then I got a flash of insight into what Dad must've felt at the end when he knew his body was letting him down, but his determination kept pushing him. It was now a case of making the most of the in-between.

Town was quieter than it had been for a long time on a Sunday. People were out, doing their usual things. Some exchanged hellos with me and all, but there was none of the bluster of the last few weeks when we'd been winning. A few looked at my face-mask and shook their heads or grumbled unintelligibly.

Two stacks of *The Tribune* sat at the front of the General Store. I stopped well before I reached them: on the front page was me, on my knees, head thrown back, face contorted in pain and masked in blood. As I got closer, I saw the big headline underneath was:

BLOODBATH!

Following that was several paragraphs saying how the Curlews had paid a heavy price for daring to challenge Little Reach. Then a tag stated the rest of the article continued on pages 2–3.

In the history of *The Tribune*, only once had football made the front page: when the Curlews beat the Scorpions in the grand final eighteen years ago – that picture that hung in our lounge, and would've hung in the homes (or the work places, if not both) of all the players who'd played that game.

Now I picked up a copy of *The Tribune* and went inside to pay for it. Margie England rolled her eyes at the sight of me, and when I didn't say anything, she sighed this big, big sigh that had the few other shoppers in the General Store checking to see if she might be suffering a heart attack. I shrugged, because I didn't know what to say, but was sympathetic to what she must be feeling.

'Those bastards,' she said. 'They'll get theirs, mark my words!'

'I hope,' I said.

'They will! What've you got written up there, on the top?' Margie leaned over the counter to get a closer look. '"Take a chance",' she read. 'What's that supposed to mean?'

Trying to explain this to Mum was one thing, but trying to explain it to Margie – who I only really knew in passing – was something else. Amanda's message was going to naturally draw all sorts of attention, given it was right out there in the open. I needed a cover story, one that wasn't so personal but would satisfy everybody.

'It's a reminder for when I play,' I told Margie. 'To take the game on and stuff.'

'Oh. Good on you!'

I took *The Tribune* outside and flipped the page. The first things that leaped out at me were the collage of pictures: my mark over Rankin, Ronnie caught doing his dance, Percy holding his hand limp, Sean spoiling Murray Verne as he attempted to mark, and Nigel sitting up looking stupefied after he'd been hit.

I leaned against the wall of the General Store and read how a possible grand final preview had erupted into a bloodbath – although it was unclear whether Little Reach had panicked and taken aggression too far, or they'd purposely gone the fist because they had no other way to stop us. Then it talked about how the vitriol had spilled into the crowd, reflected by the attitudes of the Little Reach faithful.

'"Banter is part of the outer",' I read quietly. '"Ask any player about the barbs they're subjected to during a game. However, with Little Reach, it became ugly and personal, and then racial – attitudes that are provincial and have no place in today's society, let alone in a game of football".'

The rest of the article covered the match – Adam's brilliance, as usual, and how in the second half the rest of the players followed his example and showed that they could match it with the Scorpions, so surely they'd relish another encounter, given the chance.

'Hey!' Amanda bounced up to me, and before I could even begin to think how I should behave, she kissed me, then nestled into me to see what I was reading. 'What do you think?'

'It's great. Makes you think. And your first front page, too.'

'It's a start,' Amanda said.

Amanda didn't know how true her words were: a city newspaper picked up her article, and scoffed at the barbarity of outback footy, as if this happened out here all the time. It generated lots of feedback: people from small towns all over the country wrote in to support local footy.

We didn't know this immediately, though. Monday night, me, Percy, and Amanda – Amanda driving, since Percy couldn't with his bandaged hand, and me going for moral support – drove out to Mollongong, where the offices of our football league were based, so Percy could appear at the tribunal for hitting Schwartzer.

The offices were part of the Mollongong clubrooms, although these were opulent, because Mollongong was the biggest town around here. Every year, a representative from each town was voted in to administrate the league, although usually it was the same group of people until somebody dropped off. Our representative was seventy-year-old Callum Peck – he'd actually played in the Curlews' premiership prior to the last one, forty years ago.

The door to the office opened and Ozzie Rowan, looking weird in an oversized suit with big square shoulders, called Percy's name. Percy hauled himself up. Ozzie offered a handshake; Percy held up his bandaged right hand to show he couldn't. They compromised by shaking left hands. Ozzie ushered Percy in, nodded at us, then closed the door.

Amanda and I sat in the lobby and waited. And waited. Amanda tapped her foot on the floor, while I stared at the pictures on the wall from Mollongong's triumphs. A string of flags hung from the ceiling – the premierships they'd won: ten of them, although they'd played in thirty grand finals, often coming second to Little Reach. But nobody celebrated being runners-up.

The glass doors opened and Rankin, Verne, Bell, Schwartzer – his head bandaged up – and a number of other Scorpions all came in, dressed in suits. They walked past us like we weren't there, and took seats opposite us. Several of them – most notably Schwartzer – leered at Amanda. I tensed up and she put a hand on my arm. Then the office door opened and Percy came out. He stopped at the sight of all the Scorpions. Rankin got up and offered a handshake. As he'd done earlier, Percy held up his bandaged right hand to show he couldn't reciprocate. He didn't offer his left hand, as he had with Ozzie. Unfazed, Rankin clapped Percy on the shoulder.

'No hard feelings, huh?' Rankin said. 'Just part of the game.'

'No, Claude,' Percy said, 'it's not.'

Percy led us out and in the car on the drive back home told us he'd gotten eight weeks – later, we'd learn it was the biggest suspension dealt out from that game. All those Scorpions we saw would get penalties anywhere from two to four weeks.

'Eight weeks!' Percy said.

'At least it'll give your hand time to heal,' Amanda said.

The next morning we learned that Amanda's article had continued to cause a kerfuffle online, lots of people commenting about the merits of country football, some arguing that it was primitive and a throwback to an unacceptable era. Then Percy wrote in as the coach of the Curlews, saying this game had been an aberration, and if anybody wanted to come out on a Saturday afternoon, they could enjoy a great day out between two teams who'd fight it out tough but fair. That pretty much seemed the end of it. By Thursday, the talk was fading, and by the time we faced Warrambatta on Saturday, it was forgotten – or at least it was as far as we knew.

Warrambatta sat fourth on the ladder and had been undefeated since we'd trounced them in Round 6, so people expected a close match, especially since we missed Percy as a player – as he was both suspended and injured – and Nigel, and other players were still sore and a little bit toey, probably fearing that first collision of bodies. I could sympathise. When I took off my face-mask and jogged out, the bridge of my nose felt heavy, like something had been wedged in that didn't belong. The first three contests where I clashed with opponents, I checked my nose, worried something might have jolted out of place. Even Adam seemed distracted, constantly looking over his shoulder and down at the far goals. When the siren went to end that first quarter, the score was us 2.4.(16) to Warrambatta 4.0.(24).

Percy marched out from the bench and gathered us in a huddle around the wing. 'Okay, we still have our minds on last week,' he said. 'We need to let that go. There's only today now.'

The crowd roared as somebody in one of our jumpers leaped the railing and charged out to our huddle – none other than Matt. A couple of cops (Constable Brackie one of them) patrolled the boundary, but did nothing to stop him. Matt threw an arm around Percy and heaved for breath.

'Matt—' Percy said.

'Rankin's here,' Matt said.

'What?'

'In that far pocket with his generals,' Matt said, and pointed – right in the direction Adam had been looking that whole quarter.

'What's he doing here?' Dean said.

'I wanted to …' Matt's jaw clenched. 'Never mind what I wanted to. I'm a little bit on notice with our finest. But they didn't mind me telling you. Apparently, he's scouting – has a notebook and is jotting away.'

'Scouting?' Percy said.

'Yup.'

'He's scared,' Adam said in a low, flat tone.

'Sca—' Harry said.

'That's right!' Percy said. 'He's *scared*. He's scouting us because he recognised last week we *are* a genuine threat. If we'd laid over, that would've been the end of it. But we came at them. We might've lost, but we came at them, and because of the furore about what happened last week, they won't be able to get away with that crap again.'

That message ran through each and every one of us, galvanised us, and – through the second quarter – reconnected us. I hit a few more packs, spoiled the ball, and came down convinced my nose would remain intact. From there, I recommitted myself with gusto – just as everybody did. We ran hard, we hit hard, and we played with the purpose that had directed our winning streak.

Adam was even better. Like he was trying to compensate for that quiet first quarter, he exploded. He kicked only five goals himself – *only*, like that's some small feat – but he was everywhere. One moment he'd be in defence helping Sean and me out, then he'd be on the wing, then he'd be up forward. Blink, and he'd be somewhere else.

When the siren sounded to end the game, signalling us fifty-three-point victors, Warrambatta's fans applauded us. There had always been a close relationship between Ulah, Warrambatta, and Shandeen Bank. When we weren't playing against each other, we supported each other's teams. It was the neighbourly thing to do, and *easy*, since none of us had the ego of Little Reach. But this was gratifying, especially after last week, because it showed us sportsmanship still existed.

We jogged off as other fans ran on – parents with their kids, or teens eager to kick around the football. On the boundary, Percy and Amanda were in conversation with two men, one with wispy grey hair and wearing a brown suit, the other with a bulbous nose and wearing this outrageously bright red woollen pullover.

'Adam!' Percy said. 'Adam!'

Adam slowed down, and then his shoulders came up and rolled. He lowered his head and wandered over.

Percy introduced the two men: brown suit was Colin Perrine, the city editor who'd picked up Amanda's article, while bright red pullover was Josh Carson, an independent scout who'd been contracted by several clubs to provide reports on players from more remote leagues.

'When I got hold of that article,' Perrine said, 'the first thing I did was go back through previous editions to see if this bad blood was a regular occurrence out here. In the end, it didn't matter because it was such a good story. But I was curious. And while I learned it was a once-off, what *did* stand out were reports of your brilliance.'

Carson grabbed Adam's hand and shook it, although Adam's hand – and his whole arm – remained limp. He took a small step back, but it was enough to signal his distance. Carson grimaced, gave up the attempted handshake, lifted a hand like he was going to pat Adam on the shoulder, then decided against that.

'I thought the articles had to be exaggerating,' Carson said. 'But you were brilliant. Unbelievable! How old are you?'

'How old do I look?' Adam said.

'I don't know,' Carson said. 'What? Twenty-five?'

'Sounds good.' Adam gestured to the clubrooms. 'I'm off to shower.'

'You can't just go like that!'

Adam twirled and grinned. 'I just did!'

Despite Carson's repeated attempts, Adam wouldn't engage with him. By the time we'd made our way to the Ulah'lah, everybody was talking about the possibility of Adam being recruited. I had no doubt in my mind age wouldn't matter as far as Adam was concerned.

'You should give it a shot,' Nigel said, as we crowded around our usual corner table, the guys with beer, me with my water.

'A shot?' Adam said.

'You're sweet!'

'I'm too old.'

'It doesn't matter when you're as good as you are,' Percy said.

'How many guys my age debut in the AFL?'

'A few have done it,' Percy said.

'I wouldn't want to leave my family behind either.'

'Take them with you!' Harry said.

'They're not for the city. Me neither.'

'Think about the money you'll make,' Sam said.

'Guys would kill for this shot,' Percy said.

'I'm *not* interested,' Adam said. 'I like the quiet life.'

'I would sell my soul for a shot,' Nigel said.

'Don't say that.'

'Brother, you're the best damned player I've seen.'

'Solid, mate,' Dean said.

Amanda waved at me from the bar. I gulped down my water quicker than I should've and got up.

'Gonna get another drink,' I said.

'You're going through those like they're water,' Sean said.

'Haha.'

I went to the bar as the guys continued to prod Adam and slid my glass over to Amanda. She clasped my hand. I'd never had a woman touch me like that – just to make contact. Then she took my glass and poured me another water.

'Things look tense over there,' she said.

'Guys think Adam should be giving this scout a shot.'

'Not interested?'

'Nope.' I sat on a bar stool.

'Then he's going to hate what I have to propose.'

'What?'

'The city editor …?' Amanda said.

'Yeah?'

'He wants me to write a piece on Adam. He wants to call it "Country Magic".'

'"Country Magic"?'

'Don't worry about the title. Think about what this could mean for me.'

I wasn't sure what the journalistic route was, but having an editor of a city newspaper commission a piece seemed as good a place as any to start.

'I can write the piece without Adam's help,' Amanda said. 'But it would be better if I could interview him. He won't sit for an interview, though, will he?'

I didn't want to be the one who said it aloud and made it real.

'*Will* he?'

Adam shot to his feet, his chair screeching back across the floor. 'Forget it, okay?' he said. 'I don't want to hear anything more about it.' He stormed out of the Ulah'lah.

'I guess not,' I said.

Questions ...

Over the next few days, things settled to the way they had been. On Tuesday night, I showed up at training on a clear evening and expected a bit of tension. We kicked the ball around, laughing and joking, when the curlews wailed. Adam's head bobbed up from the embankment, then he hopped the railing, and jogged over to join us.

'Hey, fellas!' he said.

That was it – whatever had happened at the Ulah'lah stayed at the Ulah'lah, and we enjoyed a sharp training run. Nobody brought up Adam's opportunity. The evening unfolded like any other – except for Matt joining us at the end of the night, when Percy called us into a huddle.

'Given Rankin watched us last week,' Percy said, 'I've been thinking it wouldn't be bad to scout our opposition – just in case, so Matt's volunteered.'

Lots of sidelong glances were exchanged, and the applause that came from the huddle was scattered and tentative. Matt nodded his head and held up his hand, then opened his mouth like he was going to say something, but then thought better of it.

Percy sent us to the showers after that, and when I was done, I dressed and found him in his little office – I think originally his office must've been a big storage closet. Now it contained a tiny desk cluttered with lots of paper and folders – God knows what else. Boxes – archives from previous seasons and coaches – were piled wherever there was space. None of us ever bothered ourselves with whatever administration Percy had to do to keep the team going. Who knew what we'd do once Percy decided to call it quits?

'What's up?' he asked.

'About Matt—'

'You're thinking we don't need him – we've been doing okay without him?'

I nodded.

Percy leaned back in his chair – not that he had a lot of room before he backed into the wall. 'Matt's looking for a bit of purpose,' he said. 'I don't think he has much else. So it helps him out, and maybe he can help us out.'

'I'm worried …' I took a deep breath. 'He used to be coach before you and didn't do such a good job of it.'

'I think he's grown up a bit since we've improved – he might've scoffed originally, but he can't argue with the results. Give him a chance. He's been around a while. He mightn't show it, but he knows his stuff. And he wants to be involved in some way.'

'Oh, okay. Sure.'

It was logical enough and made me think about what happened when your career was done. Dad had Mum and the farm. Matt was a plumber, but divorced, and he only ever saw his daughters every other weekend. I guess he didn't have anything else to fill those hours now that football was gone. I didn't feel so unsure about the appointment anymore.

Outside, Amanda waited for me on the bench. She got up, and kissed me.

'Walk a girl home?' she said.

'Home?'

'Come on.'

I fully expected to end up back at Percy's house, but Amanda walked me up the road to where a string of bungalows sat: originally, they'd been intended as rentals for people passing through – not that we had many of them. So locals rented them out – usually to kids getting out of home for the first time.

Amanda brought me to the bungalow in the middle, number 5, unlocked the door and led me in, switching on lights as she went.

I'd never been in one of these bungalows, having only heard stories about how they were dens for partying, drinking, and worse – stories that probably came about because some kids graduating high school would often rent one, party the whole night and trash it. Sean, me, and others, did all our graduation partying at the footy ground.

Amanda's bungalow was neat and simple: the lounge was sparse, with a small TV, a two-seat couch, a minuscule coffee table (which might've been an end table), and a laptop on a tiny metal desk by the window overlooking the footy ground. Cut-outs of her articles were stuck on one wall, a few of them framed. The adjoining kitchenette was so small that if you turned, you could get wedged in there. A short hallway led to her bedroom and bathroom.

'This is yours?' I said, twirling around to take it all in.

'Yep.'

'Since when?'

'A couple of weeks ago. Dad doesn't want me to tell anybody yet – in case I change my mind. Sit down. I want to show you something.'

I sat on the couch and Amanda joined me after she'd grabbed her laptop. She stuck her feet up on the coffee table, and her fingers blurred across her keyboard; then, she dumped the laptop on me. A white screen blared at me, along with lines and lines of text.

'Read this for me?' she said.

The piece was about Adam – how this brilliant Aboriginal player had emerged from the night and shaken up the entire league with his brilliance. Amanda detailed some of his highlights, and the way that Adam had defied Little Reach and all their attempts to stop him.

'What do you think?' Amanda said.

'It's good …'

'*But* …?'

'It's good but it's really just about Adam as a player, which is fine, but the city papers are talking about real players from the AFL, so what makes Adam stand out?'

Amanda frowned. 'That's a good point.'

She was distracted the rest of the evening, and Wednesday I barely saw her. Thursday, she was again waiting outside the clubrooms following training, and since neither of us had eaten we decided to go to the Ulah'lah. We found a booth in the corner and, over dinner, Amanda told me what she'd been up to.

'I worked on my piece all of yesterday and sent it to that editor,' she said. 'He liked it, but he basically said the same thing as you: what's the hook? What makes this one guy stand out and be more than a novelty? "Why should this story demand space?" That's what he said to me. I need to make it more than a novelty.'

I picked at my steak. It was rare. I hadn't wanted it rare, but that was Willie McKenna's cooking. You never knew what you'd get, and it wasn't like you could blame his drinking – sometimes he cooked at his best after a few. It was accepted that you took what you got at the Ulah'lah.

'How do you do that?' I said.

'Well, it can't be about him being good. It's like you said – they're writing about real AFL players in newspapers, so why's Adam going to bump them off the page?' Amanda picked at her salmon salad. 'I had a different idea: a story about a guy with a young child who's come to Ulah, and even though he's this brilliant talent dominating the competition and wowing this scout, he refuses to pursue this opportunity.'

'That could work.'

And it could: I'd kill for an opportunity like Adam's. What motivated him to stay out here, in the middle of nowhere? Even a couple of seasons on an AFL list could set him and his family up for life – although Adam had more than enough talent to forge a career.

'But, of course,' Amanda said, 'there's the problem he won't do the interview.'

I cut down the centre of my steak. It bled onto the plate. This was going to drive me to drink.

'I figure maybe if I explain myself, he'll come around,' Amanda said.

'Do you really believe that, given the way he's responded so far?'

'I have to try – you understand that, don't you? This could be my springboard to something bigger.'

I looked up. That's exactly what I'd thought about myself and footy – that it'd be a springboard. Exact same word.

'What?' Amanda said.

'Nothing. I understand. I do.'

'All right then. I need to ask him then. Will you come with me?'

'Where?'

'To talk to him. It might put him at ease if you're with me.'

'I'll come, but where?'

'His house.'

'Which is *where*?'

'Don't you know?' Amanda asked.

'Why would I know?' I abandoned the steak, and refocused on my vegetables.

'Haven't you ever asked him?'

'What for?'

'Because you play footy together.'

'We play here.' I used my fork to push aside two chunks of tomato, and impaled a slice of cucumber. 'We don't need to go to his place.' It was a horrible explanation, but it had never occurred to any of us to ask him his address.

'So you have no idea where he lives?'

'He said he's got a farm somewhere on the border of Ulah, Warrambatta, and Shandeen Bank.'

'You're hopeless. Dad should know. He keeps track of all the players. I'm going somewhere quiet to call him.'

'Now?'

But Amanda had already slipped from the booth and was taking her phone from her pocket. I had a few minutes to finish what I could of my meal – the green vegetables, some chunky chips, and the edges of the steak that had cooked. Then Amanda slid back into the booth.

'He doesn't know. He said the same thing as you. Dad's memorised everybody else's address, their phone numbers at work and home, their mobiles, but with Adam all Dad said was Adam just shows up.'

'Ask him next training session.'

'Surrounded by everybody?'

'So?'

'You saw the way he reacted when everybody was pushing him. I'm thinking he'll respond differently if we get him out of this environment – you know, have a casual chat, rather than one pre-game, or post-game, or whatever.'

'Fair enough.'

'Tomorrow we're going to find him.'

'How?'

'How many farms can be out there right where all those borders meet?'

The next morning, I met Amanda outside her place. The sun was out, although there was the occasional gust that snatched our words from the air.

Amanda kissed me on the lips and squeezed my hands in her own. 'You ready?'

'I guess.'

'Let's go.' She swatted me on the butt.

I lead the way to the footy ground, not knowing what to say. I was here for the company, not the investigation. But Amanda's mind was ticking. Like a bomb. About halfway across our ground, she blew.

'Have you ever thought about Adam?' Amanda asked.

'What?'

'Have you ever thought about Adam?'

'I don't know what you're asking me. I *know* what the question means. Of course I've thought about him. Who hasn't? We've all seen how good he is.'

'How do you get that good?'

'I don't know. It's something you're born with, then you work at it to make it better.'

'How've we never heard about somebody this good?'

'He said he hadn't played for a while.'

'So he picked it up again like that? Or is this his first year competitively? Unless he trained in a shed for fifteen years, he has to have played somewhere else. Where, though? For who?'

'He said he came from Western Australia. Maybe he played up there.'

'Maybe – if that's where he comes from.'

'You think he lied about coming from Western Australia?'

'I think there's more to this than meets the eye.'

She really had the character of an investigative journalist – she was a snoop. We were all curious, but she was the only one doing something to find out *more*. Everybody else was … what? Respectful? Or apathetic? Around here, maybe they amounted to the same thing.

The creek was high, as we'd already had heavy rains. But the faces of stepping stones peeked out from the water, and we hopped across, although Amanda stumbled on the last one. Her right foot sunk into the water up to her ankle, and I reached out to steady her. She rose up and shook her right foot, soaked now to the hem of her jeans.

'You okay?' I said.

'A bit wet, but fine.'

On the other side of the creek, Ulah opened up to rolling grasslands that dipped and rose and then ceded into scatterings of gums, rising up like unruly hairs waiting to be plucked. We began to pant as the hours tumbled by, and my thighs and calves ached

– not something I expected, although I guess this was a different exertion to football. The trees grew thicker with every step, until a towering line of red gums rose up to our right. We were skirting along the edge of the bush that separated us from the long main road that went all the way up to Mollongong.

Amanda stopped, and put her hands on her hips. 'We'd be in Shandeen Bank about now, wouldn't we?'

I nodded.

'We must've missed it.'

'I don't think there's any point going on,' I said.

'You're right. Let's go back.'

But, thanks to Amanda, we didn't head back but took a high course in the opposite direction of the red gums. Before long, we saw a herd of cows in a pen. One of them looked up and mooed almost belligerently. Amanda straightened up – until I told her that the farm belonged to Gavin McGrath, the former coach of Shandeen Bank. Still, she didn't relent and we pushed on as the occasional gum began to appear, forlorn at first, until more and more of them marched in and they towered all around us. The wind howled forbiddingly through their leafless branches.

'You hear that?' Amanda said.

'The wind?'

Amanda craned her head forward. I was sure she was imagining it, but then I did hear something: a *thud*, then another, then another – something metallic hitting something soft and yielding.

'What is that?' Amanda whispered.

It grew dark and cool as we slipped deeper into the gums – like the branches had reached up to shield the sun and lock us away from the world outside. The *thuds* echoed now until voices rose up – not loud enough to understand, but loud enough to be heard.

'Amanda—' I said.

'*Sshhh.*'

She moved from trunk to trunk, taking cover like she was a sniper scampering for a better vantage point. Fallen leaves crunched underfoot and the wind whipped around and raised goosebumps on my skin. The gums began to open up, so we had to jog from one to the next. Several trees had been chopped down and stacked: in front of them, a cluster of figures leaned against a familiar battered van parked on a dirt road, although the road was no more than two tracks beaten into the earth. It took a couple of moments for it to register in my head that the van was Rankin's. Then I picked them: Rankin, big and hulking in his denim jacket; Bell in slacks, a blue shirt, and a tie pulled low; Verne in cargos and a t-shirt. Each of them drank a beer, although Bell held a second in his other hand. Schwartzer, his head still bandaged, and in a set of greasy coveralls, stood in a knee-deep hole. He lifted a pickaxe and drove it into the dirt.

I shivered – I couldn't help it, the shiver coming all the way from low down until my shoulders shook. Amanda, almost mesmerised, leaned forward to head for the next closest tree, although it would've been impossible to do so without being spotted. I grabbed her wrist and she blinked, then nodded.

'What do you think they're doing?' I whispered.

'I know Rankin has investments around here,' Amanda said.

Of course – Rankin owned land. This could be his property. So that side of things made sense – or at least *could* make sense. But I didn't get the digging, although I'm sure there could be plenty of logical explanations. The problem was I couldn't think of a single one right now.

I tugged at Amanda's wrist but she became deadweight, so we stayed there, crouched behind a tree, and watched. Nothing happened, though – well, nothing more than what we were already seeing: they drank beer, and would alternate who did the digging. When a hole would become deep enough, they'd move the site, somebody else would take over, and the digging would start all over again. They talked – bits of conversation and the occasional guffaw – but the wind scattered their words so we couldn't make anything out, and it was too risky to try to get any closer.

'We should head back,' I said.

My hand tightened around Amanda's wrist and we crept away, again moving from gum to gum, often peering back over our shoulder to make sure we weren't being seen. When we couldn't see Rankin and the others anymore, we hurried from the bush and back out into the sun, standing there to let the warmth and light bask over us. It was like we'd slipped from a dark and incomprehensible hallucination and back into the real world.

'That was weird,' Amanda said.

'Yeah.'

'What do you think they were doing?'

I shrugged.

'We should've tried to get closer—'

'Any closer and they would've seen us. We got too close as it was.'

'Maybe, but …' Amanda shook her head. 'Why would you dig in the middle of nowhere? Did you notice some trees had been cut down?'

I nodded.

'Are they going to build something? A house? A cabin?'

'If that's what they were doing, that's about the most slipshod way of doing it – four guys standing around while one guy does the digging.'

'Unless they were having like some groundbreaking ceremony.'

'I don't know.' I squinted as I looked around. 'I know this area, by the way. There's nothing out here, at least not Adam anyway.'

'Are you sure?'

'Buzz O'Connor lives out that way,' I said. 'Dad deals with him a lot. There's nothing else – not for a while. Adam's definitely not out here.'

'Maybe he lied,' Amanda said.

'Why would he lie?'

'Maybe he knew all the fuss he'd create, so he prepared in advance – you know, in case …'

'In case of what?'

'In case somebody did what we're doing now,' Amanda said. 'He knew the publicity would come, so he prepared for it.'

'Maybe he lives in Mollongong,' I said. Mollongong was the town furthest from Ulah – about a twenty- to thirty-minute drive, and a killer walk. 'And came to play for Ulah to throw everybody off track.'

Amanda punched me in the arm. 'Don't make fun of me.'

'Well, then, what do you want to do?'

'I guess I'm left with the straightforward approach.'

'The straightforward approach?'

'Asking him when I see him.'

I decided not to answer that. One punch was enough.

... and More Questions

Tuesday's training session was subdued as Percy monitored us, Matt constantly behind him. It felt odd to have Matt there, although he clapped and shouted and encouraged – so that was something. He mightn't have liked the hard training when he participated in it, but he relished being vocal, and shouting at players if they did slack off. I wondered if this was a sign of the newfound maturity Percy talked about, or if Matt enjoyed the power.

Amanda watched us from the boundary, notebook in hand. The moment Percy called it a night and dismissed us to the showers, she ran on, charged through the players, and chased Adam as he headed across the ground to that far wing. Torn between following the other guys and her, I went back and forth, then decided she'd never forgive me if I didn't support her, so cantered after her.

'Adam!' she called. 'Adam!'

He slowed down – probably more out of courtesy than anything – and she sidled up to him. I kept my distance – close enough to hear what was going on, but not close enough to intrude.

'The paper – the city paper that is, *not The Tribune* – is really interested in a story—'

'No thanks,' Adam said.

'I want to explore how you've decided to stay—'

'Not interested.'

'But it's a human interest story!' Amanda said. 'You're giving up a chance—'

'All I'm interested in is being home and at peace with my family.'

They reached the railing on the other wing and stopped. Amanda bounced on her feet. I could feel the excitement and frustration in her. Adam leaned against the railing with his elbow.

'That's it?' he said.

'They want me to write this story regardless—'

'If that's true, you're free to write what you want, but I won't be involved. See ya.' Adam threw his hand up at me. 'Luke!'

I waved. 'Adam!'

He leaped over the railing and disappeared down the embankment as I drifted up behind Amanda and folded my arms around her. We didn't see Adam come up the other side of the creek – it was too dark.

'Well?' I said.

'Well, what?'

'What's your next plan?'

'I'm thinking about it.'

I nuzzled my face against her ear. 'Maybe you should let it go.'

'Luke?'

'Yeah?'

'You really smell.'

She laughed, broke free, and I chased her all the way back across the ground.

Thursday's session felt normal – no more questions about Adam, and one of the advantages of having Matt running around shouting encouragement and barking orders was that it allowed Percy to participate in the physical drills of training, although he had to do it all one-handed. Still, it helped him keep his fitness up.

Saturday, his pre-game speech was different to his usual speeches that were all about hyping us up until we bounced off the walls and out onto the field. Now – using the info Matt had gotten watching Grasstree's previous game – he broke down tactically what we had to do.

'Watch out for number thirty-two,' he said.

'Jay Collins,' Matt said.

'Matt says he won't even go for the ball – he'll block and hold the whole game long. We know he's going to go after Adam, so we have to get in there, block him back. Sean, their full-forward—'

'Wayne Kelly,' Matt filled in.

'—is quick on the lead, but he likes to double back, get in behind you.'

There was more stuff like that, and it gave the pre-game build-up a different feel, one that was almost professional, something that I would've expected in the bigger leagues. It helped, too – we knew which of their players to look out for, what they might do, and how they played, so we weren't just relying on us outplaying them. We set up the strategies to minimise the impact their best players could have. Rankin and his generals sat in the crowd watching, as they had for our last game. I wondered what they thought.

After the game, I sat in the Ulah'lah, nursing my water, while the others drank and celebrated. Matt was in there, too, coming back from the bar with jugs of beer. Now I had to concede he was a different person – not the Matt I'd known, who'd always been surly and standoffish. I guess finding a way to contribute helped him fit in – something he'd struggled with as a player as he got older. He and Sean partnered in pool and monopolised the table, winning game after game, even though they drank more than anybody.

Because I now was with Amanda, I had to wait until closing. That made not drinking harder since it was all around me. Some of the guys ribbed me, offered me beers, or shoved glasses in my face. I remembered I used to treasure this camaraderie like it meant something *because* of the beer. As the players stumbled out into the night, I didn't envy the way they'd be feeling come the morning. Once they were gone, I waited until Amanda had locked up, then walked her home.

'That can't be easy for you,' she said.

'What?'

'Sitting there, while the other guys drink.'

'I haven't given it a single thought.'

'Right. I work there. I know how hard it gets as everybody around you gets drunker and drunker, and as they get drunker and drunker, how they think they get cleverer and cleverer and funnier and funnier.'

'It's okay.'

'You think it might tempt you to get back into it?'

'I know where I want to get to.'

Amanda smiled. 'You played well today.'

'Thanks.'

'Even scored a look from Rankin.'

'What?'

'I went down to where Rankin and the others were standing – to see if I might overhear anything.'

'Oh, of course.'

'Rankin had a set of binoculars. He watched Adam pretty much the whole game – except when he swapped the binoculars around with the generals.'

'I guess they're trying to work out how to stop our best player.'

'Maybe. But it was weird.'

'What're you thinking?'

'Nothing,' Amanda said, although quite obviously something was bugging her about it. 'Nothing at all.'

We reached her little bungalow. She rose up on the single doorstep and put her arms around my neck. I held her – maybe tighter than I should've, but she felt good to hold. She kissed me – once, lightly, her mouth tugging on my lower lip. Then she grabbed my sleeve.

'Come on,' she said.

She unlocked the front door and led me in – right into her bedroom. My heart thumped faster than when I'd had to line up on Rankin. *Rankin.* He definitely wasn't who I wanted to be thinking about now. The light from the clock radio – with its digital red numbers – provided this eerie glow, like I was entering some den of foreboding. The thought leaped in, then was gone. I don't know why it had come up – why any of these thoughts had popped in.

Amanda must've sensed my anxiousness. She sat me on the bed and we kissed until I started feeling comfortable again. Those thoughts slipped away. I was okay. It was just Amanda and me now. Just us. *Us.*

'You all right?' she whispered.

I wanted to say something witty to show how relaxed I was, but didn't trust myself – at least, not entirely. I nodded.

Amanda reached over me, opened the bedside drawer and grabbed something from inside. 'I got these … well, you know, in case,' she said, tearing open a condom. 'But I want you to be prepared from now on – don't leave it all up to me, okay?'

'Okay.'

'I mean it.'

'I'm listening.'

After we were done we lay there, holding one another, and everything else was forgotten – my nervousness, football, and the rest of the world. This is what felt right and secure – not because of the sex, but because of the closeness Amanda and I had developed.

The next morning I woke to her on the phone. She sat on the bed, and nodded, while saying stuff like 'Uh-huh' and 'Okay'. Finally she hung up, glanced back at me and saw that I was awake. She slid back under the covers and cuddled up to me.

'That was the city editor,' she told me. 'I told him I was going to have trouble with this piece, but still wanted to take a shot at it. He's left it open with me – told me to take as long as I need. It takes some of the pressure off – I don't need it right away. But I don't want to keep him waiting indefinitely.'

'Adam doesn't want the article.'

'You heard him – he said I was welcome to write it without him.'

I wasn't sure I liked the sound of that.

The next fortnight, my world continued to change. I spent most of my time at Amanda's now. We'd get up together, then go do our separate things during the day – usually for me, I'd train and read. Some evenings, I'd sit on the couch and Amanda would thrust her notebook or laptop at me and ask me to read whatever she was writing. The only times I ducked home were to try to catch up on my chores, to have the occasional meal, and Friday nights – I always slept at home the night before a game because it was part of my routine, and also because I didn't want any distractions.

At first, it didn't seem any different, other than for the fact I had a girlfriend. But one evening, I came out of our fields – bare now, wheat harvested – so the emptiness swallowed me up. The house was mostly a shadow against this bloody sky marked by a string of charcoal clouds. Home had once been permanent, and now it felt temporary. I was a lodger. This wasn't where I was going to be forever.

Matt continued to deliver his scouting reports – credit to him, he knew how to identify a team's strengths and weakness, revealing a hidden talent for analysis. We beat the Shandeen Bank Bunyips by sixty-two points, and then the Baden Creek Eels – now with Nigel back in the side – by fifty-three points. Again, Rankin and his generals – still serving out their own suspensions – sat in the crowd for both games, although the few times I could check them out proved Amanda right: they weren't watching the game, but Adam. Rankin's face was ashen, and that vein in his temple throbbed. When the siren went following that Bunyips' match, Rankin and his cronies got up and walked off as our fans hooted them. Amanda – from where she watched on the boundary – and I exchanged a quick look.

Later, in the usual post-match celebrations at the Ulah'lah, Matt jumped up on a table and held a jug of beer high up. 'With that win,' he said, 'it means we are definitely playing finals this year!'

The cheer that went up had me covering my ears. We were second on the ladder and, while we could drop to fourth depending on the results of our last two games, mathematically we couldn't fall out of the final five.

'The Scorpions are going to know we're coming!' Matt said.

'Easy, easy, easy!' Percy said. 'Scorpions are undefeated this year!'

The cheer morphed – mid-cadence – into a boo.

'You can hate them,' Percy said, 'but never, ever stop respecting them – the moment you do, they'll have you.'

The night unfolded the way those nights did, and I sank into a corner table with Adam, Sean, Nigel, and Dean, each with a beer, while I nursed my second water.

'We could play in a grand final!' Sean said.

'We still have to get there first,' I said.

'We'll get there,' Sean said. 'Right?'

He lifted his glass for a toast. Adam, Nigel and Dean were quick to lift their glasses and I recognised this wasn't the place for my wariness. I toasted their glasses with my own, and we each drank – Sean until he'd finished his beer in one gulp. He slammed his glass down.

'Who's up?' he said. 'Luke?'

I got up and headed over to the bar. Amanda was pouring two jugs for Matt and rolled her eyes at me. I sat on a stool to wait. Her notebook lay folded behind the bar. I picked it up, thinking she wouldn't mind me taking a look at what I believed was the match report for *The Tribune*.

But it turned out to be about her article on Adam. In red, she'd written notes to herself:

- check on Adam's farm with real estate agent
- ring around about Adam
- ask Rankin about Adam

There was more, but I couldn't get past that one line:

— ask Rankin about Adam

Amanda snatched the notebook from me and tossed it under the bar. 'Do you mind?' she said.

'You've always got me reading stuff anyway.'

'When *I'm* ready.'

'Okay.'

'We'll talk about it later.'

It was an anxious wait until the Ulah'lah closed, and then I drifted out with everybody and said my goodbyes. The guys split their separate ways and began the stumble home – all but Adam, who loped towards the footy ground.

I started to go back into the Ulah'lah, but a car engine rumbled. A big crimson Ford – lights off – emerged from an adjacent street. The car pulled out onto Main Road and trailed behind Adam – a predator stalking its prey. I jogged down the street.

'Adam!' I said.

He turned now, the car right behind him. I pulled up alongside it. The windows were tinted, so it made it hard to see in. All I saw was a face shrouded in white. The tyres screeched and smoked as the car lurched forward, swerved around Adam, and sped off.

'What was that about?' Adam said.

'I don't know.'

'Probably somebody just gammin',' he said.

'Gammin?'

'You know – joking.'

'I know what that means. What I meant—'

'I'll see you at training.'

And off he went, down towards our footy ground. I watched him walk away until the night had swallowed him. Then I returned to the Ulah'lah, trying to puzzle out what happened. I didn't know much about cars, but I did know that car didn't come from around here. Amanda waited by the front door of the Ulah'lah, arms folded across her chest.

'Where've you been?' she said.

I told her what had happened as we walked back to her place, hand in hand. Amanda shivered next to me and I put an arm around her. She folded into me, but she remained stiff as I finished my story.

'Who do you think it was?' she said.

'I don't know – I couldn't get a proper look. It was like the guy had a mask on, but something white.'

'Why would you wear a white mask?'

'I don't know.'

I couldn't settle, even after we got back to Amanda's bungalow, and we cuddled in bed. For a while, we were quiet, our little argument we'd had in the Ulah'lah over her notes forgotten. But then her voice punctured the darkness.

'You know I want to write this story.'

'But now it's like you're prying into his personal stuff.'

'If he's not going to talk to me, what choice do I have?'

'What about wanting to talk to Rankin?'

Amanda shuddered against me, and I ran my hand up and down her back.

'The way Rankin looked at Adam ...' she said. 'Well, it wasn't just Rankin, it was all of them – Verne, Bell, Schwartzer—'

I sat up. 'Oh.'

'What?'

'*Oh.*'

'*What?*'

I lay back down. 'The white mask of the guy in the car – it wasn't a mask. It was—'

'—Schwartzer with his bandaged face.'

'Yeah.'

'What're they doing out here?'

I couldn't think of a single logical reason, which left the illogical ones: watching Adam during a game and trying to work out how to nullify him was one thing, but following him in a car was something else entirely.

'You think they want to hurt him?' Amanda said.

'They could've run him down if they wanted to hurt him.'

'Something's going on here, Luke. I'm waiting for a few calls back—'

'A few calls back from who?'

'Don McKay, for one.'

About ten years ago, there were three real estate agents who took care of the towns out here: Don McKay, Dave Cronwyn, and Murray Verne. Verne had bought his business from a friend responsible for the real estate in Ulah, Warrambatta, Shandeen Bank, and Little Reach. Being an idiot, Verne had run his business into the ground. Cronwyn, on the other hand, had been a shark, but as he got older he'd become forgetful, and would try to sell the same properties twice and stuff like that. In the end, Don McKay bought out Verne and Cronwyn, hired some staff, and now took care of all the real estate out here.

'I really want to find Adam's farm,' Amanda said. 'But you know what? I don't think it's out there. I don't think he has a farm at all.'

'So … what? He disappears into the night?'

'Don't be silly. But think about it – an unbelievable footballer pops up out of nowhere. He tells us he's got a farm out there, but we can't find it. He shies away from the media. You know what I think? I think he's hiding.'

'Who would he be hiding from?'

Amanda shrugged. 'But if you were going to hide, wouldn't this be the perfect place? It's the middle of nowhere, it has no ties to the city, it's a black hole in the outback. You come here, you've disappeared.'

'The point of *hiding* is to keep away from attention,' I said, 'and Adam's done anything but that.'

'Yeah, he's drawn *our* attention, but that stays localised to here. Who else has heard anything about it? Who would've heard about him if that article I'd written about the bloodbath hadn't been picked up? When's the last time that's happened?'

Never. There'd been fights before in games, but nothing like the violence in that match with all the reports, suspensions, and injuries it contained. It was going to get attention, even if it had occurred in some backwater league. But that was it – just that one time in the history of our league.

'See, you know there's something here. I was thinking of maybe following Adam home after a match, or maybe after training.'

'You can't do that,' I said. 'If Adam *is* hiding from something, has it occurred to you maybe that's the way he wants it to stay?'

'Well, yeah ...' Amanda said. 'But aren't you curious?'

'It's still not right.'

'Okay, I'll tell you what: I'll wait until I hear from Don McKay. I'm betting there's no farm out there. If there is, even if it's in Mollongong, then I'll drop the whole story. If it isn't out there, then you're coming with me when I speak to Rankin.'

'Me? Why me?'

Amanda rolled on top of me. 'Why do you think?'

She kissed me and I had no resistance.

Rankin

We struggled in our penultimate game for the home and away season, trailing the Verdune Cobras by a couple of goals for the first three quarters.

'What is it today?' Percy said, asking a question that had been common to his addresses throughout the match. 'These guys are second last! You got your eyes on finals? You not thinking about *now*? We *can* still drop from second, finish as low as fourth – that's an elimination final. Lose and we're out. This isn't form to be taking into the finals!'

The last quarter wasn't pretty – I felt like we waited for it all to click, and we'd overrun them. It didn't happen. With about ten minutes to go, we were sixteen points down. Percy swung me to full-forward and I was lucky enough to take a couple of marks and kick both goals. The deficit was now four points. For the next couple of minutes, Verdune tried to waste time, diving on the ball when possible, and when they had possession they kicked it around. But it came undone when an errant kick landed on Sam's chest on the wing. He kicked to me, I sidestepped my opponent, and handballed to Ronnie, who snapped to put us in front. Adam then won the clearance from the next bounce, streamed away, and kicked one of his trademark long goals, so we now led by eight points. The siren went shortly after.

Percy waved us to him as we trotted off. 'Remember this!' he said. 'You take nothing for granted!'

Unfortunately, our final game – against the Harwood Platypuses – was little better. We led the whole game, but it was always only by two or three goals. This time, at each of the breaks, instead of querying us, Percy encouraged us to focus and keep moving the ball forward. We did, but it didn't get much prettier, and the Platypuses got a couple of late goals to cut our lead to six points. They had a shot at drawing level, too – their full-forward led wide and deep, and took a mark on the boundary. His shot looked in all the way, only to graze the post. Sean kicked out long to me, I kicked to Sam on the wing, and he kicked to Ronnie. Ronnie marked, evaded two opponents, and – as lackadaisical as you like – snapped a goal. The Platypuses realised that was it. The fight back was over. At the next bounce, Adam roved the ball and kicked long. Again, Ronnie was there – he punched the ball down to Nigel, who handballed to Dean. Dean ran into an open goal and kicked truly. The siren went not long after – the seventeen-point victory flattered us.

After the game, we sat in the clubrooms, waiting to hear a round-up of the other matches. Both Warrambatta and Shandeen Bank won to cement fourth and fifth spots – the only time Warrambatta, Shandeen Bank, and Ulah all finished in the finals in the same year. It was a bit of a financial boon – there's not much in the way of an economic climate around here, so a derby involving Warrambatta and Shandeen Bank in the elimination final, and us in one of the others in the first week would skyrocket sales of alcohol, junk food, and stuff like that. You mightn't think it's a lot, but to little towns like ours it's like winning the Olympics.

Mollongong won their last game against Baden Creek by a solitary point, cementing third position. Although we'd beaten them previously, given their experience they still loomed as a legitimate threat, especially the way we were playing.

Then we heard Little Reach had obliterated this season's wooden spooners, the Verdune Cobras, by 152 points. That kept the Scorpions on top with a record of twenty-two games played, twenty-two wins – the undefeated season Rankin had always wanted. We finished with eighteen wins and four losses, with three of those losses happening within the first five rounds before we got serious. It was our best season in the history of the competition.

The Ulah'lah rocked with celebrations that night – people drank, sprayed each other with beer, and broke out into chants of *'Ulah Curlews!'* Whenever there was a lull, it was filled by boasts about how we'd smash Mollongong in the qualifying final, face Little Reach in the second semi, and get our revenge.

'Keep your minds on the job!' Percy said. 'Keep your minds on the job!'

Matt and Sean and several of the players splashed him with beer, which sent up another chant of *'Ulah Curlews!'* I sat in my corner, wishing I could get out of there. Amanda arched her brows at me, sceptical of what was going on. Then Matt and Sean fell into chairs opposite me.

'Lukey boy!' Matt clapped my shoulder. 'You excited?'

'We're gonna be premiers!' Sean said.

'I'll be excited *when* we're premiers,' I said.

Matt shook me, finished his jug, then blinked in surprise at it being empty. 'Be right back!' He stumbled up and zigzagged to the bar.

Sean leaned back in his chair and sighed.

'You're spending a bit of time with Matt,' I said.

'He's offered me an apprenticeship,' Sean said.

'Yeah?'

Sean nodded. 'Apprentice plumber. Get this: he said since he started scouting, he's talking to a lot of people at the other games, and he's been generating lots of work. So he's giving me a chance.' He grinned. 'And I'm taking it. This could help set me up.'

'Yeah.' I lifted my empty glass. 'Congratulations.'

Sean toasted me with his jug. 'Thanks!'

I wasn't sure what else to say – or what to think. Sean was happy to put down roots here, and that was fine. He had a plan. I wondered about my own future. Getting together with Amanda had occupied my mind. I needed to work out what I was doing. I thought back to my conversation with Amanda about going elsewhere to be discovered. Did I have the courage to do that?

When the Ulah'lah finally closed an hour later than it should've, Amanda and me walked back to her place. Lying in bed, I kept thinking about where I'd be this time next year, and where I'd be in ten years. Wherever it was, it wouldn't be in Ulah. I drifted off trying to find the courage in myself to commit to that jump.

Early the next morning, Amanda's phone rang from the bedside drawer. She rolled onto her back and grabbed it. I buried my head under the pillow while Amanda held a short conversation, although it was muffled to me. When she was finished, she hung up, and pulled the pillow off my head.

'That was the real estate agency,' she said.

I stifled a groan. She'd been waiting for this call – waiting so long I thought it wouldn't come. I'd hoped this business with Adam could be buried and left in peace.

'And?' I asked.

'Adam has no farm.' Amanda rolled on top of me. 'They haven't sold a farm for two years.'

'So you were right,' I said.

'They haven't sold *any* property out there in two years, Luke.'

'Maybe there's a place out there they don't handle.'

'Come on, get up.' Amanda slid off me and got out of bed.

'What?'

'I told you, if Adam had a farm out there I'd drop this. He doesn't. He has *nothing*. So we're going.'

'Where?'

'To talk to Rankin – remember? You're my chaperone.'

'Oh, great.'

While Amanda showered, I fixed a breakfast of toast, eggs, freshly-squeezed juice and tea. Then she washed up the dishes while I showered. It wasn't long before we swung around to her parents so we could borrow Percy's ute to drive to Little Reach.

The morning was blustery, winds so strong that you could hear the branches of the gums creak, while the clouds were thick and bulging, struggling to hold back a deluge. The streets of Little Reach were grey and bleak, like somebody had leeched the life from them. Rankin's house was a little weatherboard thing lined with meticulously trimmed roses, their blooms so bright they almost seemed to be pulsing, and their front lawn as neatly manicured as any football ground.

'Come on,' Amanda said.

'You better go alone,' I said. 'He mightn't talk in front of me. I'll watch from here. If there's any trouble, I'll be out like a shot.'

Amanda considered that, then nodded. 'Okay, good thinking.'

She got out of the ute, ran up to the front door and rang the bell. A small woman answered – Rankin's wife, although nobody heard much about her given she was always eclipsed by his notoriety. She was neat and well-kept, as if she'd never known a wrinkled dress, a stray hair, or even an errant thought. A short conversation followed – I couldn't hear what they were saying, but it looked nice enough, two women having a Sunday morning chat. Finally, Amanda returned.

'He's at the church,' she said.

'Sunday,' I said, then realised, 'Services are on.'

'Uh-huh.'

'Rankin goes without his wife?'

'She said he took up going weekly after he became coach. Never knew that about him, did you?'

'No. I always thought of Rankin as ... well, you know, godless.'

'That's terrible, Luke.'

'So what do we do?'

But Amanda had already started the car.

The church was only a couple of minutes from Rankin's house – it was probably only a couple of minutes from everything in Little Reach. A driveway ran down the side of the church, and into the lot at the back, only we couldn't find any parking. I did notice Rankin's battered blue van parked in the corner. Amanda drove back out front and found a spot across the street outside a little coffee shop, The Koala Kiosk. The sculpture of a wooden koala sat above the door, a cup – presumably coffee – in hand.

'This is the plan?' I asked.

'Unless you can think of something better.'

'How about we leave it?'

'How about you grab me a coffee?'

I slipped out of the ute and into The Koala Kiosk – it was tiny inside, with only a handful of chairs. Pictures hung on the wall – some were of wildlife but, unsurprisingly, most were of the Scorpions during various premiership victories. A display cabinet boasted an extensive range of pastry. Lots of it looked exotic, with different icing, different powdered sugars, different jams – I didn't know so many different pastries could exist.

'What can I get you?'

The man behind the counter was thin and middle-aged, with ruddy cheeks and a nose that belonged on a taller man – a giant, maybe. I wondered if this guy was at the games we played against the Scorpions, and if he'd booed and hissed and screamed out all that hateful shit.

'Two coffees – to go,' I said. 'A couple of chocolate doughnuts would be good, too.'

'Coming up.'

As he fixed the coffees, he glanced at me several times. I kept my head down, pretending to read a newspaper – *The Chronicle*, which covered this area – that had been left on a table. The front page had a picture of the Scorpions walking off the ground following their most recent victory, along with the headline, 'March to Greatness!'

'You look familiar,' the guy behind the counter said, 'but you're not from around here, are you?'

I shook my head.

'You play football, don't you?' He clicked his fingers and pointed at me. 'For the Curlews, yeah? You're that centre half-back. The lefty!'

I smiled guiltily, but half expected he would now spit in my coffee before he put the lid on the plastic cup.

'Good game, that last one,' he said, using a set of tongs to deposit two chocolate doughnuts into a paper bag. 'Don't think it had to turn out the way it did. We panicked when you came at us, and Claude loves his heavies. I still think we've got your number, though.'

'I hope not.'

He chuckled and pushed the coffees and bag of doughnuts across the counter. I slid my hand into my pocket. He waved at me.

'On the house,' he said.

'I couldn't—'

'I insist.'

I grabbed the coffees and the paper bag. 'Thanks. I appreciate that.'

'Hope you have a great day.'

'You, too.' I turned for the door.

'That blackfella of yours is amazing – one of the best I've seen.'

I stopped, unsure if he was purposely being racist or if he had no idea of what he was saying. 'Yeah.'

I waited for something more, some form of clarity, but when it didn't come, headed out the door and back into the ute. Amanda was rubbing her hands together, which she now wrapped around her cup. I told her what had happened as I offered her a doughnut. Given the way the guy in the coffee shop had spoken, I'd lost the taste for mine.

'Bet a lot of them are casually racist around here,' she said. 'Probably not even aware they're doing it.'

'Feels sometimes like the whole world out here is frozen in time.'

Amanda finished her doughnut, then had mine while we drank our coffee. I found a bin for the rubbish and we kept what felt a useless vigil. The clouds burst, hitting the ute with big fat raindrops that splattered across the windshield and bounced onto the road. Cars whooshed past, headlights beaming, and it grew so cold that several times Amanda had to turn the engine on and pump the heater to warm us up.

Around midday, the first of a handful of people spilled from the church and, jackets pulled up over their heads, charged around the back. Amanda switched the ignition to accessories, so she could turn the wipers on. They squelched away, but even they seemed resigned and the windscreen remained bleary. It made it hard to identify people as they emerged from the church. Husbands were sent to get cars while wives and kids waited in the foyer.

'It's gonna be hard to recognise Rankin in this rain,' I said.

It must've taken half an hour for all the cars to come around from that back parking lot, let their passengers in, and pull out onto the road. The rain didn't care and beat away, until nobody was left to come, and the church stood dark and forlorn.

'Did we miss him?' Amanda said.

'Wouldn't be surprising,' I said. 'Although ...'

'What?'

'We didn't see his van pull out.'

Amanda started the ute, hooked across the road – several cars beeping her – and into the church's driveway. She drove around to the back parking lot. Sure enough, Rankin's van sat alone there now. Amanda pulled up alongside, got out, and pressed her hands against the passenger window. Then she waved to me.

'Come on!' she said.

'Where—?'

She was already running down the drive, so I had to chase her until we got back around the front. We took the stairs two at a time and plunged into the foyer, pulling up to show some decorum, and pat the rain from ourselves as best as we could, the way a dog might shake the water from its fur.

Despite the monstrosity the church was on the outside, inside it was standard: rows of pews, stained glass windows, a dais – things you'd expect in a church. But what gave it resonance was its age. It was more than one-hundred-and-fifty years old. Over its storied history, convicts, settlers, British, and your average Australian, had all come here. It was impressive if you thought about it. I guess that's why Little Reach had such solemnity – not so much because of the church itself, but because of the history it'd seen. In a way, it was a landmark. I only really got that now.

Rankin – in a dark grey suit – sat in the second row, staring at the crucifix at the front of the church, while kneading something in his hands. As we got closer, I saw it was a set of rosary beads made from burnished wood.

'Mr Rankin?' Amanda said.

Rankin was scary on the field; in life, there was a crushing grimness about him. When he played football, his eyes burned with passion and energy, but now they were that cold metallic silver; the lines in his face were chiselled, like his face was slotted together from jigsaw pieces of flesh. Here was a guy who'd dedicated his life to small-town football, and now I felt almost as if he regretted it, but was powerless to surrender his obsession.

'What're you two doing here?' he said.

'I want to ask you about Adam Pride,' Amanda said.

Rankin smirked and looked at me. 'He's *your* teammate.'

'I noticed *your* interest in him when you came to some of our games,' Amanda said.

'You noticed that, huh?'

'Yeah.'

'Yeah, so what?' Rankin said. 'I'm a coach. I've got to figure out a way to stop him.'

'And that's all there is to it?'

'You don't know with these guys. You don't know what they're capable of.'

'That's a provincial attitude.'

'What do you want me to say?'

'Did you follow him the other night?' I said. 'With Daniel Schwartzer? Coming out of the Ulah'lah?'

'Now why would I do that?'

'I don't know – that's why I'm asking.'

'Don't know what you're talking about.'

'So you're lying in a church.'

Rankin's face grew hard. 'I'm not lying.'

And then I realised he was telling the truth – no, he personally didn't follow Adam with Daniel Schwartzer. But of course he knew about it, because he'd probably ordered it.

'How about how racial you get?' Amanda asked.

'Not me,' Rankin said.

'Your fans, too.'

'It's the way of things.'

'The *way of things?*' Amanda's eyebrows shot up.

'Again, what do you want me to say?'

'You tell me.'

Rankin laughed and clicked his fingers as realisation hit him. 'You're the girl who writes the match reports for *The Tribune*, aren't you? Yeah, I was trying to place you. Percy's daughter! You stood next to us when we watched a couple of your games.'

Amanada stiffened. She must've thought she'd been discreet but, no, Rankin had seen her. It shouldn't have been surprising, though. Rankin didn't seem the sort of person who'd miss anything.

He smiled, and the condescension radiated from him. 'So, you figure there's some story here? And you *figure* I know *something*. You want to know what *I* know?'

'Yes,' Amanda said, her voice flat, eyes unblinking.

'No, you don't – you really don't. You stay young and pretty and stupid and dream your dreams of how amazing your life can be.' Rankin's grin broadened, but his face was hard, if not pained. 'Unfortunately, shit happens, and you don't get what you want. You get what you have to deal with.' He rose to his feet and loomed over us. 'Some things, you don't want to know.'

His lips pressed into a thin line, and he looked us up and down, dismissively, as if we didn't deserve to be in his company. Amanda and I stepped back, and he slid out from the pew, scrunched his rosary in one huge fist, and walked from the church.

The Trail

'Well?' Amanda said on the drive back.

It was impossible to dispute that something was going on now. It was a question of *what*.

'I don't know what to say. Maybe we should tell somebody.'

'Tell them what? That we have some suspicions that something's not quite right? We need to find out more.'

I was afraid she was going to say that, but it became something buried in the back of my mind as a new set of worries came in – our final against Mollongong. Percy pushed us hard on Tuesday, but we all fumbled and shanked kicks; it was like we were training ankle-deep in water. Thursday wasn't any better, and at the end of it all Percy called us into a ring around him.

'Well?' he said.

He moved from player to player, looking us each in the eye, challenging us to articulate what was going on. When he got to me, I wanted to give him an answer. But some things are indefinable – form is one of them.

'Go hit the showers,' Percy said.

While we trudged off – Adam going the other way – Percy and Matt stayed on the ground, deep in conversation. They were still there after I'd washed up, changed, and come out of the clubrooms. It was an odd sight, these two middle-aged men – and I saw now that they were like Dad, battered and weathered by time – talking about our fortunes.

In bed that night, our poor form even took precedence over Amanda's investigation into the mystery behind Adam. She lay on her side, head propped up on one hand, her other hand tracing little circles on my chest.

'Do you think it's the nerves?' she said. 'You're a pretty young side. Except for Ronnie and Dad, most of you don't have much – or *any* – finals experience. Not in the Seniors, at least.'

'That could be it. But our form slipped a few weeks before the season ended.'

'Maybe when you march out there Saturday, it'll click.'

'I *hope*.'

That hope didn't seem likely pre-game, gathered in our rooms as Percy paced back and forth, and tried to rev us up, when Nigel jumped up, ran to one of the toilet cubicles and vomited.

'You okay, Nigel?' Percy said.

Nigel vomited again, then flushed the toilet. The stench wafted over us and we cringed. Matt cranked open some of the windows. Nigel sat down.

'I'm sweet,' he said.

'Look, I know we're all nervous – a lot of you haven't played in finals before,' Percy said. 'It's daunting. I understand that. I've been through it. Like Matt has. And Ronnie. We've had a—'

Sean bounced up and bolted to the toilet. It was almost like you could hear every individual chunk of vomit hit the toilet basin.

'We've had a good season,' Percy said. 'We've trained hard. When you get out there—'

Sam was next, then Nigel again, then Harry, and then five other players – each of them rotating through our toilets. It kept interrupting Percy's ability to build any real momentum, and it wasn't long before we'd all pulled the collars of our jumpers over our noses, although that didn't help. Matt opened the door to the club rooms (the crowd cheered, anticipating we were coming out), then walked around with a lighter, like that might burn away the stench.

'When you get out there,' Percy went on, 'it becomes about muscle memory. You've trained hard. Each of you knows how your teammates play and can anticipate where they'll be. You know the game we play. Let yourself go: it'll come back to you!'

It didn't – the game unfolded in a blur. My legs felt heavy, my body uncoordinated, and I was always a step behind my opponent. I wasn't the only one. Sean's opponent kicked eight goals on him. Our midfield struggled to get their hands on the ball, and what chances our forwards did have, they blew. Adam was as good as always, but it was never going to be enough wen the rest of us were so bad. Mollongong were ruthless. They'd been in finals often enough to showcase a composure that carried them from the first siren through to the final siren. When the game ended, Mollongong had won 18.8.(116) to us 8.24.(72).

We ambled off, while the Mollongong supporters in the crowd cheered and celebrated and waved their royal blue and yellow flags. Our fans were stunned. Then a set of familiar faces pushed their way to the front: Rankin and his players – at first, I thought it was just his generals, but the whole Scorpions squad lined the railing, jumped up and hurled abuse at us.

'Too bad, boys!' Rankin said.

'You're crap!' Murray Verne said.

'Front-running sucks!' Terry Bell said.

'Welcome to the big leagues, boys!' Schwartzer said, leaning so far over that he could wiggle his fingers in our faces.

'Screw you, Danny,' Adam said as we walked up the player's race to the rooms.

Schwartzer stuck a finger up at Adam.

'Not a good game – obviously,' Percy said once we were back in our rooms. 'I'm not going to sugar-coat it. But let's put it down to nerves. I think this has been building a while. Now remember what this feels like; pack it up, scrunch it up really tight,' he demonstrated, wringing his hands together, 'and keep it as motivation for the next game. Got it?'

Nobody responded, and to Percy's credit he didn't push it.

The Ulah'lah was sombre that night. Not many supporters showed up, and those who did left quick. The rest of our guys sprawled across the pub. Some played pool. Others sat in booths and watched television. A few of us sat in the corner the way we usually would, but quiet.

Matt came over with two jugs of beer and poured refills for the guys sitting with me – Adam, Sean, Nigel, Dean, and Percy. He poured himself one and plonked himself down in a chair.

'How about those Scorpions?' he said.

'Bastards,' Nigel said.

'Couldn't believe *all* of them were there,' Dean said.

'Psychological warfare,' Percy said. 'Wanted to make us feel as low as possible.'

'It worked,' Sean said.

'No,' Matt said. 'They wouldn't have done it if they weren't afraid of us.' He lifted his glass. 'It's not over yet.'

'That's right.' Percy lifted his own glass. 'We're still in this.'

'Gives you an extra week to get yourself right, too.'

'That's right, Coach,' Adam said. 'One more week with the suspension. How're the knuckles?'

Percy opened and clenched his hand. 'Feels good.'

'To next week,' Matt said.

We toasted and I finished my water, then excused myself to get a refill. I sat on a stool at the bar while Amanda served Harry, Sam, and a couple of the other guys. I watched the beer pour from the tap, splash into the glass, and foam. One beer would be okay – especially given the circumstances.

I pushed the thought from my mind. I'd made a commitment. Now I'd see it through, one way or another.

Once Amanda was finished with the guys, she poured me a water, slid it in front of me, and leaned against the bar. 'Well?'

'Well, what?'

'You coming with me?'

'Where?'

'Tonight's the night.'

'The night?'

'You *know*.'

Amanda rolled her eyes in the direction of where Adam was seated in the corner.

'You're serious?'

Amanda nodded.

'You can't do this.'

'I am. The question's whether you're coming or not.'

Nothing I said was going to change her mind. Now, either I didn't go and that would show my disapproval of the plan – and I *did* disapprove of the plan – or I went to make sure Amanda was safe. That's what I told myself.

Come closing, Amanda rushed through locking up as the guys spilled outside. They milled there the way they always did saying their goodbyes, and I felt a weird separation, like I was coming apart and losing something. Next week, if we lost our final, our season would be over. There were no more chances.

'I'll see you all Tuesday,' Percy said. 'Let's not hang onto this, huh?'

As they spread to go their own way, Amanda emerged from the Ulah'lah. She had a black jacket on – which she'd buttoned up – as well as black pants, so she'd dressed the part. She closed and locked the front door.

'Ready?' she asked.

'As I'll ever be.'

It was a bright night – a full moon that hung low and large over the far side of the creek, like the beam of a lighthouse wanting to bring us home. Adam was amazing; he must've put down twenty beers at the Ulah'lah. Anybody else would've been zigzagging. Not Adam. He was graceful as he crossed the oval and hopped the railing. The curlews were out because they shrieked, their cries echoing. Then Adam disappeared down the embankment.

Amanda and I jogged across the ground to catch up – I managed it easy enough but Amanda puffed so loud I was sure Adam would've heard her. We felt our way down the embankment, picked our way across the creek on the stepping stones, then clambered up the other side. Adam was a silhouette against the moon, keeping this undeviating line. We walked until the gums appeared, swaying like they were welcoming Adam. We had to jog again to try keep track of him. The gums grew thicker until they blotted out the moon, a monochromatic darkness falling over us, and the wind whispered through the gums' naked branches, rising up into a low, shrill howl. Now we couldn't see Adam, but we kept going straight as he'd done. Amanda stopped and I bumped into her.

'You know where we are?' she said.

I was about to ask how she expected me to know – especially in the dark – when it hit: these were the trees where we'd seen Rankin and the others.

'Can you see him?' Amanda asked.

I shook my head, and we tread forward step by step until my legs grew heavy. We might have stepped into another world here, one that was cold and dark and wrong. The best thing to do would've been to turn back, but I felt a pull to keep going; Amanda must've felt it too, because she started to pick up the pace. I took her hand. Her palm was clammy.

A wall appeared in front of us – at least that's what I thought it was at first, a solid black barrier. As I got closer, I saw it was a stack of felled trees – last time we'd seen this, there'd been only a handful. Now they were head high, and as we crept around it, it was evident that a large section of the bush had been cleared. My heartbeat thumped in my ears. Amanda's breath grated. Mine had stopped.

Amanda stumbled and fell. My grasp on her hand broke. She shrieked and was swallowed up into blackness. Then her blonde head came up. She hadn't fallen onto the ground, but *into* the ground, inside a hole about the length of her body. Holes were everywhere, like some demented feral bunny had run amok.

'Luke—!' Amanda said.

A blur shot out in front of me. Then a streak of silver. I ducked instinctively. Something *whizzed* over my head. Then wood splintered. Other figures rose up, wraiths that appeared from the ground, dark and sinewy. Two beams of light blazed directly across my line of vision. I blinked and lifted a hand to shield my eyes. A familiar denim jacket flapped in front of my face. I dropped back a step. It was Rankin. His hands were wrapped around the handle of a pickaxe, the worn blade buried in one of the fallen trees. His battered van was parked opposite me, headlights cutting through the night. The shadows weren't wraiths but his usual crew. Schwartzer stood by the van, his hand snaking through the driver's window – he'd been the one who'd turned on the headlights.

I grabbed Amanda's wrist, hoisted her out of the hole and shoved her behind me. 'Are you crazy?' I said.

Rankin shook his head like he was a sleepwalker coming out of a daze. 'You're trespassing.'

'Trespassing?' Amanda said.

'This is private property,' Rankin said. '*My* property.'

'What's with the holes?' I said.

'I've been developing. Clearing it out. Been at it the whole year. Building a house back there and everything. What're you doing?'

'We're taking a walk in the moonlight,' Amanda said.

'Yeah, right.' Rankin yanked his pick from the tree. 'Get off my property or I'll have you prosecuted.' He led the others back through the trees.

'What the hell was that about?' Amanda said.

My gaze fell on the fallen trees and my breath caught in my throat.

'Luke?'

I pointed.

Blood trickled from the puncture Rankin's pick had made in the fallen tree.

Facing Adam

We hurried back, afraid the night would yield some new threat, although now it was peaceful out here – dead quiet once we left the gums behind, and the wind didn't have their branches to whip through. The moon coated everything in a luminous gloss, and I felt a peculiar displacement that nothing was real. We bounded across the creek, and the familiarity of the footy ground embraced us, assured us we'd be okay, although it wasn't until we were huddled on the couch in Amanda's lounge – lights on, each of us with a tea in our hands – that things felt normal again.

'What happened out there?' Amanda said. 'Do you think they thought we were Adam? Do you think they were trying to kill Adam?'

'For what?' I said. 'Over a game?'

'Over whatever's between them.'

'Maybe it's what Rankin said – that he's protecting his land.'

'Swinging a pick at somebody's head is pretty extreme.' Amanda pursed her lips. 'And what about the tree? It bled, didn't it?'

'Some trees bleed, don't they? Like ironbarks?'

'I don't know. Anyway, that was a gum.'

'Maybe we should go to the cops.'

'And say what? Rankin will tell them that trespassing story and that'll be the end of it. They have no reason to dig deeper. We need to talk to Adam again.'

'About …?'

'Whatever's going on. Tuesday, training, I'm going to talk to him.'

We went to bed shortly afterward, and slept restlessly until the alarm buzzed. The covers were twisted around our feet, and the sheet dislodged. Amanda sat up and rubbed her eyes. I put my hand on her arm.

'Why don't you take the day off?' I said.

'I'll be okay once I get moving,' she said. 'Late lunch today?'

'Sure.'

'Cool. About two.'

After we had breakfast, Amanda headed off to work at the Ulah'lah, while I went to the General Store and picked up a copy of *The Tribune*. Margie shook her head from behind the counter.

'I hope we don't see a repeat of yesterday,' she said.

'So do I.'

As I walked through Ulah, others queried me. Constable Brackie asked, 'What happened there?' I shrugged. Mick Jacobs, loading up his ute, said, 'You guys need to get your head in the game – like we did, way back when.' I nodded and smiled because it was the polite thing to do. Adrian Granger sat on a bench in the little park opposite the high school feeding bread crumbs to the sparrows. 'You've surely got better than that in you?' he said. 'Surely,' I told him. Everybody had an opinion or query that made me miserable, and I couldn't have felt more relieved when I left the town behind me.

The front page of *The Tribune* was a story about milk prices. The match report – only about half a page – was buried deep in the sports section. It didn't say anything I didn't know – that it seemed nerves had gotten the better of us, Mollongong had smelled our vulnerability and been ruthless in response, and now we had a chance to redeem ourselves – but it did make me appreciate how amazing Amanda was: she watched the game, belted out an article for *The Tribune*, and then went to work at the Ulah'lah. And through it all, she kept chasing this story that she believed would help her get out of here. I needed to learn a lesson from her.

Home looked small and empty – this little house that might've sat on the edge of the world, backed by nothing but a boundless blue sky. Mum – a silk scarf tied around her head – was on her knees, spade in hand as she dug her garden bed. She didn't look up as I approached.

'Hello, stranger,' she said.

'Hey, Mum.'

'Disappointing game.'

'You said it.'

'Cruel, isn't it?'

'Cruel?'

Mum leaned back so she was kneeling, and wiped her wrist across her brow. 'You've been so good the whole year – one more bad game, and that's it. You're done until next year and have to go through it all over again.'

'Thanks, Mum.'

'It bears thinking about – a little, at least.' Mum nodded her head in the direction of Dad's shed. 'Your dad could do with some help.'

'Sure.'

Dad was heaving sacks of manure from the shed to his truck. His shoulders were bent low, his upper back a bulb – like he was becoming a hunchback. I'd never noticed that before. He nodded at me, but kept going. I followed him into the shed and grabbed a sack.

'What happened yesterday?' he said.

'Not really sure myself,' I said, as I tossed the sack into the back of the truck.

'Everybody thought you'd beat Mollongong,' he said.

'I know.'

'Don't lose it,' Dad said, as we headed back into the shed.

'What?'

'You may never get another shot at this, so make the most of it.'

I tensed up. He took a deep breath – sweat poured from him – and then he picked up a sack of manure and slung it over his shoulder. I followed his lead, although once I was moving I realised that had been an opening to talk – to ask him what finals were like, and how he dealt with the pressure. The opportunity was now gone. I helped him through the morning until we were done. I was sweaty and sore, but the labour had helped me forget about my unease.

I went into the house, showered and changed, then used our computer – this dinky desktop that sat in the spare room – to go online, and scour the *White Pages* directory to make a list of football clubs I could call, although I had no idea what I would say to them. I needed to be proactive. I couldn't keep floating out here. By the time I'd listed the contact details for every VFL club, it was time to meet Amanda, so I headed back into town and found her at the bar.

She kissed me and signalled to one of the other bartenders that she was taking her break. 'How was your morning?'

'Everybody's asking me about the loss.'

We found a booth in the corner and sat down.

'That's all they're talking about here,' Amanda said.

'Feels like people are jumping off us, or like they think we fluked getting this far and that's the end of it.'

'They're preparing themselves for the worst.'

'For the worst?'

'We don't have much success here, Luke – you know that. I think people are scared to invest now things look shaky.'

We kept making small talk – nothing about Adam, and I didn't tell her about my list. I didn't want to share that until I felt there was something to share. So we talked about the Curlews, about how far we'd come, and things we'd talked about before, which kept us busy. It wasn't much different after work, and from the outside looking in everything might've seemed normal, but we had another sleepless night.

On Tuesday, I swung by the Ulah'lah to meet Amanda. When I hugged her, I could feel how tight her back was. We didn't say anything about what came next. It hung there, a bandaged wound that was about to be stripped and exposed.

Adam was already at the ground, sitting on the doorstep leading into the clubrooms. He leaned back against the jamb, legs extended, like he might've been enjoying a picnic outing.

'You're early,' Amanda said.

'Am I?' Adam gave us one of his easy-going grins.

'You usually show up right on time.'

'Life's full of little surprises.' Adam stretched and got up. 'You two look like you have something on your minds.'

'You know, don't you?' I said.

'Know?'

'I want to write my article,' Amanda said, her words tumbling into one another like she wanted to get them out before she could lose her courage. 'And I thought I could talk to you at your place – away from all this and everybody else. So we ... well, *I* ... decided we should follow you home – just so we knew where you lived.'

Adam waved at Nigel and Dean, who headed down to the ground, joking and laughing.

'But, well, we lost you, and found ourselves out in the bush out there. Rankin was there.'

'With his generals,' I said.

Amanda nodded. 'He swung a pick at Luke. Nearly took Luke's head off. I think Rankin must've been waiting for you.'

'With a pick?' Adam said.

'I'm just telling you what happened.'

It was growing busier, more players arriving and making for the clubrooms. Adam led us down the concrete apron and to the railing. He leaned against it, his face wistful.

'I guessed you might try following me home one night,' he said. 'Doesn't bother me.'

'So you bought a farm out there?' Amanda asked.

Adam lifted his head and chuckled. 'Still the reporter!' He straightened up. 'I never said I *bought* a farm. I said I *got* a farm out there. And, yeah, you're right, I don't want to tell anybody where it is because I don't want the hoopla.'

'What about Rankin?' Amanda asked.

'A man's got the right to defend what's his,' Adam said.

'With a pick?' I said.

'You take what's at hand.'

'There were these trees, too – Rankin hit one with his pick and it bled—'

'Probably sap.'

Percy and Matt – each with a football in hand – emerged from the clubrooms, strode past us, and onto the ground. Other players followed. Some waved at us or nodded their heads in acknowledgement.

'And Rankin?' Amanda said. 'Something's going on between you two, right?'

Adam grinned that big grin, and hopped over the railing. 'If something was, wouldn't I be worried?'

'You *should* be worried – I really think you should.'

'Some things, don't question them, don't try explaining them, don't even try understanding them. Just accept them.'

'Just accept them?' Amanda said.

'Uh-huh.'

He spun and jogged away.

Gloria

'We're going to do something different tonight,' Percy said. He held his arms outstretched. 'Two groups – one to either side.'

We did that, until we were evenly split. Percy joined the side I was on, while Matt joined the other side. We waited for Percy to give us instructions – to split us into smaller groups, or queues, or whatever the drill might be. But he twirled his football in his hands and kicked it long to the other group. Matt, on the other side, did the same, kicking his ball back to us.

'This is it!' Percy said.

It took longer than it should've to sink in: this was the extent of training – there was no other agenda. Some of the guys hung back and didn't try too hard to participate. As the evening wore on, others even sat – or lay – on the ground and chatted. Nobody thought about skills or routines or pressure, and we enjoyed the night to unwind, joking and laughing as we jostled with one another, flew for marks, and kicked the ball around. Thursday was the same – if not more relaxed – and come Saturday afternoon, the mood was different in our rooms than it had been for that first final.

'At the start of the season,' Percy said, 'if I'd claimed we'd finish second and look a genuine chance for a flag, everybody would've scoffed. I wouldn't have imagined it in my wildest dreams. We hit a bump last week, but we're still here. Now let's not worry about flags. Let's not even worry about this game. Let's go out there and have a good time!'

For much of the first quarter, we were as sloppy as we had been against Mollongong, but we were also full of energy. We attacked the ball and harassed Warrambatta, but we were inaccurate, kicking 0.5. Then Warrambatta cleared the ball from their defensive arc, chipped it through the centre, and kicked long to their full-forward. Sean spoiled and the ball flew loose. My opponent picked it up but I tackled him and dispossessed him. One of their small forwards pounced on the ball and snapped a goal – like that, they were in front. The game felt a breath from unravelling, tangling up the season with it.

But in the ball up, Harry tapped it down to Adam. Adam snapped it long to Ronnie, who marked, played on, sidestepped one player, spun around another, and kicked a goal. Then he did his little dance as we swamped him. Something fell away then – the malaise of the last three weeks, where we'd struggled to find any synergy. We were good enough and just had to let go and trust in ourselves. From there, we dominated. While the first final against Mollongong had been a blur, this one whizzed by because it was so enjoyable, and from that point on everything worked. The final siren couldn't come soon enough for Warrambatta, as we marched out winners, 20.10.(130) to Warrambatta's 7.8.(50).

Percy tried to keep it low-key in the rooms, although there was a lot of hair-tousling and back-slapping and hands shook, with some of our fans even pushing in to congratulate us. But then Matt charged in and waved his arms for quiet.

'I just got off the phone!' he said. 'Little Reach won – by one-hundred and thirty-four points.'

That shut up everybody quick – regardless what we'd done, the Scorpions were still out there and they were formidable in every way a football team could be. And we had to get through Mollongong in the preliminary final before we could worry about

Little Reach in the grand final. That was something Percy brought up in the Ulah'lah later, when he stood up on a table to interrupt a chant of, *'Ulah Curlews! Ulah Curlews!'*

'Let's not get ahead of ourselves!' he said. 'Let's focus on the now. I don't want to be a killjoy, but let's keep a little bit of perspective, huh?'

I was worried that somebody might spray him with beer, and then everybody else would jump in, showing that while they might be listening to his words, they weren't going to live by them. But then Ronnie jumped up on a chair by Percy's table.

'Coach is right!' Ronnie said. 'We got back to winning today. We have to do it two more times! And before we can do it twice more, we need to do it next week.' He lifted his glass. 'Let's have a good time – but let's not get carried away either!'

It was an edict that seeped through the whole town. I'd see people on the street or in shops, they'd grin and open their mouths like they were going to boast or something, but then they'd clamp their lips shut. It wasn't too long ago they'd been cocky. Only last week they'd been dubious. Now they were warily optimistic – almost like they were worried saying the wrong thing would curse it. Football bred fickle attitudes.

We played Mollongong over at their home ground, the crowd packed with not only their fans, but also people from Warrambatta and Shandeen Bank. When we ran out, a week's worth of waiting finally gave voice to a roar. The reaction to Mollongong's emergence was tame in comparison – right then, I knew we had them. Mollongong might've gone into the finals as hopeful as always – and that might've skyrocketed after they'd beaten us – but now their confidence was broken and scattered, courtesy of how Little Reach had pulverised them last week. Mollongong knew that no matter what they did today, they had no chance next week, and it showed in a listless performance.

We raced to a twelve goal lead by half-time. From there, Percy rotated players through the interchange bench to give them a good rest. About the only player Percy didn't take off was himself – this was his comeback game, and being out for two months had left him rusty. But he ran hard, took a few marks, and kicked three goals – not bad given how long he'd been out.

The final siren sounded to signal us 80-point winners, and immediately the *'Ulah Curlews!'* chant went up. But a pocket of our fans behind the goals shouted something else. At first, it was all garbled in the mishmash of voices, but other fans picked it up, until the chorus spread, pulsating all around the ground: *'You're next! You're next! You're next!'*

Faces were pointed one way – aimed at Rankin and his generals in the front row. He scowled and tried to make a dignified exit, but fans jumped in his way, waved their fingers and hands and flags in front of his eyes, and laughed and crowed at him.

In the rooms, Percy tried to make a speech but was so overcome that he hugged everybody instead. Other guys patted one another on the back. Matt jumped up on a bench and pressed his hands down, to signal that we shouldn't let the victory get the better of us.

'Next week!' he said. 'Let's keep focused for next week!'

It wasn't so much a warning but a timely reminder, so instead of celebrating, we showered and changed, before Percy gestured for us to all come together again. We formed a ring around him.

'A grand final next,' he said. 'We have the game to challenge the Scorpions. Each of you know that in *here.*' He thumped his chest. 'You can be nervous, but don't doubt yourselves. I'm proud of each and every one of you for carrying us this far, and I know you'll do me proud one more week, whatever happens.'

Once he'd hugged each of us again, I drifted outside with Sean, Nigel, and Dean, prepared to make the drive back to the Ulah'lah. Then I saw Amanda sitting in her dad's ute, typing away on the laptop, the brightness of the screen ghostly across her face. She snapped the laptop closed and got out. The other guys didn't even bother waiting for me.

'You're still here?' I said.

'Obviously. I'll give you a lift.'

We got in the ute. Ahead of us, Sean pulled out of the spot where he was parked, but Amanda swerved around him and gunned the ute towards the exit. The tyres screeched as she pulled out onto the road.

'Easy,' I said.

'I'm already late for work – you took a while getting changed.'

'Why did you wait for me?'

'I needed to ask you something: Rankin used to have a fourth guy who was always with him, didn't he?'

'Kevin Dunbar.'

'He was the one who took his own life?'

'Yeah.'

'He was good, wasn't he?'

'People say he was second only to Rankin for talent, and that he knocked back an offer to go to the AFL. Why?'

'Why'd he kill himself?'

'Financial pressures – that's what I've heard.'

'You believe that?'

'I didn't know the guy, Amanda.'

'I've been thinking of that arrangement of guys Rankin's got with him as his generals. They're all different, aren't they?'

'Different players, yeah.'

'I mean different people.'

'I guess. Where are you going with this?'

'I've been thinking about them, and about how friends are made.'

'How friends are made? It's a footy team, Amanda.'

'I know people are bonded because they're in the same team, but that doesn't knit them together as friends. It's like, you're friends with Sean, but you're not really friends with Ronnie—'

'Come on – Ronnie's like twice my age.'

'Or how about Sam? Sam's only a couple of years older. It's a strange group Rankin put together.'

'Do you think?'

'Schwartzer's the Little Reach mechanic, right?'

'Yeah.'

'And Terry Bell?'

'He's an accountant, I think.'

'And Murray Verne? He used to be in real estate. What's he do now?'

'Now? I'm not sure – I think he's been in lots of jobs. He was an editor at *The Chronicle* for a bit, then went into landscaping, then printing, then – last I heard – he was labouring.'

'What about Kevin Dunbar?'

'He was a primary school teacher.'

'Right. And Rankin lives off investments and his celebrity. Then there's their ages. Rankin's forty or something? The others are younger? Schwartzer's like thirty-two, isn't he? Kevin Dunbar would've been what now? About thirty if he was still alive? How different are these guys? In every way, how different are they? Take the footy out of it, and they have very little in common.'

'But footy's the thing. The generals are meant to represent the different kinds of players in the team, as well as the different age groups.'

'I might believe that if they changed over the years *with* the team, but they've been together for, what, ten years?'

'Yeah, about that.'

'Look, when you make friends you do that with people who are like you, like you and Sean. But those guys with Rankin ... what if there's another reason they're friends?'

'Like?'

'What if they were thrown together?' Amanda asked.

'How?'

'I don't know. Some common bond.'

'And Kevin Dunbar?'

'Maybe it's why he killed himself.'

'How serious would this have to be that Dunbar killed himself over it?'

'I don't know.'

'You don't have evidence for any of this. You're trying to take what little you know and make it fit into this scenario.'

'Maybe, Luke. But I've been thinking – I've been thinking a lot.'

'About?'

'That night we tried to follow Adam home and ran into Rankin. It doesn't make sense. *Of course* it doesn't make sense. You have Rankin and three grown men lying in wait. If they really thought we were trespassers, they could've easily incapacitated us. There's four of them, all built like giants. Rankin took the action he wanted to take.'

'Then you're suggesting he wanted to kill Adam – that's …'

'What? Insane? Look at the way Rankin swung that pick. If you hadn't ducked, he would've taken your head off. You're lucky.'

I hadn't even thought about that – about being lucky. I'd been too caught up in the things that had followed: the tree bleeding, the finals, and researching VFL clubs. But Amanda was right.

'You know what I think now?' Amanda said. 'I think Adam planned this – he's out here goading Rankin and the others.'

'But why? And what's he want to get out of it?'

'That I don't know.'

We got back to the Ulah'lah before any of the team on account of Amanda's driving. Of course, the pub was busy – as it always was following a win. People clapped me on the back when I came in. The wariness was gone. They wished me the best for next week and assured me we'd smash them. I smiled and said all the right things, all the diplomatic things – like, 'They're still the team to beat' and 'We'll do our best' – and pushed my way through until I got to the bar. All the stools were occupied, but somebody got up and offered me their seat. Amanda poured me a beer and slid it across to me.

'What's this?'

'You look pale. I thought you could do with it.'

'I'm fine.'

'Nobody would begrudge you a single beer.'

'No,' I said. 'Next week after the grand final, I'll drink myself silly and you'll have to put me to bed, but for now, no drinking.'

'You sure?'

'Yeah.'

Amanda picked up the beer and downed it in one gulp. It was the first time I'd seen her drink beer. She sipped at the occasional glass of wine here and there, but never beer. I'd assumed she never touched the stuff.

'You drink?' I asked.

'I work in a pub; it becomes unavoidable. I guess I wanted to steel myself.'

'For what?'

'I want to talk to somebody who knew Kevin Dunbar.'

'Who? Rankin again?'

'No, somebody outside that football circle. Kevin Dunbar was married, wasn't he?'

'You want to talk to his wife?'

Amanda nodded.

'And say what? *Excuse me, why did your husband kill himself? We're curious.*'

'Don't be snide.'

'She's not gonna want to talk about her husband killing himself.'

'We don't know that.'

'Would you?'

'I don't know. We don't know anything unless we try.'

We had to drop it as the first group of players arrived. Then they all began pouring in, and the celebrations for us making the grand final started in earnest. It ended up being a late night, despite Percy's repeated cautions. He might've worried about players overdoing it, but he overdid it most of all, and by 2.00 am he was slurring and starting up chants of *'Ulah Curlews!'* Others joined in and the beer continued to flow. Sean fell asleep on a table shortly after, and a couple of players ended up on the floor. Although its license was only until 1.00 am, that night the Ulah'lah closed at 4.30 am. We had to rouse players and fill them with enough coffee to wake them and send them bleary-eyed into the grey dawn, the ravens groaning that their morning had been disturbed.

Amanda and I didn't get back to her place until after 5.00, and I thought we'd sleep in until well past noon, but she was out of bed at 9.00, and using her phone to check the *White Pages* online to look up 'Dunbar'. There were eight listings in this area, but only one 'G. Dunbar'. Amanda made the call.

'Is this Gloria Dunbar?' she said.

Although I couldn't make out the words, I could hear a measured voice on the other end.

'Hello, Mrs Dunbar,' Amanda said. 'I wanted to inquire about your late husband—'

The voice now rose so that Amanda had to pull the phone away from her ear. I couldn't make much out, but it didn't sound good.

'I wanted to discuss his time with the Little Reach Scorpions,' Amanda said. 'It's for a retrospective on the Scorpions' success—'

Amanda's voice halted. I opened my eyes. She gaped at the phone, then put it on her bedside drawer.

'She hang up on you?' I said.

'Uh-huh.'

'Well, I guess they're the breaks.'

Amanda pounced on me and shook me, then kissed my head. 'Come on!' she said.

'What?'

'We're going out there to talk to her.'

'Out where?'

'Mollongong.'

'Mollongong?' I couldn't believe what she was proposing.

'I guess that's where she's moved.'

'She doesn't want to talk to you.'

'Maybe, but if I talk to her in person she can't hang up on me.'

'She can slam the door in your face,' I said.

'Well, we'll see.'

'I wish you'd thought of this yesterday when we were in Mollongong.'

'They're the breaks.'

Amanda got up and stripped the covers from my body.

We showered and ate, then drove out all the way back to Mollongong. The houses here were small and neat, sandwiched together, neatly-trimmed thickets of brightly coloured flowers rising up from their garden beds. Ferns dotted the street. Only a couple of kids were out to enjoy the morning, kicking a football around. They reminded me of me and Sean when we were kids, dreaming of one day playing for the Seniors.

'It's number sixty-two,' Amanda said.

We spotted how out of place the property was before we saw its number: the house itself was like the others around it, but the yard was overgrown, the garden beds unruly, and weeds stuck up from between the tiles of the path that ran up to the verandah. A kid's tricycle lay upended in the drive.

Amanda pulled up to the curb and pursed her lips.

'Well?' I said.

'Here goes nothing.'

I followed her out to the front door. She lifted her hand, paused, then used the knocker. It echoed through the house. I imagined inside it was cold and empty and sad. What had Dunbar's suicide done to his wife? She'd moved out here – maybe she'd done that to get away from the memories of her husband in Little Reach. Amanda used the knocker again, and now we heard footsteps. Then a lock jangled, and the front door swung open.

Gloria Dunbar was only in her twenties, but her ginger hair was thin, and her face lined. A redheaded boy – couldn't have been older than nine or ten – peeked out from behind an archway at the end of a hallway. Another kid, a much younger girl – it made me think that Gloria must've gotten pregnant only shortly before

Kevin took his own life – with a bundle of messy red hair and dragging a purple teddy bear behind her, came out of a room and gaped at us.

'Miss Dunbar?' Amanda asked.

'Who wants to know?' Gloria's voice was tired, like she'd had enough of everything life had thrown at her.

'I called earlier this morning, about your husband Kevin.'

'And I hung up on you.' Gloria slammed the door closed.

Amanda clenched her jaw, challenging me to say something. I didn't need to be a genius to work out that wouldn't be the smart thing to do.

'Please, Miss Dunbar!' Amanda used the knocker again. Then she shrugged at me. 'I *know* what happened.'

The door opened and Gloria almost jumped out. We fell back onto the first step of the verandah. She pulled the door closed behind her so the kids couldn't see or hear her, and leaned towards us.

'I don't care what you've heard!' she said, her voice a hiss. 'My husband didn't kill anybody! Now let him rest in peace!'

Then she darted back inside and slammed the door.

The Newspaper Archives

Amanda's hands tightened around the steering wheel as we drove home. 'Killed,' she said. '*Killed*. Who could Dunbar have killed?'

'His wife said he didn't kill anybody.'

'Who could he have been *accused* of killing?'

'Since Adam's involved somehow, it would have to be somebody mutual to them both.'

'Or somebody in Adam's family?'

'No. *No.*'

'What?'

'Can you really imagine that Dunbar killed somebody close to Adam, and Adam's revenge is to come back and play football?' I asked. 'I know Little Reach take their footy seriously, but that's about the worst revenge ever.'

'Yeah, I guess you're right. Unless something happened and Adam saw it.'

'Why not go to the cops?'

'Maybe he did and they didn't listen – you know, given Rankin's reputation.'

'I'm sure something like that would've gotten out. Everybody knows everybody's business.'

'Okay, let's think laterally. How did Kevin Dunbar do it?'

'Hanged himself. Why?'

'Maybe he didn't,' Amanda said. 'Maybe Rankin and the others killed him.'

'You serious?'

'Maybe it was an accident, and they made it look like suicide to cover it up. And maybe Adam saw whatever happened.'

'You're really reaching to connect everybody.'

'It makes sense, doesn't it?'

'Didn't you suggest before that the thing that bonds these guys is whatever happened?'

'Yeah …?'

'Dunbar died five years ago. That group of generals has been together ten years.'

'Oh.'

'And if Adam saw it, where's he been the last five years—?'

Amanda thrust her foot onto the brakes. The ute fish-tailed as it juddered to a halt. The seatbelt snapped across my chest and ribs, and yanked the breath from my lungs.

'Which way's Baden Creek?' Amanda asked.

'That way-ish.' I pointed as I braced myself. 'Why?'

Amanda checked for traffic, threw the ute into reverse, and floored the accelerator.

'What the hell are you doing?'

Amanda didn't answer, concentrating on the road behind her.

'Amanda—!' I looked left and right to make sure cars weren't coming from either side.

The ute screamed into the centre of the intersection. Amanda jammed the gearshift and stomped the accelerator. Smoke spewed up from the tyres as they screeched on the road. Then the ute lurched forward.

'There's a newspaper morgue in Baden Creek,' Amanda said.

'A … what?'

'It's the archives where they keep all the old papers for this area, from Ulah to Mollongong—'

'To Little Reach. What do you expect to find?'

'Anything unusual.'

'Such as?'

'I don't know. But you said these guys have been together ten years. Let's start there.'

'You want to check every paper for the last ten years?'

'It won't have to be every paper. If something happened, I bet it happened between Kevin Dunbar's suicide and when these guys first got together.'

'This is a lot of guesswork.'

'It's a hunch.'

Although we took a couple of wrong turns along the way, we eventually got into Baden Creek around lunchtime. Amanda ducked into a coffee shop to ask for directions to *The Chronicle*, the newspaper that covered Baden Creek, Piper's Hill, and Little Reach. It turned out to be not far down the road, a nondescript two-storey building nestled between a florist and a taxidermist.

The offices were long, with desks – overflowing with paper and old computers, cords tangled like rampant webs – crammed up against one another. As it was a Sunday, the only person in was *The Chronicle*'s editor, Ed Goddard. He emerged from his office – a box partitioned with a glass wall at the very front – and ogled Amanda. I might as well have been invisible next to her. He had this frizzy black hair that probably hadn't seen a comb for years, and an odd plumpness about his waist, like every bit of fat had congealed there. It made him look like one of those inflatable dolls that always righted itself when you punched it to the floor.

'I'm a cadet for *The Tribune*,' Amanda told him following introductions. 'And I wanted to check the archives in your newspaper morgue.'

'How old?'

'Ten years, or so.'

Goddard frowned. 'We did have a morgue – a warehouse where we kept all that stuff. But it's gone – electrical fire destroyed most of it.'

'Oh.'

'But we scanned all the newspapers prior.' Goddard switched on one of the computers and, as it booted up, told us how they'd digitally catalogued everything, and were the first of the towns to do so. Then he signed into the computer, and logged into their archives. 'You should be able to find anything you want here.'

'Thanks.' Amanda sat down.

'Help yourself to coffee or whatnot.' Goddard pointed to a tea station in a corner.

From his vantage point, he glanced down the front of Amanda's blouse longer than he should have, then realised I'd seen him. He grinned – it wasn't apologetic or anything, but more as if to say, *What do you expect?* I clenched my fists, but he was oblivious.

'If you need anything, shout,' he said, and plodded back into his office.

Amanda grabbed me by the wrist and pulled me down into the chair next to hers.

'The nerve of him,' I said.

'What?'

'The way he looked at you,' I said.

'It's no different to what happens at the Ulah'lah.'

'That doesn't mean it's right.'

'Calm down. I can take care of myself.'

Her fingers raced across the keyboard as she used the SEARCH feature, typing in 'Adam Pride'. Nothing came up. She typed in 'Claude Rankin', but the only hits were a couple of years old.

'That doesn't make sense,' she said. 'Rankin would have to be in older newspapers.'

She went through the newspapers manually, until one stuttered onto the screen, the text furry, the pages murky, some of them just the littlest bit crooked.

'Damn,' she said.

'What?'

'When he,' Amanda gestured over her shoulder in the direction of Ed Goddard's office, 'said they scanned the newspapers in, I thought they'd be scanned in as documents. These are pictures.'

'What's that mean?'

'It's like somebody took a photo of each page – that means you can't search for text in them, because each page is one big image. We're going to have to look through them manually.'

The computer whined, almost resistant to loading up pages – or maybe they were resistant to loading up the past. It took so long that Amanda ordered me to make her a coffee, and as I fixed her one (and a tea for myself), she went back to *The Chronicles* that were twelve years old – twelve to be safe and make sure she didn't miss anything.

She searched for just over an hour, checking every page of each edition of *The Chronicle*. Like *The Tribune*, the bulk of *The Chronicle*'s content was stories about what people were doing, or businesses that had functions on, and stuff like that. Or it was stories reposted from the other papers, which was the same collection of minutiae.

'This is hopeless,' I said.

'We're just beginning.'

Another hour's search still yielded nothing. Amanda began to yawn, but her eyes were unblinking as she scrolled through page after page, speed-reading each headline and the first paragraph or so of the subsequent story. My stomach grumbled, and my back tightened up from sitting around for so long.

'I'm hungry,' I said, getting up to stretch.

'Why don't you duck out and grab something for us?' Amanda said. 'I'll keep going with this.'

I glanced over at Goddard's office. He typed away at his computer. 'Sure,' I said.

I thought the coffee shop where we'd stopped for directions would be good place to grab food, but along the way I passed a store called 'Odds, Ends, and Never Agains.' The windows boasted knickknacks – little statues and trinkets, as well as books. But what drew my attention was a small leather journal, along with a fancy crimson fountain pen. It screamed at me *Amanda*, and her birthday was coming up. I ducked in, bought both, and had the clerk wrap them up. Then I stuffed them into my pocket, hoping I could hide them from Amanda and keep them a surprise.

At the coffee shop – The Golden Wombat – I bought a pie, a couple of ham and cheese focaccias, and two bottles of orange juice. I ate the pie on the way back, and was starting on my focaccia when I got back to the offices of *The Chronicle*. Amanda waved me over.

'Quick, come see this!'

There was an announcement in the sports section that Little Reach, in their first game under new captain-coach Claude Rankin, had beaten the Ulah Curlews by forty-four points. A picture showed a much younger, fitter Rankin taking a strong mark in front of none other than Dad. I looked at him and saw myself – young, strong, and hopeful. I was a kid then, maybe seven or eight. What had Dad seen for his future? Was he happy with the life he had built? I'd never really questioned that.

The article itself featured an interview with Rankin who promised that, under his tenure, he would do everything in his power to ensure the Scorpions were successful. This snapshot into the past was interesting – perhaps most of all because it showed how little Rankin had changed – but it did nothing to enlighten us on what might be going on.

Then, splashed across the Monday edition of *The Chronicle* was the following headline:

LITTLE REACH STARS SURVIVE VAN WRECK

The story told how Rankin had been driving his van home after the match, hit a red kangaroo, lost control, and just missed a tree. Rankin's passengers had been four guys hitching a lift home after a game – names we now knew all too well: Kevin Dunbar, Terry Bell, Murray Verne, and Daniel Schwartzer. They'd escaped without serious injury.

'This is where it began,' Amanda said. 'This is what brought these five together, and has kept them together.'

'They hit a kangaroo – it's hardly a conspiracy.'

'But this is the first reference of them as a group.'

'Okay. So what's it all mean?'

She kept rifling through the newspapers as she ate her lunch. The computer whirred and the screen flickered, taxed perhaps not by the duty it was being asked to perform, but Amanda's sheer determination. But even she began to slump. She got up and stretched, and I took over.

'There's no reason Adam should be in these papers,' I said.

'I know.'

'So what're you thinking now?'

'I don't know, but I'm convinced we're on the right track. It's a question of finding out *how* Adam's involved.'

Goddard came out to fix himself a coffee. I asked him to fire up another computer for me – something he did begrudgingly. Then I checked editions of *The Chronicles* from five years ago, going back to the time of the kangaroo accident, while Amanda continued from where she was.

I wasn't as thorough as her, skimming headlines, because this was beginning to feel futile. Outside, it grew dark, and we became mindful of Goddard. He came out a couple more times – the second time he told us he was closing up about seven, as he was on top of his work.

Now we raced through newspapers, although I don't think either of us expected to find anything more. I also dreaded that maybe I'd missed something in my impatience. But then a small headline nestled into the corner of a page caught my eye:

MYSTERY OF MISSING
LOCAL MAN SOLVED

The story – contained in a small article nine or ten paragraphs long – recounted the disappearance of Adam Pride, his wife Jilli, and their four-year-old son, Tabulum. After finding farming in Ulah not to their liking, they'd moved back to Western Australia to restart their lives – a fact only discovered three months later when their farm had sold. The article was reprinted from where it originally appeared in *The Tribune*.

'Look at the date,' Amanda said. 'A year after they hit the kangaroo.' She checked her computer – she'd already made her way five years past the accident. 'I don't know how I missed that.'

'Must've been while you were yawning.'

'I should've done better.'

'Lucky you've got me, huh?'

'I guess you are good for something.' Amanda frowned. 'But if the article's nine years old, how old does that make Adam? Do you know?'

'No. I assumed mid-twenties.'

'He'd have to be at least thirty.'

'He could be.'

'Okay. Let's say he's thirty – so he's twenty-one when this article is written, by which time he's already married, has a four-year-old kid, and owns a farm.'

'It's not impossible.'

'No, but it's improbable. Also, it doesn't make sense – if he sold his farm, what did he come back to? He said he didn't buy one.'

'Maybe he had two.'

Amanda arched a brow. 'It says he doesn't like farming.'

Something else bothered me about the article, although I couldn't pinpoint it. The answer danced out of reach. It was always the way – the harder you tried to remember something, the harder it was to recollect it.

Goddard lumbered out of his office, jingling his keys. 'I'm sorry, but I've got to head off.'

Amanda got up. 'That's okay. I think we've found out about as much as we can.'

'You know, we're looking for a cadet here,' Goddard said. 'If you're interested.'

'Thanks for the offer. I'll keep that in mind. But I don't know if I want to work for such a leery boss.'

Goddard spluttered, like he wanted to refute that, but the surprise of the accusation had robbed him of speech.

'You know you are,' Amanda said. 'You should have a little more respect.'

She turned and left. I grinned at Goddard.

'A lot more respect,' I said, then followed Amanda out.

She drove fine on the way home, but it felt like her attention was anywhere but on the road – she was trying to put all this together, like she could force an answer through willpower alone.

'What now?' I asked.

'There's a few things I want to check on.' Amanda had that look in her eye that meant she was planning her next line of attack, not that she'd tell me – well, not before it was ready anyway. 'You okay?'

'Yeah. Why?'

'Just checking.'

Questions needed to be answered – that much was obvious. I shuddered. It didn't feel right – like we were delving into something we shouldn't, into something that was trying to keep us out.

I couldn't help feeling we were inviting trouble.

The Fourth Quarter

Make or Break

The sky blazed with a fire that shone from the goalposts like beams of white light, sparkled off grass that was emerald green, and flecked my skin like I'd been dipped in glitter. I felt peaceful – none of the nerves or excitement I usually had before a game. And it didn't seem at all strange that there wasn't a single fan in attendance, or that curlews covered the entirety of that far wing.

In the middle of the ground, his back to me, Adam swayed on the spot, a shadow shimmering around him. I knew if he turned, I was going to see something I didn't want to see. Now I felt the first tightening in my stomach, the first irregular heartbeat.

Facing Adam was Rankin, shoulders broad, face chiselled and etched in slivers of flame. Flanking him were all his generals: Schwartzer and Bell on one side, Verne and Dunbar – Dunbar's face cold blue, his eyes sunken, and dirt all over his jumper and on his fingers and under his nails – on the other side.

The absurdity of it all poked through my unconsciousness. This was a dream. Of course it was a dream. But that was no reassurance. My mouth dried up until each breath felt like sandpaper down my throat. The siren blared and the grass fluttered. Adam clapped his hands and began to pivot, to gesture to me that *this was it*. The curlews wailed, and their chorus rose up into a shriek that was wholly human.

I jolted from my sleep and sat up. That shriek hadn't been in the dream – it sounded like Amanda. She wasn't in bed. Somebody must have broken in – Rankin. And his generals. It was addled thinking because I wasn't fully awake, but I shot from the bed and found Amanda, in her bathrobe, in the kitchen. She threw her arms up – something glinted in her hand: her phone.

'What?' I said. '*What?*'

'I spoke with Colin,' Amanda said. 'He said he's been following my stuff in *The Tribune*. He really likes it – he likes the way I break down the games and am always finding something new to say. He wants to see me this Tuesday.'

'See you?'

'To talk about a cadetship!'

Amanda squealed and ran on the spot, then hurled herself at me. I caught her and swung her around, then kissed her on the cheek.

'That's great!' I said. 'Congratulations.'

'I can't believe it – I really can't believe it. I should put a folio together of my stuff – although, he's read all *The Tribune* stuff. But that would be professional, wouldn't it? And I have other stuff that *The Tribune* hasn't published. I have to be prepared. Don't I? I'm not sure what I'm meant to do next! All I've done is obsess about a moment like this, and now that it's here I don't know what to do.'

I guided her to the couch and sat her down. 'Take a deep breath, and think about it. Better yet …' I grabbed the notebook and pen that sat on her computer desk and handed them to her. 'Write a list of what you think you need.'

'Okay. Good idea. Thanks.'

While she did that, I slipped into the kitchen, grabbed some eggs and ham from the fridge, and began to make an omelette. Rain spattered on the roof, and the window revealed nothing but grey. I was happy for Amanda – I really was. But I was also envious. I thought about that list of contact details I'd found for VFL clubs waiting for me back home. If I couldn't get somebody to look at me, what then? I had to go with her, didn't I? And there were other clubs – in even lower leagues – where I could begin. I needed to stop *thinking* about this, about idealising this, and make it *happen*, as Amanda had made her dream happen. Now, I wanted to be out of here and on the phone.

I shredded the ham into a bowl, cracked four eggs in after it, whisked it up, and fried it in a hot pan. I also made a cup of tea and poured some orange juice. This was as gourmet as I got. I brought the lot over to Amanda, expecting she wouldn't be hungry, but she devoured it in a few mouthfuls.

'If this works out,' Amanda said, 'I'll need somewhere cheap to stay – somewhere close to the paper hopefully, so I won't need a car. Cadets make nothing. We're going to have to live frugally for a while.'

I must've blanched or something, because Amanda's eyes fixed on me.

'You *are* coming, right?' She put down her empty plate and grasped my hands. 'We're in this together – and we can work out what we do for you next.' She smiled. 'It'll work out. Everything's been working out since Adam got here.'

'Let's worry about you for the moment,' I said.

'You are okay with this? You don't want to stay here, do you?'

'No ... but I guess I've been dealing more with the fantasy of all this rather than the reality.'

I could've told her about looking up the VFL clubs. She would've been proud of me. But now she had something real. When I broached this with her, I wanted to have something real, too, so we were going down this path together equally, rather than her having to carry me.

Amanda was distracted the rest of the day going through her writing. There was tons of stuff she'd never shown me – pieces on small-town life, profiles on Percy as the coach of the Curlews, explorations on the history of rural football teams. I skimmed through it, impressed by how thorough she was. It wasn't long before printouts of all her writing tiled the floor and, at that point, I decided it was best I get out of her way. I made a tactical retreat, went home and stared at my list.

I didn't sleep well that night, thinking that come Monday, I had to start ringing. As I lay in bed, I rehearsed approaches, but knew I'd never be so eloquent. The ravens woke me, shrieking as if they were heralding what I had to get done, but because it was too early to make my calls, I fixed myself some breakfast, then helped Dad around the farm. Around lunch, I excused myself, grabbed the phone, and – my back against my bed – sat on the floor.

'Hi, could I speak to whoever's in charge of recruiting?' I said to the woman who answered my first call.

'In charge of recruiting?'

'Whoever's in charge of the club's list,' I said.

'The list manager works for our AFL affiliate.'

'Oh.'

'You could try ringing them – I can give you a name and number?'

'Sure.'

I jotted down the new number, called, and asked for the name I'd been given. I was transferred a couple of times, then finally got through to who I needed.

'Who are you?' he said, once I introduced myself.

'I play for a football team – a country football team, the Ulah Curlews.'

'Ulah?' He sounded puzzled. 'Where's that?'

'On the border—'

'You have to go through the national draft if you want to be picked up.'

'I wasn't expecting to be picked up as an AFL prospect. I thought you might need, like, top-up players for your VFL affiliate.'

'Oh. Okay. Trying to come through the ground floor, huh?'

'I guess.' I didn't like how sly he made it sound.

'So what do you expect me to do?'

'I thought – if you were free – you might come out and watch me play. Our grand final is this week—'

'Might be better if you film yourself, cut together a package and mail it to me here.'

'Oh. Sure.'

'Sorry I couldn't be more help.'

That was one of my better conversations. Others knocked me back flat. A few quizzed me about the league, wanting to get a handle on how good it was. Most of the time, I was transferred back and forth and around and around. A few times, I was given other numbers to call – to VFL administrators, or to independent scouts. I'd finished all my original list, and had gone through the bulk of the new numbers when I got a familiar voice.

'Josh Carson speaking.'

I went through my spiel. I'd made so many calls that I'd distilled it to a pitch, although I didn't have the enthusiasm of earlier calls. It was impossible. But now Carson cut me off the moment I told him about our league.

'Ulah Curlews?' he said. 'Why do I know that name?'

'I'm not sure—'

'I saw you play – that's right!'

Now I picked the voice, although I should've recognised the name – he was the scout who'd come down to watch Adam.

'Didn't click straight away – you don't know how many clubs I watch play week to week. I remember you, too. You're the centre half-back, aren't you? The left-footer.'

I held my breath. He remembered me!

'Yeah, you looked okay. Stood out – well, as much as I noticed you next to that other guy. Andrew, wasn't it?'

'Adam.'

'Amazing talent. You know, I'll come down, give you a look. I can't promise you anything, obviously. I don't do the recruiting. I'm a scout. But I remember you, so that's a good thing, and I know some clubs are open to lateral recruiting, particularly with later picks, and with rookies, where they can find guys with potential who could excel in their system. Give me the details.'

Once I was done, I almost bounced around the house. Dad was asleep in his chair, and Mum was hanging clothes on the indoor clothes rack. Her eyes narrowed as I appeared in the archway.

'What's up with you?'

I opened my mouth, then closed it. I wanted to tell them, but I wanted to tell Amanda first, so I excused myself and went outside.

It was drizzling, this persistent rain that had turned the dirt road to slush and had soaked through all my clothes before I'd even begun to consider it wasn't such a good idea to be out here without an umbrella. But still I ploughed on until I reached our ground. The sight of the surface an inch or so underwater stopped me and drove my news from my head. I could hear the torrent of the creek – no doubt it'd be flooded.

I ran a hand through my hair, and drifted into our clubrooms. Percy was in his little office, going through paperwork.

'Luke!' His head shot up. 'What the hell are you doing?'

'What?'

'You trying to land the flu before the grand final?'

'I'll be okay,' I said. 'The rain's not going to affect the grand final, is it?'

'Why would it affect the grand final?'

'Our ground's like an inch underwater.'

'Little Reach have drainage and a curator – they'll be fine. We have greater concerns than rain.'

'Like …?'

'I wonder about the sort of game it'll be, given the way it was last time. That fan going after Adam, I can't tell you how that shook me.' Percy's jaw clenched. 'I can't believe how long that's been going on, but I'm only now seeing it. Sometimes, you get inside something, and you become blind to it. No more.'

'No more?'

Percy snorted. 'Don't worry about it. You go home and get changed.'

I didn't go home, but instead went to Amanda's and knocked on the door. She opened it and gaped at the sight of me, bedraggled, dripping on her WELCOME mat.

'What the hell are you doing?'

'I've got to tell—'

Amanda grabbed me by my collar, guided me through the minefield the floor had become with all her articles – I dribbled on a number of them – and into the bathroom. She plugged the tub and turned on the taps.

'What the hell's gotten into you?' she said.

'I've been calling scouts, asking them to come have a look at me,' I said, shivering. 'That scout who came to see Adam, he said he'd come watch me in the grand final – he couldn't promise—'

Amanda threw her arms around my neck and kissed me. 'That's great! That's ... that's ...' She kissed me again. 'What're the odds, too? The same guy!'

'I called pretty much everybody there is, so I guess I was bound to get him, but he said he remembered me.'

'Luke, I'm so ... well, I'm not just happy and excited, but I'm *so* proud! And you're freezing, aren't you?'

I nodded.

She ushered me into the tub and I submerged myself until I warmed up. A little later, she joined me. The rain pounded the roof, but here we were safe and warm. I wanted the moment to last forever, but knew it wouldn't because things were changing. Life was changing.

'Regardless of what else happens,' Amanda said, 'you'll need a job.'

'I don't know what I'm really qualified to do.'

'I wonder if they'd fix you up – if they took you on.'

'I don't know. I don't know how any of this works.'

'Scary, isn't it?'

'Yeah.'

'Because it's new. I know we'll make it, Luke – one way or another we will.'

We kept talking, going over everything and rehashing it until the water grew tepid. We refilled the tub, then thrashed it out all over, examining every angle, until we pruned and decided that was a good time to get out. Amanda went back to organising her portfolio. My stomach rumbled, reminding me I hadn't eaten anything since breakfast, so I made sandwiches. We finished the night holding one another on the couch, having the same conversations all over, as the television blared in the background.

The next morning I was out of bed before Amanda. I made her breakfast as she showered and dressed, putting on a blazer that might've been Percy's, a shirt, and a pair of tan slacks. It was an odd assortment that she made work.

'You sure you don't want me to come with you?' I asked, once I saw her out to Percy's ute. The rain had stopped but the roads were slick, and hills of charcoal clouds hung low until, in the distance, they seemed to merge with Ulah itself.

'You have training tonight,' Amanda said. 'I'll be okay.'

'Drive carefully.'

'You know me.' Amanda smiled and kissed me through the open driver's window of the ute.

'I'm serious.'

Amanda saluted me, and eased the ute out of the drive. Then she drove down the street – sedately, to her credit.

I stood there watching until she was out of sight.

An Important Discovery

I jogged home and hurled myself into my chores. It wasn't that they needed to be done right now – and the wet made them unpleasant – but it was a good distraction from the upcoming grand final, the possible move into the city, and the mystery surrounding Adam and Rankin.

When I finished, I went into the house, dried off, and flopped into Dad's recliner in front of the TV. I picked up the remote and flicked through the channels. Mum, who was in the kitchen making lunch, came in to look at me.

'Luke, that's irritating.'

'Sorry.' I flicked without even thinking about it.

'Luke!'

'I'm sorry.' *Flick.*

'Are you purposely trying to annoy me?'

I put the remote down on the armrest, and put my hands on my lap.

'Thank you. You worried about the grand final?' Mum started for the kitchen.

'Amanda wants me to move into the city with her.'

Mum spun back around.

'Try my luck with one of the feeder clubs the AFL might look at – I've got an independent scout who does profiles for a few clubs coming in to watch me for the grand final.'

'You've been busy.'

'I really think this is what I want to do.'

'Luke, you're old enough to make your own decisions, but consider it.'

I looked back at her to show her that I had, that this wasn't a whim.

'You're not taking a job, you're not going to study, it's not like you've even been invited to try out at one of these clubs.'

I nodded, not that I meant to be humouring Mum, but I braced myself for the assault of reason.

'You'll need a job.'

She waited, as if I was going to contest that. I didn't.

'A place to stay.'

Mum was renowned for her pauses when she lectured. It was her way of making sure that everything sunk in, not to mention you couldn't turn away when she was staring at you.

'You'll need to take care of yourself. And juggle a relationship.'

If I'd been hearing this for the first time, it would've killed my dreams, but Amanda and I had brutally dissected it so we knew what we were getting ourselves into.

'You'll be fighting every step of the way.'

'I know, Mum.'

'You've thought this through, then.'

I nodded.

'Okay.'

Mum returned to the kitchen, but that wouldn't be the end of it. Right now, she was digesting what I'd told her; then she'd talk to Dad – although I wasn't sure if he'd say much. Mum was the one I talked to about the big things. When she had everything clear in her mind, she'd come back.

I went back to flicking channels.

It drizzled throughout the afternoon, and grew heavier for training. Lots of people gathered to watch – families, friends, as well as fans. Harry walked down the concrete apron with his two-year-old son in one arm, and four-year-old son in the other. He set them down when he reached the ground, and – to the applause of his kids, his wife showing up with an umbrella to shield herself and them – jogged on to join us. His kids shrieked and threw their arms up in the air. It reminded me of when I used to watch Dad.

Because of the wet, Percy ran us through a light session, which was just as well because most of us were horrid. It wasn't that the ball was slippery but everybody was jittery – everybody but Adam. He handled the ball as if it was dry, and was as sure-footed as always.

It was then I realised he'd come up to training the usual way – right across the creek. When I had the chance to chase a ball in that direction, I checked on the water-level. The stepping stones were buried under a deluge. What had Adam done? Swum? He might've crossed at one of the bridges, but followed the line of the creek and come up the embankment the same way he always did. I was suspicious – Amanda's influence was making me question everything, even things that didn't need to be questioned.

At the end of the session, some of the fans ran onto the ground to kick the ball around. Harry's sons also waddled on, wearing bright yellow raincoats. Harry lumbered over and handballed the footy to them. Watching them, it clicked what had been wrong with that article in the morgue. Adam had said he had a four-year-old son. The article referred to a four-year-old son. But the article was nine years old. It didn't make sense, unless the son mentioned in the article had died (I imagined Amanda's conspiracy theories about how he might've died) and Adam and his wife had had another.

I turned to locate Adam, expecting he'd already be all the way across the ground and on his way home, as he always did right after training. But he was right by my side, face wistful, as he watched Harry kick the ball around with his kids. Adam must've sensed I was looking at him, because he flashed that grin at me, although now it was flat.

'Your family coming out for the grand final?' I asked.

'Told ya, I think, wife's not big on football.'

'What about your son?'

'He likes it okay.'

'He's four, yeah?'

'Yeah.'

'You never told us their names.'

Adam's lips pursed. He must've known I was snooping, although I tried to be casual. Maybe I did a good job, or – in the end – he didn't care.

'Jilli and Tabulum,' he said.

'That's cool,' I said.

Tabulum – the *same* son.

'I should be going home to them,' he said.

'Sure.'

I raced through my shower and let myself in at Amanda's, throwing a frozen pizza into the oven. She got home not long afterwards. We stood there, me in the kitchen, her in the lounge. Her expression gave nothing away, and I feared that after coming this far, this was all going to come apart.

Then she smiled. 'It's mine,' she said.

I hugged and kissed her, and over dinner we discussed her plans, although pressing at my mind – caged and wanting to bust out – was the new information I'd found out about Adam.

'I'm looking at moving in December,' she said. 'But I'll make a few trips beforehand to get everything organised – find a place and all that. Colin had a few suggestions. I had a quick look at them – they're nothing special, not much more than this, but that's about all we need. You'll come with me, right? To have a look?'

'Sure. That sounds good.'

'What's wrong?' Amanda asked. 'You're not excited?'

'It's not that.'

'Then what?'

'I was speaking to Adam after training,' I said. 'He said he has a four-year-old son – Tabulum. That's the same son mentioned in that article.'

'Why didn't you tell me this straight away?'

'I didn't want to spoil your news.'

'But this … this is something. What does it mean?'

'It can't be the same son,' I said. 'So it has to be another son with the same name – like maybe they lost the first son—'

'Do you think …?'

Although Amanda's voice trailed away, I knew what she was going to ask – we were becoming *that* in tune over this: *Do you think Dunbar was responsible?* But again, it came down to the same thing: if Dunbar had been responsible, was this really the revenge Adam would take? Playing football?

'Would you name a son after one you lost?' Amanda said.

'I wouldn't … but who knows?'

'That would be creepy.'

'I'm not sure what else it can mean. Does …?'

'What?' Amanda said.

Does it matter? That's what I was going to ask. Amanda had her cadetship. She no longer needed this story. And if I said that, that might've been the end of it. We might've had to concede we didn't need to pursue this any further. But I needed to know now.

'You've had a big day,' I said. 'How about we go to bed?'

'Sure.'

Wednesday, we had clear skies during the morning. I surprised Amanda with breakfast in bed, and the gift of the journal and the fountain pen.

'Happy birthday,' I said.

She opened her gift, whooped, then hugged me until she choked me. We kissed, which led to other things as storm clouds grew thick outside. Afterward, I made a fresh breakfast. We ate and showered, and then sat on the couch. Thunder rumbled through the bungalow and rain hammered the roof as we used Amanda's laptop to check places for rent. We marked down several to get an idea what we'd be looking at. Then I checked the job sites – most of my choices were in telemarketing or sales – while Amanda went into the bedroom to make some calls.

For dinner, we went to the Ulah'lah, where news of our eventual departure had already begun to spread – I don't know how it had gotten out so quick. I suppose Amanda had told Percy and he'd told whoever, and it had gone from there. A number of people interrupted our dinner to wish us their best. We thanked them and ate quicker, a bit uncomfortable with the attention.

The rain continued through Thursday, until the creek overflowed all the way up to the embankment and our ground was ankle deep in water. Matt suggested a group of us – me, him, Sean, and Harry – drive out to Little Reach, where we strolled across their ground. The drainage had done the best it could, but puddles had still formed. When we got back to Ulah, Percy said if this kept up on Friday, he'd give Rankin a call to discuss the match and whether it should be postponed.

Despite the downpour and our feet sploshing through water, the evening training session was full of energy. Again, lots of people had gathered to watch, although all you saw was a ceiling of brightly-coloured umbrellas. But our fans cheered us and clapped and shouted encouragement until we were done. Then Percy called us into a circle and we gathered around him, arms interlocking. The rain continued to drive at us and lightning flared. We could've taken this into the clubrooms where it was dry but, somehow, it seemed right to do it out here, to brave the elements, and to stand defiant.

'Life's about change,' Percy said. 'Everything changes. It's constantly changing, from moment to moment. For us, this is the last time this group will stand together like this. As I'm sure you've all heard, Luke's leaving us come the end of the year.'

Nigel and Harry – who were to either side of me – patted me on the back, while everybody shouted some form of simple encouragement, like, 'On ya, Luke!' and 'Good luck, Luke!' and 'Go for it, Luke!' I was embarrassed, but also overcome by the goodwill I felt from everybody.

'We don't know where we'll be tomorrow,' Percy said once the comments had died down, 'so it's important to value the time that we do have together, to value our opportunities while we have them. We've come a long way to get here, so I want you to all take a moment to think about what Saturday means to you.'

'It means the end of Little Reach!' Dean said.

Some of the guys laughed. Others cheered.

'We could be premiers!' Sam said.

Everybody roared and punched the air.

'It means a chance to go down in history,' Harry said.

'And it means victory!' Nigel said.

'It means beer and fans!' Sean said.

'Fame!' Nigel said. 'And fortune!'

Again, laughter, at the silliness of Nigel's suggestion.

'It means – if just for a moment – we can stand above everything we've ever known, ever been, perhaps ever will be,' Adam said, 'and we can become immortal.'

The silence that fell over us was reverential. Chances at flags weren't so common around here that we should take them for granted, and it only began to sink in now that this might be it. This opportunity may never come again – and it never would for this same group since I was leaving. Maybe that's what made Little Reach special – they didn't take it for granted. They kept pushing and pushing to stay at the top.

'It means,' Percy said quietly, 'we're faced with a choice: we can fall as individuals, or we can stand together.'

'Together,' I said.

'Together,' everybody else echoed.

'You know, Little Reach will try to rattle us,' Percy said. 'You know they'll hit hard. And you know that all those dropkicks who support them will jeer us and call us names and shout out

a lot of that racial shit. I want you to think about that. I haven't
– I've never really thought about the crap that people say, and
I've played this game twenty-five years. But it hit me, that last
game we played, the way we accept things, the way we accept that
Little Reach dominance, their arrogance, their pride, as the way
things are. You're going out there to not only do yourself proud,
but also every one of your teammates. I want you to think about
that, because that's how we stand together.'

'Together,' we said again.

The Big Dinner

The next morning it rained, but by afternoon, sunshine broke through and the clouds scattered. The ground was still covered in water, but at least now it'd have a chance to settle. If the weather could remain clear, we'd have a wet and slippery grand final, but at least we'd have one.

That evening, the Ulah'lah threw us a team dinner, the players the guests of honour. I dressed in jeans and one of Dad's blazers, met Amanda at her bungalow, and walked down to the Ulah'lah. A long table had been set up at the front of the pub – Percy sat there, along with Matt, Ronnie, and several of our previous premiership players, although there was no sign of Dad. The current players – minus Adam – had been assigned tables to share with their partners and families. Chatter droned between everybody until Matt grabbed a microphone and got up.

'If I can have a bit of quiet,' he said. 'Thank you! First, a toast.' He lifted a glass of orange juice. 'You'll find there's no beer here tonight – given what's going on tomorrow, we're running dry.'

Some people tittered. Nobody complained.

'But, despite that, we can still have a toast,' Matt said. 'So, to how far we've come!'

Everybody raised their glasses and toasted whoever was closest. It was a melody of glasses clinking against one another.

'I'll try not to bore you,' Matt said, 'but I will say this: when Percy instituted this new training regime, when he said he wanted to take football seriously, my body told me it was time to get out. It couldn't cope. That's the way of things. And I thought he was wrong, but here we are. So credit where credit is due.' He clapped Percy on the back. 'To Percy!'

Everybody rose and applauded for a full minute. Percy's eyes grew misty, and he held a hand up in acknowledgement. Amanda also grew teary. We sat down and I put an arm around her.

'Next,' Matt said, 'I'd like to introduce our last premiership coach, Henry Wickers, to have a word.'

Henry was old when he was coach. Now he was an antique, more lines in his face than there was smooth flesh, and his shock of white hair slicked back, the style a holdover to a generation with which we had no connection. He doddered out with the support of a cane. His eyes – this unnatural opal blue – sparkled behind his thick horn-rimmed glasses. Matt handed him the microphone, although Henry didn't really need it – his voice was so deep and hoarse it grated through the Ulah'lah.

'Our time don't come around often,' he said. 'We've always struggled to make it, for one reason or another. But it's our time now. Don't take that for granted. You're not only going out there to represent the Curlews, but the town of Ulah. People will tell you it's only a game. It is. It's a game of football. At the beginning of the day and the end of the day, that's what it is.'

Sean took hold of his orange juice and, under the table, poured a dash of something clear – probably vodka, or tequila – in it from a flask he pulled out of his pocket. I sighed.

'But in between,' Henry said, 'it's a war. And nobody wants to lose a war.'

Some of the guys cheered, and a few clapped until everybody was clapping.

'You do what it takes to win,' Henry said. 'Don't let anybody ever tell you different. You don't cheat. You don't play dirty. You don't go the fist. You do what it takes by playing your football. You play your football against their football. You beat their football with your football. And even if they do you wrong, you stick to your football because, at the end of that war, you know you've done everything you can, and you've done it *right* to win that damned game.'

Again, we got the roars and the applause, as Matt took the microphone, and the Ulah'lah staff began to serve the meals.

'I want to take this opportunity to introduce the players who'll be representing us tomorrow,' Matt said. 'You know them – of course you know them. But I think they each deserve some individual acknowledgement.'

Matt introduced each of us – whoever's name he called would stand up and be applauded. On and on it went. Ronnie got one of the biggest ovations. And then me, some people even shouting, 'On ya, Luke!' Of course, Adam's name wasn't called because he wasn't here, but I frowned that nobody mentioned his absence. Matt didn't address it; nobody queried it.

Once the introductions were done, we got down to eating – a choice of steak or chicken, accompanied with vegetables and chips. We ate and had our orange juices refilled. I saw Sean sneak another shot into his drink. After we'd finished eating, he got up to go to the toilet. I followed him, and we stood side by side at the urinal.

'What a night, huh?' he said.

'Yeah.' I took a deep breath and braced myself. 'You're slipping some vodka into your drink?'

Sean's jaw dropped, but then he laughed. 'I've only had a couple – so nervous. Don't worry, not going to overdo it.'

I wasn't sure where to take this – I didn't want to nag, but I knew Sean was prone to having too many. He shook his head, as if reading my thoughts.

'I won't – promise. Anyway, I'm not the only one.'

I zipped up and splashed my face at the sink. Here we were, at the end of the season, on the eve of the most important game we've ever played, and this was happening. I gripped the rim of the sink. Sean walked past me, slapped me on the back, and washed his hands at the adjacent sink.

'It's okay,' he said. 'Unwind a bit.' He smirked. 'I'm gonna miss you.'

'What?'

'When you go – I'll still be a Curlew, but you … I hope you make it.'

He hugged me and I felt the bonds of our friendship stretching over the last fifteen years. But we were also so distant. I don't even know how that had happened. Was it because I got together with Amanda and didn't spend as much time with him? Or because I'd started taking footy seriously? Like my relationship with Dad, it had come undone without me even noticing it. With Sean, though, I knew this was it: whatever happened, we might promise to keep in touch, we might even do it for a while, but even if it didn't work out for me and I came back to Ulah, things were never going to be the same between us. I hugged him back.

When we went out to re-join the others, we found that everybody was up and chatting in groups, although a few players had left. I wanted to be out of there, too, but Amanda wasn't at our table. I checked around, only to spot her behind the bar on her phone. She waved at me and I went over. She hung up, and leant over the bar.

'Do you want to go?' she said.

'Sure.'

'Feel like a road trip?'

'A road trip?'

'Come on.'

We said our goodbyes, and started the short walk back to her bungalow.

'That was Don McKay on the phone,' she said. 'We found Adam's farm.'

'What? How?'

'We were on it.'

'What ...? You mean where Rankin almost took my head off?'

'Yeah. If you go back another fifty metres, there should be a house. It used to be Adam's farm. Rankin bought it after Adam moved to Western Australia. But that's not the worst of it.'

'What, then?'

'There's no record of Adam owning it, and the only record Don McKay has of Rankin buying it is the deed in Rankin's name.'

'Wait. You're confusing me. If there's no record of Adam owning it, then how do you know it was his?'

'Okay. Don McKay was curious why there was no record of who Rankin bought the farm from. So he tracked it down to the previous owner, Barry Hammond. McKay spoke to Hammond – actually rang him and spoke to him. Hammond's in a home now, pushing eighty, and his memory's not the greatest, but he remembered this. He said he sold the farm to a young Indigenous couple about eleven or twelve years ago. He said the couple were in their twenties and had a son, maybe two or three-years old.'

'Adam.'

Amanda nodded. 'Hammond remembered him by name.'

'And that would make Adam about thirty or so?'

'Yeah.'

'It's a stretch, but he could be – he could look young for his age. Why's there no record of the sale ...?' But even as I was asking, I knew why. 'This would've all happened when Murray Verne took care of the real estate.'

'Right. For some reason, Murray Verne got rid of the records.'

'A cover-up. But why?' I said.

'I don't know. Could it be that they ripped Adam off? Maybe Rankin's investments are based on fraud.'

'So we're off Dunbar killing somebody?'

'I'm thinking aloud.'

'Fraud might explain things from back then, but what about Adam's son, who hasn't aged? Or Adam – how old must he be? Or where they're living? Or Rankin's fascination with him? Or what Dunbar's wife said?'

Amanda shrugged. 'I want to see this farm.'

'What do you expect to find?'

'I really don't know.'

We reached the bungalow. Amanda took her keys out and unlocked the driver's door of the ute parked out front. I looked at the ute, the bungalow, and back at the ute again. Amanda had already sunken into the driver's seat.

'Amanda, I've got a grand final tomorrow.'

'Come on, you baby. It's only nine-thirty.'

How could I argue with that?

We had to take the main road out, the one that ran all the way up to Mollongong, then find a gravelly turn-off that wound through the gums and came out the other side of where we'd seen Rankin. The high beams of the ute blared through the night, and our anticipation ebbed away to confusion as the gums thinned, scattered, then fell away into a hill that rose up and dead-ended at the raging creek.

'We must've driven past it,' Amanda said.

We backtracked, slower now, and found another detour – a pair of tracks barely visible in the earth. The gums grew thick now and branches slapped at the windshield, almost like they were trying to discourage us: *Go back! Go back! Go back!* I kept getting the feeling we were falling into some inescapable darkness, but then a vast clearing opened up before us. The ute's headlights splashed onto the fresh skeleton of a house, although that was all you could see – everything around it was black. Amanda hit the brakes.

'This it?' she said.

'This is new – Rankin had told us he'd been building a house, remember?'

We got out of the ute, the cold like a knife on our skin, our breath misting. The quiet felt like a mausoleum, some place you shouldn't speak. I grabbed Amanda's hand.

'I think we should—' I said.

Another set of headlights ignited from opposite us. Amanda and I lifted our hands in front of our eyes and fell back a step. A figure wandered into the headlights and shuffled towards us – the silhouette of a bulky man carrying a rifle.

'What're you two doing here?'

Rankin – now close enough that the light splashed from his face, his eyes slits. The rifle trembled in his hands. Rifles aren't unusual out here. A lot of farmers keep them to shoot vermin. That still doesn't mean you want to be confronted by one – especially if the man holding it is shaking.

'You're trespassing, you know,' Rankin said, voice thick and slurring, like he'd had a few drinks. '*Again.*'

'This your land?' Amanda asked, a tremor in her voice.

'I told you that the other night.'

'This was where Adam Pride's farm used to be, wasn't it?'

Rankin snorted. 'You know, don't you?'

'Know what?' I said, getting in front of Amanda – not that it meant anything. If Rankin fired at this range, the bullet would go straight through both of us.

Rankin's gaze searched me, perhaps trying to work out whether I was bluffing or not. I braced myself, expecting him to shoot. What would he do then? Bury us out here? But he lowered the rifle – not entirely, but enough to show he wasn't going to shoot.

'Get out of here,' he said.

I grabbed Amanda's wrist and tugged her back to the ute. I was worried she'd come up with another question but then she was stumbling past me and jumping into the driver's seat. I scampered into the passenger seat. As rain spattered across the windshield, she thrust the ute into reverse, and slammed the accelerator. The high beams shone like spotlights on Rankin.

Rising up behind Rankin was a shadow – a wraith that lifted its arms to embrace him. Then the light hit its face: Adam. Amanda braked. Adam disappeared – not like he ducked behind Rankin or stepped out of the light, but evaporated. Rankin shuddered – you could see it, wriggling from his shoulders down to his ankles – and his head snapped back so he could check over his shoulder. Amanda hit the accelerator and reversed until the ute fish-tailed. She braked, hurled the gearshift into DRIVE, and then thrust her foot back down on the accelerator.

Dad's Game

The ute swerved onto the gravel turn-off. Gums blurred past, branches flapping as if they were taunting us. I sat back in my seat, trying to work out what had happened. Amanda's hands tightened around the steering wheel, and her eyes kept flitting to the rear-view mirror. She swung the ute onto the main road. Out here, back in the open, on the road that intersected every town, we felt our first assurance that we were leaving whatever had happened behind.

'You saw Adam, right?' Amanda said.

'Coming up behind Rankin,' I said.

'Out of a shadow.'

'And then he was gone.'

'We didn't imagine that? We didn't jointly imagine that?'

'Maybe we did,' I said, although my voice was hollow. 'It's all we've been thinking about for a while now.'

'And we saw the same thing? The *exact* same thing?'

'What're the alternatives?'

Amanda shook her head. 'I was right about the conspiracy, though. There's no farm out there – just whatever Rankin's building. They erased the farm like they erased the record of Rankin's purchase.'

'What do we do?'

'We'll go to the police – this is fraud, so that's something. They can check into the rest.'

We drove to the police station in Ulah, a little block of a building down the road from the Ulah'lah. It had a lobby, and a couple of cells out back where the drunk and disorderly spent the night. Fortunately, Constable Brackie – the only officer we both really knew – was on duty, standing behind the counter. When he saw me, he checked his watch.

'Shouldn't you be in bed?' he said. 'Big game tomorrow.'

'We have something we need to discuss with you.'

Constable Brackie fixed us a cup of tea and we drank as Amanda relayed what she'd learned. I piped in here and there, adding bits about Rankin's attitude toward Adam. Constable Brackie nodded and took notes. When Amanda was done, he tapped his notes with his pen.

'You're sure about all this?' he said.

'Speak to Don McKay,' Amanda said.

'We'll talk to Rankin, but we've got to get tomorrow out of the way first—'

'What?'

'Amanda, it's been nine or ten years – this isn't going anywhere in a hurry. It can wait a day or two. I take this to Rankin tomorrow morning or – God forbid – tonight, they're going to accuse me of doing it to disrupt Little Reach's preparation for the grand final.'

'Screw the football game!' Amanda said.

Constable Brackie frowned at me, and pointed at Amanda. 'Does she realise where she is?'

I put a hand on Amanda's back. 'He's right.'

'I'm also going to check on this – talk to Don McKay, get whatever paperwork I can so that when I talk to Rankin, I have evidence to back up any accusations I make.'

Amanda opened her mouth.

Constable Brackie put a hand on her arm. 'I believe you, Amanda – I *do*. But I want to do this right. The best thing you could do is take Luke home.'

Amanda sighed. 'All right. But you *are* going to check?'

'I promise you, I'll ring Don McKay first thing in the morning. Okay?'

'Sure.'

Amanda drove me home and pulled up outside the front door. The light was on in the kitchen, and around the side of the house I could see the light on in the shed – Dad fiddling around with something, no doubt.

'You okay?' she said.

I searched my thoughts, my feelings, and felt only a lack of tension and anticipation. Questions still needed to be answered about Adam, but now that it had been handed over to Ulah's finest, I didn't need to worry anymore – at least that's what I told myself.

'I think I'm relieved,' I said.

'I have to admit, so am I. Sorry for keeping you up so late.'

'I'll be okay.'

'Good luck tomorrow – I know you'll be great.'

'Thanks.'

I kissed her, got out of the ute, and watched her drive down the road until her taillights had disappeared into the night. Then I went into the house.

'Honey?' Mum's voice sounded from the kitchen. She sat at the table, sewing the strap back onto one of Dad's overalls. 'Oh, it's only you.'

'Yep, only me.'

'You should be in bed, shouldn't you?'

'On my way.'

'You want to grab your dad before you go? He's in the shed. God knows how long he's been in there.'

I went out to the shed, feeling the security of home wash over me – it was a contrast to what I'd felt out there with Rankin. I'd miss this feeling. But I guess it came down to me – and Amanda – making some other place feel like home.

'Dad?' I called as I reached the shed.

He lay on the ground, head flopped to one side, eyes closed. A piece of timber lay alongside to him. I ran over to him and grabbed his shoulders.

'Dad?' I said. 'Dad!' Then, over my shoulder, I screamed, 'Mum! *Mum!*'

My heart accelerated like it was trying to thump its way out of my chest. The shed lurched so I took a deep breath. Panic was the last thing I needed. I had to check if Dad was okay, although I wasn't sure how I was supposed to do that. A pulse! I pressed two fingers to his neck, the way they did on television and in the movies, but I couldn't feel anything – I didn't know if that was because I wasn't doing it right, or because there was nothing to feel. Behind me, Mum's feet pattered across the yard. Then I saw Dad's chest, rising and falling steadily – he was breathing.

Mum skittered into the shed. She kneeled alongside me and caressed Dad's cheek. 'Honey, are you all right?' she said. Her voice was calm, even familiar. 'Pick him up and bring him inside.'

'What's going on?'

'He's fainted.'

'How do you know?'

'This has happened before.'

'Why—?'

'Luke, pick him up.'

I shovelled my arms under Dad and braced myself, but when I hoisted him up I almost fell – not because of his weight, but the lack of it. He used to carry me like this, so effortlessly, swinging me around the yard, or catching me up on the football ground and twirling me around as he playfully tackled me.

Mum supported his head and we carried him inside. I laid him on the couch and Mum grabbed a damp cloth and placed it over his forehead. Dad's eyes fluttered, then blinked open. He closed them again and his face hardened. One of his hands tightened into a fist.

'What's going on?' I said. 'Should I call a doctor—?'

'No,' Dad said.

'It's okay,' Mum said. 'Your dad's been on some medication for his blood pressure, and fainting's been a side effect. They're still trying to get it right.'

'How many times has this happened before?' I asked.

'A few times.'

'How many?'

'A *few*.'

But I'd never seen any. The bulk of the time I was with Amanda. Had this been happening before I'd gotten together with her? Or maybe it had happened since I'd been with her – Dad had to cover for when I wasn't around and probably overworked himself. I slumped, and all the excitement from the last week – all the plans and discussions – crashed down around me.

'This is my fault,' I said.

'Luke—?'

'Since I've been with Amanda, Dad's had to do more around here, hasn't he? That's the reason—'

'It's not the reason,' Dad said.

He pushed himself up to a sitting position. I found I had my hands out, like I was getting ready to catch him should he fall forward. He waved me away, then put a hand to his temple.

'But you can't run the farm like this,' I said. 'I can't go – I won't go with Amanda. I'll stay here.'

'Don't be silly,' Mum said.

'But how will you—?'

'We're selling,' Dad said.

I gaped at him, then at Mum. She nodded.

'Because I'm going?' I said.

'Not everything's about you, Luke,' Dad said.

He eased himself off the couch and went into the kitchen. I didn't know whether to follow him or stay here with Mum. I heard the fridge open, the unmistakeable sound of a bottle lifted from a shelf, and a top twisted off.

He's drinking? I mouthed to Mum.

She shrugged.

Dad came back into the lounge and sank into his recliner, right under that framed front page from *The Tribune*.

'We're looking at selling because we've been doing this twenty-five years and we want to do something different,' Mum said. 'Travel, maybe.'

'When?'

'Well, it won't be straight away – we have to advertise, find a buyer, all that. It'll take months – at the very least.'

'Then you need me here—'

'I don't want to hear any more of this talk about you hanging around here,' Dad said, glaring at me.

'I think I'll make myself a tea,' Mum said, and slipped into the kitchen.

Dad's gaze stayed fixed on me. 'Your mother said you want to try your luck getting a place on an AFL list.'

'I'm not that optimistic.'

'No?' Dad gulped from his beer.

'I mean, I'm not expecting to show up and get a spot on an AFL list.' I sank onto the couch. 'I was thinking about maybe trying out for some feeder club, get their attention that way.'

'You'll have to play the season with them, then.'

'I know.'

'Maybe more.'

'Yeah.'

'Lot of players running around out there.'

'I've asked a scout to come out and have a look at me tomorrow.'

'So you've talked about it thoroughly with Amanda?' Dad said.

'Yeah, Dad, we have.'

He nodded. 'You think you'll win tomorrow?'

My thoughts – which had been focused on all the discussions Amanda and me had had about relocation – scattered. I leaned forward on the couch, opened my mouth, but didn't know what to say. If this discussion was with any passer-by in the street, I'd have answers; if it was with anybody in the team, we'd talk about it analytically. But now, my head was empty.

'Think they're worried about you,' Dad said. 'Given the way they went the fist last time. Probably will again.'

'Probably.'

'But you've got something this year. People talk. I hear them talk about that Aiden fella.'

'Adam.'

Dad drank from his beer. 'I hear them talk about you – you've come a long way.'

I grinned – I couldn't help it – and looked away from Dad, embarrassed to be complimented.

'Last time we beat Little Reach was a fluke,' Dad said. '*Our* flag.' He thrust the neck of his beer up at the picture behind him. 'We didn't have a lot of talent, so Henry Wickers drilled into us this underdog attitude – us against the world, you know? But that's the way we were. That's the way we always had been. Battlers.'

And still were ... until Adam.

'That year, we ground out win after win. Games were always close, didn't matter who we played, because that's what we did. We ground out wins and stuffed ourselves doing it. It's like this town. We stuff ourselves getting through day to day.'

I'd never heard Mum or Dad say anything bad about Ulah. I'd always accepted they were content to be part of the cycle of life here. But maybe they hadn't had a choice. If I couldn't get picked up, what came next? It wasn't about what you wanted to do, but what you did with what you were given. I shuddered, realising this is what Rankin had told us back in the church.

'Little Reach have always been brilliant. People couldn't believe how good they were,' Dad said. 'That was the difference between us. People would go to watch Little Reach to see them in action. Come the grand final, everybody expected Little Reach to win. Everybody but Henry Wickers. Henry told us to stick to football.

He put it on the whole team that if anybody saw one head drop, then everybody had to rally and get that player to stand tall.'

Sounded a lot like Percy.

'The other thing Henry told us to do was to make the game ugly. Little Reach didn't like ugly, so it frustrated them to play scrappy. Whenever they found space, we'd flood and cram them up. We gang-tackled, we smothered, we kept pushing and pushing and pushing. Little Reach couldn't shake us.'

Through the archway, I could see Mum had sat back at the kitchen table. Although she was sewing, she had her head cocked back in a way I could tell she was listening.

'As the match wore on and we stayed within a kick, they panicked and took risks, trying to get their natural game going. Because this is what everybody thought would happen: sooner or later, the Scorpions would go bang, and kill us. But we weren't letting it happen.'

'They go the fist?' I asked.

'No – they didn't do that so much back then. They kept making more and more mistakes. Rankin was there. He was young then. Five minutes left, he tried this kick right across the goal-face. If it came off, the Scorpions were away. Our full forward, Matt Reynolds—'

'Matt?'

Dad nodded. 'He was an amazing talent. Kicked five that day in a scrappy game. He intercepted, kicked a goal and put us in front. You know what it sounds like when the crowd roar? Like when they cheer and that cheer sweeps across the ground and it picks you up?'

I nodded.

'There was silence. Even from our fans. Nobody could believe it. And the silence did the opposite. Just fell out of the sky and it squashed Little Reach. Flattened them. And that quiet, that deathly nothing quiet, it woke them to how wrong everything was at that moment. They were meant to be winning; they weren't.

They were meant to have shaken us loose; they couldn't. And now, with five minutes left, it got into their heads that they *might* lose. When you're the club Little Reach was – *is* – that's something you never consider.'

I knew that feeling from our winning streak.

'For the next three or four minutes, Little Reach non-stop attacked. Our whole team was camped in their forward line. Their full-forward roved the footy at one stage and snapped. Ronnie Waite leapt across, smothered it – he must've slid ten metres and rushed the ball through for a behind. I kicked out, and their centre half-forward, Bernie Wells, got the stupidest free for being held. He played for it, and got it. He was about fifty out, but straight in front.'

Dad sipped from his beer and I looked up at that framed front page, almost expecting that picture to be different, to show the Curlews as the honourable runners-up.

'Bernie *could* kick. He could kick sixty metres off one step. He'd kick a sheep over a shed if you'd let him. But this is one hundred minutes into an exhausting game. Time goes on, kicks drop short, players struggle. Rankin runs past Bernie, calls for the handball. Rankin might've been young, but you've seen the man he's become: he talks, people listen. Then there's the fact he was a gun. Probably about the best player I've seen around here.'

'What happened?' I said.

'It was *luck*. I don't know what would've happened had Rankin gotten that handball. He might've kicked the goal, might not have. He probably would've. But a guy like Rankin, I bet the not knowing bothers him most of all.' Dad chortled, shook his head, and took another drink. 'Our rover, Stan Sykes – the only Aboriginal in our team back then – was jogging past at that moment. Just pure chance. Maybe they didn't see him. He was only five foot tall. You turned and you'd see over his head. Anyway, Stan intercepts the ball – accidentally. I mean, he was so shocked he nearly spilled it. But once it clicked to him the ball was his, he ran, he ran straight down the middle of the ground, those little legs of his pumping until they were a blur. Everybody else was in Little Reach's forward line, and they ran after him. Stan gets to about centre half-forward and kicks the crap out of the ball.'

I tried to find Stan in the front page picture – he wasn't one of the premiership players I knew. Then I saw him in the corner, a clenched fist raised up, a wry grin on a face stony with age and hardship.

'Ball goes only about thirty metres, bounces and rolls and skews all the way to the top of the goal square. Stan's still running. He's forty, a big drinker like a lot of the guys were back then, a chain smoker, he died about four years later from a stroke. But he's got this one effort in him, this one moment of glory, like he's a superhero or something, and he keeps running, leading this pack like the robot bunny at the greyhound races. He kicks the ball off the ground, but he's so stuffed from all that running that it goes off the side of his boot. Ball hits the point post, but it doesn't matter, 'cos the siren goes, and we win. Stan had iced the clock with that effort and we were premiers.'

'Premiers,' I whispered.

'That day,' Dad said, 'we became immortal.'

I shivered as I remembered Adam's plea at training.

'Nothing we could do – not even another flag – could top that win. Maybe that was the problem, too. Think we became complacent. Never pushed ourselves again the same way; oh, we tried, but we never had that same fanaticism. We spent something that day we never got back. Not fully. But that was our fault, because we didn't know there wouldn't be a day like that again. We took it for granted. Sometimes, you accept things will never change, or they'll always be as good as they are in that moment, so you stop giving it your best. You accept what is and forget what it took to get you there. But at least we had that day, and in winning that match we left nothing behind.'

'Dad, why're you telling me this?'

'Lots of things have made me think lately – you and Amanda wanting to move, me and your mum wanting to see more of the world than just Ulah, and ... well, my health. Things are changing. And the stuff with my health has made me realise I don't want to lose this opportunity to talk to you, to pass this on. Maybe I should've done it long ago, but here it is.'

I felt now like I was just a kid again of five or six, sitting across from Dad and holding onto his every word.

'I was okay when I was young, Luke. A lot of people around here are. But life gets in the way, and people don't take the chances they should maybe. Maybe. You want to go with Amanda, go with Amanda. But don't leave anything behind, okay?'

'So you regret—'

'No. I love you, I love your mother, and I love this place. That's all that matters. I regret nothing, Luke. Nothing.'

'But you said about this town—'

'There's more to life than this town, Luke. There's more to this town than this town, even when you're living in it, even when it's all around you and soaked into every pore of your skin. You think it's small and boring and everybody keeps going in circles, but you know the best thing about this place?'

I shook my head.

'*This* place,' Dad said. 'No matter what you think about what you have to do, or the day to day, everybody's like this extended family. Like that game Little Reach went the fist. Matt ran out, even though Percy had basically cut him from the team.'

'Matt quit because he couldn't handle the training.'

'You're being a bit idealistic. Percy lifted the bar so he could leave the stragglers behind. He knew what he was doing. And the people who quit knew what Percy was doing to them. It was a gamble, because if you'd lost those first few games, or had a couple of average months, Percy would've been about done. But it worked out, and those guys could've had even more right to feel hard-done by, being shown up like that. Were they? They probably grumbled a bit. But what about when push came to shove? Matt was first out to stand up for Percy and the team. Then everybody else went. Not saying it's right, to get violent like that.'

'Mum said you got in Rankin's face.'

Dad chuckled. 'As I said, it's not right. But it shows you, we care about our own and we take care of our own, so no matter what happens, Luke, no matter where you get in life, never forget what we're about.'

I got up and hovered over Dad, then hugged him. His hand came down awkwardly on my back.

'I won't, Dad,' I said.

Pre-Game

I woke thinking it must be before sunrise, but when I checked the clock radio, found it was 1.11 am. Thoughts bounced off one another in my head – going to the cops about Adam, Mum and Dad saying they were selling, Dad's health, and the grand final. But overriding it all was a sense of ending – that I was leaving something behind, that I wasn't so sure now that I wanted to lose it, but knowing I was moving into the next stage of my life.

I drifted in and out of sleep until the ravens, shrieking and whining, woke me, the sky still black. How many times had I heard them in the morning and accepted them as part of my world? Wherever I ended up would be different. *New.* Dad was right about this place. I'd spurned it in a lot of ways for no real reason other than I had some lofty dream I wanted to pursue, and I thought this place was holding me back, but now I hoped that wherever Amanda and I went, we could feel that same sense of closeness.

I got out of bed, showered and dressed, and had breakfast. Nobody else was awake. The peacefulness swept over me. It began to feel almost like a farewell – the house saying goodbye to me. I'd still be in and out for the next couple of months, but only as somebody passing through. I looked at things I'd forgotten – like the jamb of the archway, where Mum had measured my height as a kid; the worn couch in the lounge, where Dad and I used to watch AFL games together; the yard before our fields, where we kicked a ball around. Memories were ingrained in every nook. I grew teary as I absorbed it all, locking it up to hold on to.

The first tinges of light poked through the kitchen window. The clouds were thick, a rolling canvas of grey tinged with black. I remembered my dream, when Adam and I had faced off against Rankin and his generals. There'd be no golden skies – it'd rain today, on and off. But what else awaited?

I took a leisurely walk over to our ground, the wind fitful, uncertain which way it should blow. Then I sat on the interchange bench and enjoyed the quiet – until a curlew wailed. I half-expected Adam to be coming up the embankment, but there was nothing. So I closed my eyes and listened to the wind, felt it on my skin, and smelled the water on the grass.

'Hey!'

Nigel and Dean came down the apron, Dean twirling a football.

'Couldn't sleep, huh?' Dean said.

'Nah, he's here because he could sleep,' Nigel said. 'Want to have a kick?'

'I'll give it a miss for now,' I said.

They strolled onto the ground – feet splashing in the wet grass – and kicked the ball around. It wasn't long before some of the others showed up – Harry, Sean, Sam, and then Percy and Matt. Percy went into the clubrooms, but Matt kicked the ball around until he started to puff. He gave up, and came and sat next to me.

'Amazing how quick the fitness goes,' Matt said. 'Not that I ever had much to begin with, especially the last few years.'

'Was talking to Dad yesterday,' I said. 'He said you were a great player.'

'Yeah, I was pretty good. Probably got by on natural talent more than anything. A lot like …' Matt thrust his chin in the direction of Sean.

'Sean's good,' I said.

'He's got a lot of talent, but it takes a lot more than talent. Talent's the easy bit. It doesn't take anything to have talent. I didn't have the commitment. Sean doesn't either – not really. It's all a bit of a laugh for him right now because it comes so easy. But you do. You have that commitment. You got tunnel vision. I wish I'd been like that. Might've gotten out of here, had some chances. It's a skill in itself that you have that dedication – it's a skill you have to push to make yourself stronger and better. Honestly, people say Allan's our best player, or our most important player, but I think it's you – you're a marshal in defence.'

'You mean Adam?'

I frowned at this recent spate of people getting Adam's name wrong. It wasn't that hard to remember, and they'd been saying it no problem all season.

'What did I say?' Matt asked.

'Allan.'

Matt snorted. 'Blame it on my age.'

'And I'm not—'

'Don't downplay yourself. I know. I've played thirty years – seen a lot of players. Adam might be freakish, Sean might have more natural skill, but you've got that single-minded determination, that presence that teammates trust and look up to – I can see why Percy made you deputy vice-captain. You've gotten so good this year, and you'll get better. Don't doubt yourself. Not for a moment. And, if you ever do, just pick yourself up and keep trying.'

I'd never seen Matt so earnest. I couldn't hold his gaze anymore, so I looked down at my feet. He clapped me on the back.

'I know I was a bit of a pain in that brief time we played together,' he said. 'I used to be even worse – and that time I was coach before Percy, forget about it. I look back at myself and can't believe the pain I was. Sometimes you need that new perspective. You understand that?'

'Yeah. Yeah, I think I do.'

Percy emerged from the clubrooms and waved an arm around. 'Hey, how about some breakfast?'

We went over to the Ulah'lah, and grabbed something to eat. I had a second breakfast – some bacon and an omelette. The guys filled themselves up on similar stuff. Nobody had any alcohol, although I doubt any of the bartenders would've served us if anybody had tried. While we ate, Percy, always the manager, arranged the seating for the trip up to Little Reach, assigning drivers, as well as who would go with each.

'What time we going?' Sean asked.

'Get there about twelve, twelve-thirty,' Percy said.

'You know, Little Reach's Under 12s and Teens are in the grand finals,' Nigel said.

'Typical,' Dean said.

'We should go down and watch them.'

'That might be something to kill the time,' Percy said.

After breakfast, I went to the bar to get an orange juice and talk to Amanda, who'd pulled an early shift. She looked even more tired than me.

'Didn't sleep so well, huh?' I said.

'There's a lot to process,' Amanda said. 'I hope you went straight to bed last night.'

'More or less,' I said.

'I wonder how Constable Brackie's going.'

I shrugged.

'Whatever happens today, you'd have to think that after the game there's going to be fireworks.'

We stayed in the Ulah'lah for another hour or so. People came in, shook our hands, wished us the best. A few chants of *'Ulah Curlews!'* started up. Then I went back home to get my stuff ready, and ate half a sandwich for lunch. I was finishing eating when Amanda arrived in the ute, Dean and Nigel crammed in the back. Mum and Dad saw me out.

'Good luck!' Mum said.

They waved as I got into the ute and as we drove off, I got a preview of what it would be like leaving home – Mum and Dad, arms around one another, waving at me, getting smaller and smaller until I couldn't see them anymore. Then it was the house, until that became a blip, and then that was gone, too.

The nerves hit – I wasn't sure why, or if it was a combination of things: the clamminess in my hands, the shortness in my breath. I wished I could be dropped right into the game so I didn't have to deal with the anticipation. The ute veered onto the main road with screeching tyres.

'Hey, Amanda, we want to get to the game in one piece!' Dean said.

'Which piece?' she asked.

'Haha!'

'We go any faster, we'll go back in time,' Nigel said.

The quips didn't have their usual enthusiasm. The tension settled into my arms and legs, and a weight built on my chest as we drove into Little Reach. Crimson and gold balloons and streamers hung from shopfronts, and people stopped whatever they were doing to jeer us.

We pulled into the lot outside Little Reach's ground, although we had to park down back, since there were already so many cars. Dean and Nigel scrambled out. Amanda leaned across and kissed me on the lips.

'Good luck, huh?' she said.

'Thanks.'

I followed Dean and Nigel to the clubrooms, where Sean, Ronnie – smoking a cigarette – and a bunch of other guys were standing out front, watching the Teens grand final. Little Reach fans surrounded the ground – had to be a couple of thousand already, staking their claim. I searched out the scoreboard and saw it was the second quarter. Little Reach 3.3.(21) trailed Warrambatta 5.6.(36).

'Be sweet if they lose,' Dean said.

'Their Under 12s won the grand final by eight points earlier,' Sean said.

'They breed them young out here,' Ronnie said. 'They'll come back – give them time.'

Almost as if to emphasise Ronnie's prediction, the Scorpions kicked a goal. Their fans cheered. Somebody screamed, *'We're coming for you, Warrambatta!'* And then a slow chant of *'Scor-pee-ons!'* went up.

Ronnie dropped his cigarette and ground it out with his foot. 'Think I've had about enough.'

He went into the clubrooms. We followed him, sat down and tried to relax as the rest of the team showed up – well, everybody but Adam. But nobody panicked. This is what Adam did. He showed up late, but he showed up.

A string of roars from outside followed over the next ten minutes; Sean finally poked his head out to check the score, then told us the Scorpions were now twenty-four points up. You could hear the confidence of their fans grow – not just that, but the arrogance, too. Individual catchcries rang out – things like, *'Back to the dung heap, Warrambatta!'* and *'You're not up to it!'* and *'Losing's too good for you!'* That superiority that was infused in every inch of Little Reach burgeoned into a hostility that assaulted our clubrooms and besieged us – this is what we had to go out to.

Players changed like they were pre-schoolers who still weren't sure how to dress themselves. Sam, Sean, and Harry hyperventilated. Nigel ran to the toilets and threw up. Then Sean did. Matt opened the windows. I grabbed a ball, got up and kicked it to Dean, but my leg felt like lead and the ball dribbled off my foot.

Outside, cheers grew louder and louder as more people arrived. At 1.15 pm the siren to end the Teens match sounded. Little Reach had won by thirty-five points. First the Under 12s, then the Teens. We hoped it wasn't an omen, but our anxiousness exploded into spot-fires of panic. Several guys lay down. Some paced. Others vomited (or vomited again).

Percy came out from the bathroom section of the change rooms. He was ready to play, but with one difference: he had black smeared under his eyes – war paint, maybe. He tossed a small red tube to me. Printed on the front was 'Eye Black', and underneath that, in a floral script, *'Reduces glare.'*

'What the hell, Percy?' Nigel said.

'You go black, you're never going back,' Dean said.

'Taking a stand,' Percy said.

'Go away,' Nigel said.

'We are going to war today, gentlemen, and we're going to show Little Reach we're going to war together. Who's with me?'

It was more than that – I knew that. It was too symbolic a gesture to suggest it was anything other than support for Adam, Dean, and Nigel. Some of the others realised that. Some didn't, and accepted Percy's challenge at face value. I opened the tube and ran it under my eyes. Dean and Nigel clapped and whooped. Sean took the tube from me.

'Now, I know we're all nervous,' Percy said. 'We'd be inhuman if we weren't. But you need only look at that last time we played the Scorpions to see they fear us. You don't believe me? Who'd they target in that match? Who?' Before anybody could suggest Adam, Percy provided his own answer. 'All of us! Because they recognise we are the team to beat! That's what you've gotta watch out for out there. Watch out they don't go the fist again! They'll do it, because they're thugs!'

A few players, sucked into the whirlpool of Percy's speech, chorused, 'Yeah!'

'Stand your ground! If they come at you, don't take a backward step. If they knock you over, pick yourself up. Do *not* – not even for a second – contemplate retaliation. Stick to our football. If any of you see *anybody* forgetting that, then it's on all of us as a group to go remind that teammate to play our football!'

On and on Percy went as everybody put on the Eye Black – even Matt. Percy built up a case for what villains Little Reach were, and how it wasn't going to be us against Little Reach, but us against the world. The players not only bought it, they invested in it. Nerves were forgotten. Adam – who Percy hadn't mentioned once – was forgotten.

'We can have this if we want it enough, if we commit to making it happen,' Percy went on. 'For years we've lived in the shadows of these bastards. We've lost because we've been too timid to realise we have it inside us to achieve great things if we push ourselves, if we realise we can accomplish above and beyond what anybody expects of us, what we expect of ourselves!'

The players roared as the siren sounded outside.

'Now when you get out there, there's one last thing I want you to remember, that I want you to tattoo on your brains: we are not only representing our football team, but our football club, our history, and the town of Ulah. Whatever happens here today, you make sure that when you walk off that ground, you know you've done each and every one of them proud! Make sure you do *yourself* proud!'

Percy had talked non-stop for half an hour. He'd taken players who were wrecks and not only made them forget what they were worried about, but pumped them up into believing they could win, and that they were going out onto a field of battle where it was a matter of life and death, and that they'd willingly give their lives to achieve victory.

At 2.00 pm, we sprinted from the clubrooms. People were everywhere: seated on the grass inside the railing that circled the ground; crowded around the perimeter; on top of cars that had been parked behind people, and then there were utes and trucks parked behind them; fans huddled on the roof of the clubhouse and anywhere that had a vantage point. Some even perched on top of the Little Reach church, all rugged up in jackets and hoods and scarves, like benevolent gargoyles. Everybody from every town had come out, maybe sensing something special was going to happen. Our own fans had even made a banner, although it only had one word on it: **WIN**.

As we ran through it, a commotion erupted in the crowd opposite us. A fight must've broken out – going on what happened last time, it was as close to inevitable as you could get. A body was thrown up onto outstretched hands. No, not a fight. It was Adam, dressed for the game. He was passed forward, from hand to hand, like a crowd-surfer, and deposited onto the ground. The people seated outside the boundary moved for him to pass through, and he jogged up to us.

'Deadly,' Adam said, taking in the Eye Black.

'Where've you been?' Percy said.

'Got held up.'

'Talk about giving a coach a heart attack.'

'Won't happen again.'

We went through our warm-up drills, the cheers whenever somebody nailed a goal overriding the boos from the Little Reach fans. Their boos were jittery. Grand finals and flags were common for them. They were expected. But now, they felt threatened. Other individual catcalls were more hateful, and directed at the Eye Black, things like, *'Borrow the old lady's mascara, did you, Perce?'* and, *'Never seen a football team in make-up!'* Laughter answered each barb – not that they were particularly funny; it was the posse mentality of Little Reach.

When Ozzie Rowan called for the toss, both teams crowded behind their captain-coaches. The unblinking eyes of the Little Reach players fixed on us. Every one of them had a target. They were trying to intimidate, and it was working. Their players looked bigger, tougher, more experienced. And this was their element.

Rankin snorted. 'Got your make-up on, Perce, but did you forget your bra and knickers?'

His players sniggered. Some made effeminate gestures.

'Settle,' Ozzie said. He threw the coin in the air and looked to Rankin. 'Call.'

'Heads,' Rankin said.

The coin landed in the grass on its side. Ozzie picked it up. 'Let's do that again,' he said. 'Call.' He tossed the coin in the air.

'Tails,' Rankin said.

It came down heads. Percy thrust his hand up towards the goals favoured by the erratic breeze. The crowd roared. We jogged back to our centre half-forward position, where Percy called us in for one last huddle. We formed a ring around him, arms interlocked over our shoulders.

'Okay, let's break it down here, guys,' he told us. 'We don't have the reputation they do, we don't have the expectations they do, we don't have the history they do. For them, winning is everything. They don't have a choice. For us, we've got nothing to lose!'

The players growled and hugged and then growled some more. Everybody had focused, and Adam's arrival had fuelled that fire Percy had stoked in the rooms. But now, I was anxious. When we broke, Percy ran over to me and put his hand on my shoulder.

'You okay?' he said.

I nodded, not trusting myself to speak. It wasn't the game. It was playing on Rankin: Rankin who'd threatened me with a rifle last night; Rankin who'd almost taken my head off with a pick; Rankin, with whom Amanda and I had developed this insidious off-field relationship.

'Luke,' Percy said, 'you've got the talent, you've got the ability, you've got the commitment. You've shown it the whole year. I don't think you realise how good you are. You've become one of my most important players, a leader of this side. I'm proud of you. I couldn't have done any of this without you. Don't overthink it now. Don't even *think*. Do what you've been doing and you'll be right, okay?'

I singled Rankin out of a group of Scorpions who were separating into position, but saw past him, focusing on the Ulah contingent that had gathered around the goals. There, in the front, was Mum and Dad. Dad waved.

'Luke? Okay?'

'Yeah,' I said, and lifted a hand in return.

'Good.'

Percy patted me on the back, then jogged away as Rankin approached. He showed no recognition for me, or what had transpired last night. Or maybe he'd left it all off-field. I offered a handshake but he slapped it away.

'Good luck,' he said.

The First Half

Rankin nudged me, and when I didn't respond, he bumped me so I stumbled. I cocked my arm, ready to elbow him. He shoved me in the side. Then he knocked me with his hip. None of this was vicious; it was irritating more than anything else. I clenched my fist. Rankin leered and waved me to him, *inviting* me to hit him.

'Come on,' he said.

A lot of jostling was going on all around me – typical before a big game. But now a healthy dose of paranoia underpinned it. Even if Percy hadn't warned us, we knew what Little Reach was like. *Everybody* knew what Little Reach was like. And we remembered the last game they'd played against us.

The siren blared. The crowd's roar was like an earthquake that sheared the ground. Rankin prodded me again and again and again. I thrust my open palms into his chest. He fell flat on his butt. The crowd exploded in a mixture of elation and anger. Rankin appealed to the closest umpire. The ump wasn't fooled by Rankin's dramatics. He shook his head.

'Take it to Hollywood, Claude,' the umpire said.

Rankin rolled his eyes. 'That's one I owe you.'

He got up and niggled me again, but now it didn't bother me, and I waved him away like I'd shoo a fly buzzing around my face.

It wasn't long ago that Rankin wouldn't have acknowledged my existence. Or he would've thumped me. Now he wanted an umpire to save him. The thought filled me with confidence. I stood tall, ready for what was to come.

In the centre square, Little Reach had Andrew Close on Adam. Close was a dour half-back flanker of little skill. He got a game because he injected grunt into the Scorpions. But he *was* a footballer who knew how to read the play, so maybe there'd be no standover tactics this match.

Ozzie bounced the ball so it sailed up straight and high. Ken Kotz and Harry collided in a tangle of knees. The ball spilled off their hands. A pack of players converged, and then Close – no less – handballed the footy out to Terry Bell, who got a quick high kick out of the centre.

I ran back with the flight of the ball as it wobbled over my head. Rankin bore down on me. Murray Verne – followed by Sean – charged towards me. I leapt, took the ball in my fingertips, landed in Verne's line and whirled to avoid his charge, expecting Rankin to cannon into me. But all that happened was his hands came down on my back to make sure I didn't try to run off.

I spun. Rankin was on the mark, arms wide. Both he and Verne had had the chance to clean me up – Rankin would've been late, and Verne would've had to deviate from his line, but it's what I'd expected.

Nope. They'd come to play.

Although that became evident quick, the realisation sank in slow, like it had to work its way through the muck. The Scorpions ran in numbers, supported one another, and moved the ball fast. A lot of our guys were caught flat-footed, or braced themselves for physical aggression that never came.

In the first twenty minutes, Little Reach pumped the ball into their forward line time and time and time again, and time and time and time again I was the one who stood in their way, although I swear the ball followed me. Whenever they tried passing to Verne,

I was there to intercept the lead; if they went to Rankin, he was wrong-sided, allowing me to out-mark him or mop up. Then I remembered, the scout was meant to be out there watching me. I'd forgotten about him with everything that had gone on. This was a good audition so far. I pushed the thought out. I had to think about the team, not myself.

Although defensively we stood up, we barely got past our own half-forward line. Kotz dominated the ruck, and Close kept Adam quiet, although Close did nothing else but follow Adam – Close had no interest in winning the footy. His game was dedicated to shutting Adam out of the match, and he was doing a damned good job of it.

As the quarter wore on, the Scorpions changed tactics – Rankin led wide and deep, taking me away from our defensive arc. Then they kicked to where I had been, their smaller forwards leading into space to take easy marks. They nailed three goals, and a fourth when Sean spoiled Verne in the goal square, and Close soccered the ball through. When the siren went to end the first quarter, Little Reach was 4.3.(27) to our 0.2.(2).

We had to brave the derision of the Little Reach faithful – some of it aimed at our failure collectively (*'This is the real thing now!'*), some of it aimed at Adam (*'You're a fluke, you black bastard!'* and *'Shouldn't you be collecting your unemployment?'*) and even some of it aimed at me (*'You'll get yours!'*) – as we formed our ring, arms interlinked, around Percy. Then their slow *'Scor-pee-ons!'* chant rose up as we tried to regroup.

'What the hell's going on?' Dean asked.

'They're playing footy,' Nigel said.

'Yeah, they're playing footy,' Percy said. 'Last time they went the fist, and now they're playing footy and none of us expected it. Come on, guys! We're running around expecting them to cheap shot us. It's not happening. I don't want to go out like this. Luke, Rankin's playing as a decoy – he's leading you out of defence. Once he runs past half-forward, you swing back into the defensive arc, play the loose man, plug up that hole they're creating. Sam, you pick up Rankin once he's out of the forward-fifty.'

'Me?' Sam blinked.

'They're not going to kick to him – he's the decoy. So, it's precautionary, and they won't be expecting you to do it. I'm guessing Rankin will stop the tactic rather than let Luke run around as the extra defender. Now, we've gotten plenty of rebound out of defence, but we're not capitalising. We need to generate more run from the midfield, present more, get those options opening up. Run. *Run* hard. Okay, let's do this!'

The first ten minutes of the second quarter were much the same as Little Reach bombarded their forward arc. Unmanned, I floated across each time and took an assortment of marks. I wasn't just confident now – now it felt as if a certainty guided my every decision, dictated my every move. As Percy predicted, Rankin swung back to man me up, but it didn't matter. I began taking chances I hadn't in the first quarter, playing on at all costs. This had a catalyst effect, getting Nigel, Sam, and Dean into the game, although Close still shadowed Adam.

We peppered the goals, but nerves still rattled a lot of the guys, and the bad conditions made it even worse. Percy put two shots on the full, Ronnie kicked three straight points, Nigel streamed into an open goal and hit the post, and Sam and Dean missed easy snaps. Twenty minutes into the second quarter, our score had eked to 0.9.(9), while Little Reach had moved to 7.5.(47). The Little Reach fans resumed their slow chant, '*Scor-pee-ons!*', a dirge that filled the ground like a mass wanting to commemorate our demise.

And then it drizzled – light, but annoying enough that it was going to make hauling in this deficit harder. Too many of our players were down, Adam not least of all. He drifted around like he was disinterested. I shouted, I clapped, I encouraged, and tried to keep our energy high.

Following the next bounce, Close won the ball and handballed to Bell, who raked a pass to Verne. Sean got his fist to it, and the ball rebounded to me. I scooped it up in one hand – one of those sure-handed gathers that's more luck than anything – sidestepped Rankin, handballed the ball to Nigel, and set off. Nigel handballed the ball back to me. I sprinted through the centre and kicked a low pass to Ronnie. Ronnie handballed the ball back to me as I whizzed by. I bounced again, and again, wrong-footed a couple of Little Reach defenders in the muck, bounced again, and kept running. As I streamed past centre half-forward I had a moment of bravado, or insanity – they amount to the same thing – and kicked the ball long over the leading forwards.

I was tackled and ridden into the ground, me and my tackler sliding but keeping our eyes on the ball as it spiralled over outstretched fingertips, bounced on the top of the goal square, and skidded through. Our fans roared and somebody shouted, '*He's your man, Rankin!*'

Percy was the first one to me. He hauled me up and hugged me; then Ronnie jumped on my back; followed by Nigel, Sam, Dean; Harry reached over the top of everybody to rub my head. Then everybody came in and jumped on me, or jumped on teammates who were jumping on me. You would've sworn the kick had won the game, but everybody was thinking the same thing: it was such a relief to get that first goal. Now we were underway!

As my teammates scattered back into position, I noticed Rankin keeled over. He'd chased me the length of the ground and now his chest heaved and his face was bloated. His arms were coated in what I first thought was mud, but then I saw it was a bright red and ran from his skin in the rain.

I felt giddy as I jogged back to position, unable to take my eyes from Rankin. He gaped back at me. I lifted my hands and saw they were also red – as were my jumper, shorts, and both legs. I patted myself down, but didn't feel any injury. I wasn't hurt. It hadn't come from me. And it hadn't come from Rankin. It must've come from something we'd done together – when he'd tackled me and we'd slid through the grass.

Ozzie bounced the ball, and Close snapped out of the centre. Instinct took over, transcended my shock, and I intercepted Rankin's lead, marking the ball in front of my chest. Everybody flooded forward. I spotted Ronnie running wide and pinned him with a pass. Then I dropped back to man-up Rankin, but he just gazed around as if he was only now becoming aware of his surroundings.

'You see it?' he said, and those normally narrow eyes were like a possum's, veins mottled in his face as he gaped at his crimson hands. 'You see it, right?'

'Yeah.'

'You can't bury some things,' he said – or at least I thought that's what he said, his voice was so quiet.

A cheer interrupted us. Somebody had snapped the ball towards goals. Adam soared above the pack, knees balanced on players' heads while his hands implored the sky. Lightning illuminated everything. His fingertips almost punctured the footy as Schwartzer attempted to spoil. Schwartzer and Adam collided; Adam catapulted into the behind post so hard the post was knocked askew, then hit the ground face first, ball still clawed between his fingers. Thunder rumbled.

Yes!

I wasn't sure if I'd heard it or if I'd imagined it, but I *felt* it from Rankin: jubilation. He clenched his right fist, and from the seam of his little finger curled into his palm, that red stuff trickled free. However fairly Little Reach were playing, a little brutality never went astray. Rankin's mouth dropped open as Adam – now smeared red – bounced to his feet.

'No ...' Rankin said.

Adam snapped the goal, and our teammates swamped him as the umpires straightened the post.

'What's going on?' I said.

Rankin shook his head.

'Tell me,' I said.

'Some things you can't escape.'

'What?'

He didn't say any more.

In the final minutes of the quarter, the match became a slugfest as players tackled opponents to the ground, and then everybody else stacked on them to make sure the ball didn't come loose. I held my breath the first few times the players disentangled themselves and got to their feet, expecting them to be covered in red. Nope. Just wet. Maybe it was a part of the ground that had done this, although others had fallen in the same sections Rankin, me, and Adam had.

Ozzie called for the ball and threw it up. Adam roved the tap from Harry and snapped it forward to Percy. Percy spilled the mark, but recovered and handballed to Ronnie, who banana kicked a goal. The next bit of play was almost identical: from the ball-up, Adam pilfered the ball and kicked it long. Percy's attempt at a mark was spoiled and Ronnie pounced on the ball. He evaded one opponent, but was tackled by a second as he got a handball off to Percy. Percy steadied and kicked, the siren sounding as the ball was still in mid-air. The ball sailed through truly, the scores for half-time Little Reach 7.5.(47) to us 4.9.(33).

'Hey,' I said, jogging up to Nigel as I tugged the hem of my reddened jumper, 'what do you make of this?'

'It's the clay,' Nigel said.

'The clay?'

'In the ground,' Nigel said. 'Rain probably brought it up.'

I clung to that. It had been raining so much, maybe some underground layer of clay had soaked up through the ground. Of course, clay was browner than it was red, and *this* was red.

We gathered at the race that went up to our rooms, waiting for the rest of our guys to join us. Fans shouted lots of things – our fans shouted encouragement, while the Little Reach fans kept up their abuse. It bounced off me until a single voice cut through it all.

'Luke! *Luke!*'

Amanda pushed through people to lean over the railing that fenced off the ground. She tugged at her jacket, then pointed at me and frowned, mouthing the words, *What the hell ...?* She could see it. I cast a glance back to the Scorpions, about to head up their own race.

Rankin's generals surrounded him, their mouths hanging wide open as they panted, chests heaving. Were they seeing it? The rest of the team huddled around them, like the formation of a Roman legion, but Rankin moved back and forth to get a clear line of vision of our players.

I didn't have to bother checking who he was looking at.

The Second Half

Percy let everybody absorb the events of the first half as he paced back and forth. The rain pounded the roof so hard the clubrooms shook. The guys settled down on benches, or sat on the floor with their backs to the wall, panting, trying to catch their breath. I sat there and stared at my reddened hands. Matt went from player to player with a tray of sliced oranges.

'All right!' Percy said. 'We took a while to settle but we *have* settled! We're fourteen points down. Fourteen points! Three straight kicks and we're in front.'

'Three-goal lead in this,' Nigel pointed at the ceiling, 'isn't going to be easy.'

'Keep doing what we're doing!' Percy said. 'It's not a day for forwards. Luke, you're killing Rankin.'

I looked up. 'What …?'

'Rankin's had …?'

'One handball,' Matt said.

'You've taken him out of the game,' Percy said. 'Sean, you're beating Verne. That's their two best forwards quiet. I don't want anybody looking too far ahead, but we can do this.'

He went on in typical Percy fashion, passionate and engaging, but I found it impossible to focus – at least on his speech. So Rankin, me, and Amanda all saw what was going on. It wasn't clear if the generals did. But it wasn't coincidence about the three of us. We were all in this together. With Adam.

He sat on a bench opposite me, the red stained into his kit, dripping from his body, and pooling on the floor. He smiled at me – not that typical big grin that came up in all of his face. He looked tired, his eyes sunken, dark, and fixed on me with a knowing that betrayed his guilt. He understood this. He understood every bit of it. Like Rankin. And somehow, because me and Amanda had gotten inside it, it touched us. The question was what *it* was.

The siren rang to signal the end of half-time, and the guys around me and Adam jumped up and roared. I'd missed pretty much everything Percy had said. Somebody grabbed the back of my collar – Sean – and hoisted me up.

'Let's do this!' he said.

Adam rose up and nodded.

We filed out, the rain like hundreds of stinging bees, the storm continuing to rage. The downpour was a wave crashing across the ground. When each drop hit the grass, tiny explosions of red erupted from the surface.

'Luke?' Percy said, when I paused before taking my first step onto the ground. 'Something wrong?'

My right foot hovered above the grass.

'Luke?'

Percy shoved me onto the ground. I was sure the surface stuck to the soles of my boots; each time I put my foot down, there was a *squelch* that made me think of squashing big, fat bugs; and when I lifted my foot it was like a bandage being ripped off an ugly wound.

Rankin looked even worse when I joined him at centre half-forward. His breath came in ragged gasps, and his left eye was a huge circle, while the other – a vein in his temple throbbing above it – was squinted down to a slit. He opened his mouth, but my face must've answered whatever question he was going to ask.

Ozzie held up the ball as the siren to begin the third quarter tried to punch a hole in the rain. Instinct kicked in, and I put a hand onto Rankin's forearm to get a bearing of where he was. He grabbed me, his fingers clawing into my flesh. I tried shaking loose, but he held firm. I started to tell him to let go, but the sight of how pasty he'd become killed the protest. I followed the line of his gaze.

Adam.

He wasn't covered in what had come up from the ground now; blood gushed from a gaping wound in the top of his head and from a cratered hole in the palm of his right hand, a finger lifted to accuse Rankin. His eyes were bloodshot, and half his chest was caved in.

Because it was raining so hard, Ozzie threw up the ball, and a pack of players converged and obscured Adam. When they parted, it was Adam again – no wounds, no blood, his eyes on the football as it came off the outstretched palm of Kotz. Bell plucked it out of the air but was tackled by Sam, both of them hitting the ground. Everybody else piled on top of them. Ozzie blew the whistle and called for another ball up.

The players dragged themselves to their feet, now covered in blood – and there it was, my acknowledgement of what it had to be. Sam, who'd laid the tackle, was plastered in it from head to toe, but gave no sign of its existence. Nor did Ozzie, who moved in to throw the ball up again. But Bell checked himself, like I had, trying to work out where it had come from.

Kotz and Harry struggled for the tap out. Their bodies collided, they bounced off one another, and Adam won the ball, sidestepping Bell – who was still checking himself – and snapped it out of the pack to centre half-forward. Percy flew for the mark, but Schwartzer punched the ball away. Both men hit the ground, slid ten feet, but were immediately back up – coated in blood – to chase the ball, although Schwartzer slowed, then stopped to examine himself. He saw it. Percy didn't. But Schwartzed *did*.

Play seesawed back and forth, both teams struggling as the rain battered us, the surface became slipperier, and players grew tired. Guys would kick the ball long to try and gain distance. Out of one pack in the centre, Bell got a handball out to Close, who booted the footy over mine and Rankin's heads. I charged back as Verne bolted at me, the ball landing between us. We collided with a sickening crunch as I scooped up the ball and spun away, keeping my feet, as Verne face-planted the ground. I handballed to Sean running past. He kicked long to Sam on the wing.

Verne thrust his hands into the grass and slowly began to push himself up. He was red all over – his chest, his arms, and his face. He jumped up and brushed himself, as if he could wipe himself clean, but all he succeeded in doing was smearing it all over himself.

'Claude!' he said. 'Claude!'

Rankin held out his hands, as if he didn't know what to say.

The only grace was because the rain was so heavy, it washed the blood away from everything but our clothes. You couldn't notice it much in the Little Reach kit, since their guernsey and shorts were crimson. But ours was mostly white, so it was damning.

I had to give it to them, though, because – after the initial shock – they stuck with the game. Maybe something like this had already happened to them – in fact, I was sure of it. And this is the way they tried to deal with it – by braving through, and committing to the contest, as if that would help them win out. Victory was paramount. This was a grand final. And Little Reach was about success. Footy and winning had become so ingrained in their character it not only overrode everything else, but it became their answer to everything.

The game devolved into a scramble. Both teams flooded into the other's forward lines to try to make it impossible to score. It worked for the most part, with Little Reach kicking 1.3 to our 1.6, taking the score to Little Reach 8.8.(56) to our 5.15.(45). We were the better team, but we couldn't put our chances away.

In the last minute, Ronnie kicked the ball long to the top of the goal square. Percy leaped for the mark. A blood-soaked Schwartzer came over the top and thumped the ball clear out of bounds. The boundary umpire retrieved it and I followed Rankin down as every player from both teams camped out in the forward-arc.

Harry got his hand to the throw-in and tapped it over his head, hoping for the best more than anything else. Then Adam was there. He sliced through the congestion like he was ice-skating and took the ball in one hand. Bell hurled his arms around Adam's waist, but Adam pirouetted and broke clear. Schwartzer dove at him, but Adam sidestepped like a matador evading a charging bull. Verne and Rankin closed on him. Adam stepped into their attempted assault, committing them, then withdrew. Verne and Rankin crashed into one another. Adam spun around their fallen bodies and banana kicked the ball through for a goal just before the siren went, bringing the third quarter score to Little Reach 8.8.(56) to our 6.15.(51). Our fans cheered, and I was shocked to see that even some of the Little Reach faithful clapping, awe on their faces.

Adam loped amongst the dejected Little Reach players and pointed out each of his attempted assailants – Bell, Schwartzer, Verne, and Rankin – thrusting his hand out like he was shooting a gun. But now, it was that bloodied, wounded Adam who did the pointing, and each one of his targets saw him as he appeared to me. They gaped, their faces white. Bell spun away, doubled over, and vomit streamed from his mouth.

Our guys jumped on Adam in celebration, swamping him, but when they parted it was Adam again.

'Come on!' Percy said. 'Come on!'

The players huddled around Percy, and I tried to get alongside Adam, but he was jammed-up front near Sean and Nigel, so it was impossible to talk to him. I lowered my head and took a deep breath as Percy's voice lifted over us.

'There's not a lot more to say to you,' he said. 'We know what it's taken to get this far. Now it comes down to the next thirty minutes. This could be the last quarter of football of our lives. Not one of us knows what awaits us after today. We can either go down as another group of valiant but unfortunate Ulah Curlews battlers, or we have a chance to make a name for ourselves here, now! Which do you want it to be?'

The players hollered and we broke into our positions.

I met Rankin at the centre half-forward position, and offered him a handshake again, like a boxer offering to knock gloves before the championship round. But there was no recognition in his face – not for the gesture, not for me, or even the game.

'He shouldn't be here,' Rankin said.

The siren rang for the fourth quarter. The crowd roared as Ozzie threw the ball up. Close roved Kotz's tap and snapped the ball in my direction. I marked it out in front and turned to check Rankin's position. He was standing where I'd left him, looking around in wonder. The crowd hooted.

'*Time to give it up, Rankin!*' somebody shouted – somebody from behind the goals the Little Reach faithful occupied.

I ran off, leaving Rankin in my wake, charged down the centre, and kicked the ball to Adam, who'd run to our centre half-forward position. He marked, and off one step snapped the ball for a goal. It was so matter-of-fact, nobody reacted immediately.

'You are kidding me,' Rankin said as I jogged back into position.

At first, I thought it was thunder that exploded, but it was our fans celebrating us hitting the lead. Even more of the Little Reach fans applauded. Adam's brilliance had won them over. Teammates from everywhere jumped on Adam. But, like Rankin, I stood there in disbelief. *Nobody* snapped a waterlogged ball fifty metres – even more, since the ball had gone another ten metres after it had crossed the goal – in rain like this. It should've been impossible.

On the next ball up, Harry tapped the footy to Adam as Adam ran past. Close's fingertips brushed the hem of Adam's jumper as Adam's long strides carried him away. Bell dived at Adam, and Adam sidestepped him and ran past centre half-forward. Schwartzer awaited, arms wide. Adam feigned a handball; Schwartzer committed to snatching the footy and Adam spun around him. Balancing, he drilled the ball for another goal. Again, both sides of the crowd erupted; again, our teammates swarmed Adam; and, again, neither Rankin nor I could believe it.

'What the hell …?' Rankin said.

On and on it went, each of Adam's feats more outrageous than the one that preceded it. Whenever he won the ball from the centre, he'd race clear and evade every Little Reach attempt to tackle him. A few times, he kicked long goals; other times he passed to teammates, but would then be a blur past them and demand the ball back. The few times Little Reach did manage a spoil and tried counter-attacking out of defence, Adam was everywhere. He'd tackle Scorpions, smother kicks and handballs, or he'd chase and pressure and regain possession.

Rankin had been anxious the whole game, but now his face grew purple, and that vein in his temple throbbed. 'This is beyond a joke,' he said, following another Adam goal, the lead stretching to thirty-two points. The fans' cheering elongated into a rendition of the Ulah Curlews club song. Rankin scanned the crowd. 'Shut up!' he said, although I'm not sure whether he aimed that at our celebrating fans, or the mesmerised Little Reach faithful who continued to clap.

As the quarter wore on, the Scorpions resorted to character: tackles became vicious, our players slung well after they'd gotten rid of the ball; whenever we went for a mark, a Scorpion would hurtle into our backs, or a spoil would be high. They were booed and heckled by both sets of fans.

With minutes remaining, Adam snapped another goal to put us in front by forty-four points. Teammates jumped on him as Scorpions dropped their heads and the crowd broke into yet another rendition of the 'Ulah Curlews!' chant.

Players moved back into position and Ozzie threw the ball up. By now, Harry and Kotz were beyond exhaustion and the ball dribbled off their hands. Sam plucked it out of the air but was gang-tackled. Ozzie blew his whistle and called for the ball.

Again and again this happened. Players had nothing left. And, with only a minute or two remaining and the margin what it was, there wasn't the incentive to find anything more.

Each time the ball was thrown up, Rankin drifted closer to the action. Unlike his players, he still swaggered, his chin lifted, shoulders pronounced. But I had it wrong. It wasn't anger that fuelled him. It was pride. Even in defeat, he wasn't going to let himself be seen as beaten.

Ozzie threw the ball up yet again. Kotz and Harry jostled for position, Kotz – the stronger – getting an arm free to palm the ball to Bell. I tackled Bell to the ground and his handball went awry to Sam. Close crunched Sam. The ball popped loose to Dean. I struggled to my knees. Jason Mason and Schwartzer confronted Dean. Dean lobbed the ball to Adam. Rankin charged in, elbows pumping like pistons.

I shot up, arms spread wide, preparing to shepherd Adam. Rankin's body crunched mine. My breath burst from my lungs, and his flailing elbow struck my temple. The inside of my head exploded. Rankin bounced off me, spinning as he fell to his hands and knees; the force of the impact drove me into the ground, my head whiplashing.

Everything went black.

Echoes from the Past

H ard, driving rain – the sort that could wash the world away –
fell across the winding gravel road Amanda and I had taken
last night. Dusk swathed shivering gums in purple, like the sky
had been bruised and was cowering into the night.

A car approached. No, something bigger – a bright blue van
with a bull-bar – rounded the bend. Headlights blinded me. The
engine rumbled and the tyres spat up gravel and muck as the van
sped towards me. I would've shrunk away, or braced myself, if I
could, but felt disembodied. The van hit me. I went through it,
and found myself in the back compartment.

Schwartzer, Bell, and Verne were there; Rankin was in the
passenger seat. They were all a lot younger – ten years younger.
In the driver's seat, pimply faced and no older than eighteen, was
Kevin Dunbar. He was a kid compared to the rest, his soft features
still untouched by that Little Reach ruthlessness. The lot of them
were drinking beers, their movements abrupt. Their speech was
high-pitched and indecipherable.

Still, I knew post-match camaraderie when I saw it. I also knew
a few too many drinks when I saw that, too. The Scorpions had
won. They'd beaten Ulah. It was the game I'd seen in *The Chronicle*
– the one that showed the picture of Rankin marking in front of
Dad. I didn't know how I knew that – how I knew any of this. I

just did. And here were five guys – probably not best friends or anything like that off-field – bound by the revelry of victory.

Rankin finished his beer, called for another. Schwartzer reached into an esky by his feet and hoisted out a six-pack. Moisture dripped from the cans as he pulled them clear from the ringlets. He tossed one to Bell, one to Verne, and two towards Rankin.

As the cans spiralled through the air, they slowed, drops breaking free and glimmering before they burst into fleeting prisms of light. Rankin caught one can in his left hand, the other in his right. His mouth twisted open in the caricature of a grin. He thrust a beer at Dunbar. Dunbar turned to take it. I could see it in his eyes then: this was about being one of the boys for him – something I knew only too well.

Through the windshield, the wipers squelched, and the road wound through trembling gums. Dunbar grabbed the beer from Rankin. Coming around a sharp curve, the road straightened. A small, old car – the front tyre reared-up on a jack – sat parked on the shoulder of the road. Standing beside the car was a woman with an umbrella, a kid – four years old, I *knew* he was four years old – cradled into her thigh. Kneeled at their feet, changing the tyre, was Adam, dressed in the same shorts and t-shirt he wore whenever he showed up at training.

Dunbar took his free hand off the wheel to snap the can open.

I tried to yell, to tell him to look out.

Rankin pulled the metal ring from his can.

Bell spotted the car. He rose to warn them, but his seatbelt reined him in.

Dunbar lifted his gaze back to the road, minute creases in his face deepening.

The scene accelerated.

Dunbar hit the brakes. The van pivoted on its front left wheel. The right wheels elevated, skidded, and the van threatened to flip. The back compartment thudded; the van jolted, shook. Metal screeched and whined. Everybody was hurtled into their seatbelts, but whipped back into place. When the van stilled, it sat at an angle, the left wheel propped up. Rain drilled the roof.

Schwartzer, Bell, and Verne groaned, rubbed their heads and blinked, trying to work out what had happened. Rankin looked around frantically. Dunbar stared straight ahead. We could see the misshapen corner of the car they'd hit from this vantage point, but nothing else.

'Everybody okay?' Rankin asked.

Time sped up, slowed down, and occasionally paused in normalcy, like it was trying to digest what had happened, but was struggling to express it.

Rankin was the first to move. He wrenched open the passsenger door and hopped out. Verne was next, sliding open the side door. Schwartzer followed him, and then Bell, although he went tentatively.

The woman was sandwiched horizontally between the van's bull-bar and the battered car, suspended in mid-air. The little boy was pinned under the van's front left wheel. The eyes of both were pulled so far open it was like they had no eyelids; their mouths frothed with blood.

'No …' The voice was weak, but unmistakeable.

Verne, Bell, and Schwartzer walked around the back of the van, to Rankin's side. Rankin towered above Adam, who lay on his back, face bruised, his chest crushed, blood pooling into the muck of the earth beneath him. He implored Rankin with his right hand.

'What're we gonna do?' Verne said.

'We've gotta call an ambulance!' Bell said.

'You're kidding,' Schwartzer said. 'They'll call the cops. We've all been drinking!'

'We can't let him die, Danny!' Bell said.

'*Danny* …' Adam said.

Then silence, except from the rain. Nobody had the courage to look at Adam. They gaped at one another, as if they hoped somebody could flick a switch and undo what had happened. Then Rankin strode to the rear of the van, opened the back doors, reached in, and came back with a pick – the blade bright, the handle burnished. It was the same pick he'd swung at me, but shiny and brand new.

'What are you going—?' Verne said.

Rankin swung the pick. Adam lifted his hand in front of his face. I couldn't look – without thinking, without knowing how it worked being in this disembodied form, I spun away. I heard a *thud*, and then the scrape of something sharp that cut through the driving rain and reverberated off the gums. And then a sigh. I knew it was Adam – an exhalation of one final breath. Then, rain, hammering leaves, hammering the trees, hammering Rankin and the others, and pinging off the roof of the van. If I was in bed, sleeping in with Amanda, it would be restful to listen to, all warm and snug. And it seemed to be the only sound now, the only expression of this reality, like this moment had become stuck in time.

Then I heard Rankin move and I dared a look to see he'd pried his pick free. I caught a glimpse of Adam, still, bleeding from the top of his head and hand. There's a cliché that dead people could be mistaken for people who are asleep. Well, maybe if the person's led a good long life and drifted off amongst loved ones. But all I could see now was a rupture in my world, and from the wound poured an irresistible endless grief that could never be healed.

Bell keeled over and vomited into the brush. That's how everything resumed – with this moron vomiting. Then cries from all around us, so everybody jumped and looked around frantically. But it was the curlews. I don't know where they were, but their wails were mournful.

'What the hell are you doing?' Verne said.

'What do you think?' Rankin said. 'That there's leniency for killing two instead of three?'

'They were an accident!' Verne said, pointing at the woman and child.

'Do you think that's going to matter?' Rankin said. 'We've been drinking! We've all been drinking! Anyway, all I did was put him out of his misery. I did him a favour.' He surveyed the van's damage; the bull-bar had spared it major structural damage, but the corner of the front left panel was dented. 'If anybody asks, we hit an animal. Kangaroo, maybe. I was driving.'

'You?' Bell said.

'It's my van. I should've been driving anyway.'

Rankin wasn't being magnanimous. He knew he had enough celebrity to protect him from anyone probing deeper. Cops might investigate one of the others, especially if they suspected alcohol was involved – and they would, given this had happened after a footy match.

'How can you be so cold?' Verne said.

'Do you want to lose everything?' Rankin said. 'Your business? Your life? The way people look at you? All of it! What do you think will happen? You want to go to jail? Over this?' He thrust a hand down at Adam. '*This.*'

'He's right,' Schwartzer said. 'There's no other choice.'

Verne lowered his head.

Bell vomited again.

Rankin snorted. 'Who'll miss him anyway? Any of them? Plenty more of them around.' He turned back to his van. 'Kevin! Kevin!'

Dunbar was still in the van, head buried in his arms, folded on the steering wheel.

'Kevin!'

Dunbar lifted his face. His eyes were red, rimmed with tears.

'We got some tarp in the back of the van? Get it out here!'

Dunbar didn't move.

'Now!'

I looked at Adam, lying in a pool of blood that seeped into the muck of the road. My chest tightened until it became a searing pain, and blackness closed in on me again. I blinked. Lightning lit up the darkness. Adam's face hovered over me. He grinned. The drumbeat of the rain was steady, the ground soft and yielding under me. I understood the blood now that I'd seen earlier – the earth itself mourning what had happened, weeping for the injustice of what had happened. Booted feet surrounded me – my teammates. Percy and Dad crouched on either side of me, and Mum and Amanda stood behind Dad.

'Thanks for taking the hit,' Adam said, 'but I was okay.'

What could I say to that?

'I killed him!'

This from a ring of Scorpions to my left. Through gaps between legs, I could make out Rankin's form lying on the ground, although I couldn't see his face. Just his left arm, flailing.

'I killed him!' Rankin said. 'I killed him!'

Percy called through the rings of players, 'He's okay, Claude!' He thought Rankin was talking about me!

'I killed him!' Rankin said.

Dad leaned in close to me. 'You okay?'

'Yeah.'

'You hit the ground hard,' Percy said.

'I black out?' I said.

'For a little, yeah.'

Adam stepped back while Percy and Dad grabbed me under the armpits, lifted me to my feet, and hooped my arms around their necks. The crowd applauded. I lifted my right hand to show them I was okay, and that I appreciated their concern. From somewhere, an ambulance wailed.

'You called an ambulance?' I said.

'Not for you,' Amanda said.

The ring of Scorpions parted to reveal Rankin gasping, his face blue, that vein in his temple thick as a cord. His left arm bucked like a cut electrical line, while his right hand clutched his chest. Not that I'd seen any heart attacks in my life, but I was sure that's what I was looking at.

'I killed him,' he said, his voice a breathless whisper. 'I killed him.'

Amanda and I exchanged a look.

'We should get you checked,' Mum said.

They helped me to the boundary, while the arriving ambulance drove onto the ground to fetch Rankin. Once they'd taken him away, the game continued for all of about fifteen seconds. That was all the time left. The siren sounded, the crowd roared, and our players hugged and congratulated one another.

Ozzie coordinated the presentations, a trophy thrust upon Percy, who made a speech about teamwork and unity. They presented a medal for best on ground – I waited for Adam's name to be called, but it was given to me. Fans crowded us, patted us on the back, shook our hands, and jumped around with their arms held up. A bright red woollen pullover on the boundary caught my eye – the scout, Josh Carson! He gave me a thumbs-up.

Adam didn't join the jubilation. Nobody else saw him. Everybody ran past him, ran around him to congratulate one another. Sean hung off me and kissed my cheek. It was a mass of people – players and fans – bouncing around and chanting, 'Ulah Curlews! Ulah Curlews!' Mum and Dad found their way through and hugged me, while Amanda hugged Percy.

I barely moved. Through the blur of people, I stared at Adam. He smiled. Although there was no joy in the expression, his face was peaceful, and those shadows had faded from his eyes. He lifted his right hand and I waved back to him, knowing I wouldn't see him again. None of us would.

Then, he left the way he came.

Full Time

A Way of Life

I was kept overnight at Mollongong Hospital for observation in the room opposite Claude Rankin's, where he was being minded by constabulary from both Ulah and Little Reach.

Before going in for a quintuple bypass, Rankin confessed to the murders of Adam Pride and his family, which prompted Schwartzer, Bell, and Verne to confess, although their accounts were haphazard and mired in half-truths. Police used all their confessions to decipher and piece together the whole story later.

The corpses of Adam and his family had been wrapped in a tarpaulin and buried on Adam's property. Verne, who'd been the local real estate agent at the time, facilitated the sale of Adam's property to Rankin. Rankin had Adam's farmhouse demolished and allowed the wild to grow over it. Schwartzer, as a mechanic, had taken Adam's car, stripped it clean and sold the parts. He'd also repaired Rankin's van, which Rankin had driven to this day – a symbol of their pact.

But little odds and ends piled up over the next year, which got people wondering – the Prides' uncollected mail, contracted utilities that went unpaid, and the enrolment of Adam's son, Tabulum, at the pre-kindergarten that went unfulfilled. Rankin and the generals created the fiction that Adam and his family had moved back to Western Australia. Verne fed the story to a girlfriend at *The Tribune*. She didn't query it. It was the typical filler that made our newspapers around here.

When Verne's real estate business wobbled, Don McKay offered to buy him out. Rankin – worried about McKay having the record of the sale of Adam's farm – ordered Verne to erase any paper trail of Adam owning a property out here. It was lies, lies, and more lies. Although none of them admitted it, police speculated that some – or all – of the group might've set the fire that had destroyed the warehouse newspaper morgue, unaware that everything had been archived electronically.

Dunbar couldn't handle keeping the secret and often confronted Rankin about confessing. Rankin always stalled him, suggesting they should see how things went. When it became clear they'd gotten away with it, Dunbar began drinking. Sometimes, he rambled about murdering somebody, and rumours sprang up. Rankin spoke to him privately. There were other rumours – just rumours, mind you – that Rankin manipulated Dunbar into killing himself.

A lot of people said guilt caused Rankin's heart attack. Others said it was Ulah's defeat of Little Reach in the grand final. Perhaps it was a combination of things. Maybe the biggest contributor was the stress of the phenomena.

Imagine it: Rankin was sure he'd killed this guy, and yet there he was, running around for the Curlews. That night we saw Rankin in the clearing, that night he almost took my head off with the pick, apparently he and his generals were trying to find the corpses of Adam and his family, to make sure that he hadn't somehow escaped.

Rankin recovered from heart surgery, and he and his generals were charged with one count of murder, two counts of manslaughter, fraud, three counts of interfering with a corpse – the list went on and on. It was the biggest news in the history of our area – news that went national.

Amanda kept investigating and found Adam Pride had been an exceptional junior footballer in Western Australia, but he'd only ever been interested in playing socially. He met his sweetheart, Jilli, when they were fifteen, and they both worked full-time for the next ten years, saving money. He was twenty-six, married, and had a three-year-old son, Tabulum, when he and Jilli uprooted their lives and moved to Ulah, where they bought a small farm. On a hunch, Amanda rifled through the Curlews archives, sorting through registrations, memos, and other notes, that had been packed chaotically in the boxes in Percy's office. She found a note from Adam which said, simply, *Interested in playing*, and left his first name, address and phone number. It was dated the day he was killed. He must've been at the game, then gotten the flat tyre on the way home. Matt would've been coach then – maybe he followed up and, getting no response, had left it. But the truth is Adam would've been a Curlew. Who knows if he was as good as what we saw, or whether some ethereal force had fuelled him – a force that touched us all.

Police excavated the property and found the bodies of the Prides about a month later – right under the house Rankin was building out there. As far as Amanda and I could figure, that's when it all began – when Rankin began redeveloping Adam's land.

The Curlews' number 8 jumper, two pairs of shorts (one white, one black), socks, and Percy's spare football boots were also found lying scattered, as if somebody had discarded them, the way you might undress before going to bed. Considered something of a novelty, they were retired and hung up in the clubrooms.

It was the only real memory of Adam, but even that was this strange, shapeless thing. Once the grand final ended, people started to forget him. Well, not entirely, but they could never recollect him accurately. He'd become smoke. You knew he was there, but try to grab him and your hands went right through him. When I think about it, that was even beginning to happen in the lead-up to the grand final – the way people kept messing up his name, and how nobody questioned his absence at the grand final dinner.

People talked about his feats, mentioned the huge goal he kicked against Little Reach and stuff like that, but you could never nail them down on the specifics. If you asked what his name was, people would respond with a blank look, think about it for a while and then offer *Ash, Alan, Anthony, Andrew, Aaron*, and so on. Sometimes they'd get it right, although that was more by accident, and even then they were never really sure.

Amanda and I remembered him. Remembered everything. I think it's because we got inside it. I don't think we were meant to be exempt; it's just the way it happened – maybe because Amanda nosed around.

We attended the funeral for the Prides. Nobody understood why. Nobody connected that the slain man and the freak who'd played for us were one and the same. By now, Adam might never have existed. It saddened me that something so tragic could be forgotten. For nights I was sleepless. Amanda was the same. Sometimes, she cried – and I'd never seen her cry; she was always so strong and resilient.

She talked to Scott Harrow at *The Tribune*, and he put her in touch with an Aboriginal Elder. Amanda explained what had happened to the Prides, and we took the Elder out to where the bodies had been found. The Elder performed a smoking ceremony: he took a coolamon – a curved wooden bowl – and filled it with brown and green gum leaves. He set the leaves alight, so they burned slowly, letting the smoke drift across the site as he spoke partly in language. He explained that this would allow the spirits to leave the earth, and it was our way of making peace with what had happened and showing remorse. It didn't seem enough that Amanda and I should carry this alone. I guess that's the way some things are unless you experience them, and see them for yourself. I wished it didn't have to be that way.

Afterwards, we took a drive out to find the spot where Dunbar had hit the Prides with Rankin's van. While the gums and foliage had changed, that curve in the road was unmistakeable. We parked and, as the curlews wailed, went through the same ceremony. When it was done, I felt some small sense of peacefulness – only a sliver, but maybe that was enough to get started. The curlews fell quiet.

About two months after the grand final, things changed in ways that told me this chapter in my life had closed, and there was no going back now. Mum and Dad put the farm up for sale. Ronnie retired as the only Ulah player to play in two Curlew premierships. Wanting to go out on top, Percy retired as a coach and player. Matt took over, and appointed Harry his captain; Sean, Dean, Sam, and Nigel his vice-captains; and set up a regimented training program. Amanda and I packed our things, said our goodbyes, and drove out of Ulah to pursue our own dreams – dreams that existed thanks to Adam.

I don't know if we'll make it. I'd like to think we've got the talent, and that talent has already gotten us so far – with Amanda's city editor for her, the scout for me. There's no bridge that exists between dreams and reality, not unless you make it yourself, and that's something you don't know you can build until you give it a try.

But I'm confident. Why not? There's nothing to lose. And I have the best grounding, and it's one that has nothing to do with Adam; one that has been there since the day I was born, and has ridden every breath of my existence.

Football – it's a way of life.

And death, sometimes.

But I wouldn't have it any other way.

Acknowledgements

This book started life under the title *Pride*.

The original draft was a 44,000-word novella I serialised for a sporting website I ran back in 2002. As a story, it flowed as it emerged onto the page, and I thought it worked out pretty well. I shudder now to contemplate looking at that draft, as the book has gone through numerous redrafts, has grown, shrunk, evolved, devolved, re-evolved, and now matured into what it is. In accomplishing that, there's a number of people to thank.

Primarily, thanks to Blaise van Hecke, who read a very early draft of this book back in 2007, and has always liked and championed it, and suggested publishing it. She's the one person who's had an unfailing belief in it, which is nice to have when you're otherwise collecting rejections. Thanks, Blaise, for your support and encouragement. For any other writers out there: never, ever take for granted somebody who believes in your work. Blaise, you're the best!

Thanks to Inga Simpson and Nike Bourke, who selected it for the Olvar Wood Fellowship in 2009 – my first real prose accomplishment as a writer. I should also thank the other participants in that Fellowship – Felicity Castagna, Paul Garretty, and Kylie Mulcahy – for their workshop feedback during the Fellowship. And, again, to Inga (author of the wonderful *Mr*

Wigg), for her structural feedback, who mentored me through a redraft back then, and more recently (2015) edited an updated draft – she was another believer in the book.

To all the publishers who rejected it (and some gave me encouraging responses), thank you. With each rejection, I looked at the book again and again, would revise and rewrite and develop this world and the story it was telling further. If it had been accepted previously, it would have been much lesser than it is today. It's astonishing how you can find opportunity where you probably otherwise wouldn't expect it.

Similarly, a big thank-you to my old laptop, which served me faithfully for a number of years, and then died as I was halfway through my latest (big) revision. The hard drive was irrecoverable, despite consulting tech heads and data specialists – a frustrating couple of weeks.

Although I usually backed up obsessively, on this occasion my most recent back-up only had one quarter of my revision. I vacillated between giving up, or starting from scratch – since so much time had elapsed, I couldn't pick up from where I'd left off on the back-up. Because I did start from scratch, I think I pushed myself harder to get the most out of it, so this book became something it never would've previously.

Thanks to my writing group – Beau Hillier, Gina Boothroyd, Tess Evans, Jasmine Powell, and (again) Blaise van Hecke – for comments on various chapters; and thanks also to various people who read *Pride* over the years previously and gave me feedback, such as Blaise (she must've read eight or nine incarnations), Beau (again, who provided an assessment for one of the publishers who rejected an early version), Les Zig (he comes up with a thing or two structurally), Tess (again), Kim Lock (who always gives great feedback), and Val Vogel. Also, thank you to JM Peace, for helping me with the charges Rankin and the others would face.

My good friend, Laurie Steed, author of the wonderful *You Belong Here*, is always a towering figure of support, and gave me encouraging feedback that helped me to feel confident about the book.

You develop your own writing community – friends who donate their time to read your stuff not for recreation (although hopefully they do get that) but to lend their expertise and provide feedback. Then you also meet new people who are willing to do the same, and ask nothing for their time. They do it out of generosity and good-heartedness.

Such a person is author Kathrine 'Kat' Clarke who read *Pride* and guided me in the etiquette and protocols of dealing with cultural sensitivities, offered me invaluable feedback on rounding out the Indigenous characters, and also fielded my countless questions with good grace. A huge thank-you to Kat! I cannot thank her enough or speak more highly of her. Any errors in this regard are mine.

To Laura McCluskey, my young and especially talented editor, and a great writer in her own right. She challenged me and got me thinking about the book in different ways, and picked up things that nobody else had.

Thanks to everybody at Busybird Publishing – Kev Howlett, for his brilliant cover, which captured the essence of the book; to Jessica Wartski, Ashleigh Andrews, Jessica Waters, Clare Millar, Anna Bilbrough, Jennifer Walker, and Tom O'Connell for their proofing (I hope you enjoyed the read), and Busybird Publishing as a whole, for taking the chance.

I always looked at *Pride* as being like *To Kill a Mockingbird*: while it told the story through the eyes of a young protagonist (in this case 18-year-old Luke, in *Mockingbird*'s case, six-year-old Scout), it dealt with serious themes and issues. In that way, I think it tweened between Young Adult and Adult.

One concern with *Pride* being Young Adult, though, is Luke and Amanda consummating their relationship. Some considered that scene too adult for a young adult market (although, hopefully, the scene dealt with sex respectfully and responsibly).

As a result, we decided to release a definitively Young Adult version, which is what you're holding in your hands. *Song of the Curlew* has trimmed away and rewritten those scenes that might've been considered inappropriate for Young Adult.

A big thanks to Sam Stevens, Anais Thornbury, Alyse Clarke for their proofing; to Blaise van Hecke for the terrific new cover; to Blaise and Sam for the book club questions; and, of course (and again) a huge thanks to Busybird Publishing!

Indigenous Literacy Foundation

The Indigenous Literacy Foundation (ILF) is a national charity of the Australian Book Industry. Our aim is to reduce the disadvantage experienced by children in very remote Indigenous communities across Australia. Our focus is to improve literacy rates and instil a lifelong love of reading. Our programs focus on creating a special relationship with reading from an early age with free books, some in First language, and through publishing stories from communities.

For more information visit **www.ilf.org.au**

Find **ILF** on social media:
    Facebook: **@The Indigenous Literacy Foundation**
    Twitter: **@IndigenousLF**

About the Author

Lazaros Zigomanis has been interested in telling stories all his life.

It began as a teenager, when he handwrote his first book (the beginning of a fantasy epic) through two A5 exercise books. He gradually progressed onto a typewriter, and then a computer.

In the ensuing years, he's written short stories, books, articles, screenplays, and one poem. He's run his own sporting website, and written for other sports websites about his passion for Australian Rules Football.

He's had short stories and articles published in various print and digital journals, screenplays optioned, and placed in awards for his writing.

The Shadow in the Wind

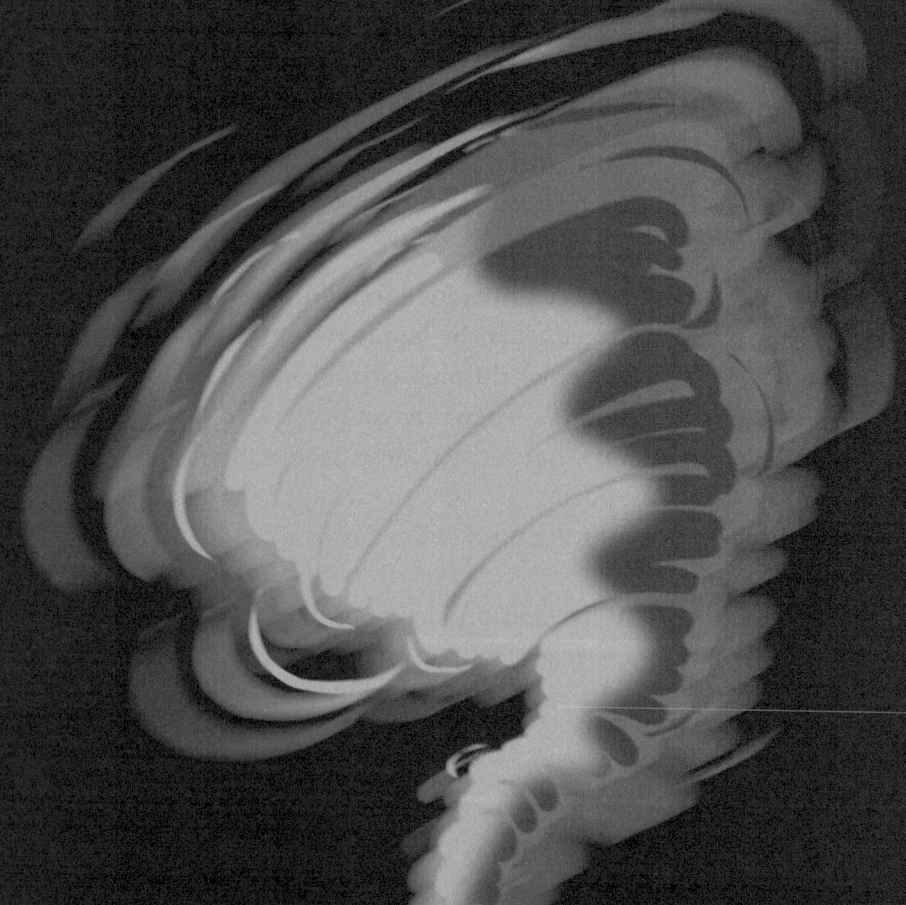

Lazaros
Zigomanis

The Shadow in the Wind

There's always hope.

At seven, almost eight, Keene can't understand what's wrong with Mum. She lies in bed in the spare room, wasting away, even though she's hooked up to a bag that is meant to make her feel better. Dad describes Mum's illness like 'a darkness inside her'. But Keene's sure something else is responsible.

He's sure it's the shadow that's killing her.

So, one stormy day, Keene decides to go on an adventure into the bush with just his Border Collie, Bunch, in tow – an adventure he's sure will save Mum.

But even Keene is not prepared for the dangers he faces.

The Shadow in the Wind is a story of adventure and magical realism as Keene deals with and learns to reconcile events he's too young to fully understand.

> 'Inspired, unexpected and moving, *The Shadow in the Wind* is a delight.'
> Ryan O'Neill
> *Their Brilliant Careers*
> Winner of the 2017 Australian Prime Minister's
> Literary Award for Fiction

Questions for Discussion

1. A mysterious figure turns up in town and things start to change for the Curlews. Can you identify a turning point, or was it a culmination of events?
2. Luke Miggs likes football and hanging out with his teammates after training sessions for a beer at the pub. What happens to modify his thoughts about drinking and step up his training?
3. Amanda Hunt has ambitions. What are they and how do they carry the story forward?
4. As the story progresses, secrets start to emerge. Have you had a secret that impacted your life? How do you feel about what happened to Adam Pride and his family?
5. How do you think the fact that Adam and his family were Indigenous affected the decisions that Rankin and his 'generals' made?
6. The town of Ulah has a strong community. Is community important to the health and wellbeing of people in general?
7. Why do you think Little Reach held very different views to the community in Ulah? Can you think of a community or town that has different values from where you live?
8. Australia is often accused of being casually racist. What does that mean and does that have any bearing on this story?
9. Many people might see football as 'just a game' and not a worthwhile pursuit as a player or audience. How do you feel about it? Does it contribute to wellbeing or is it just mindless entertainment?
10. Australian sport has a big drinking culture. How do you feel about alcohol? How is it different to other forms of drugs? Is the culture too blasé about drinking and has it become socially unacceptable not to drink?

11. How do young people find ways to not get swept up by their peers? How does Luke hold strong to his convictions?"
12. How did each of Rankin's group react to the choices that they made? Were they realistic? Is it fair to say that conscience plays a big part in how we might deal with something after the fact?
13. Friendships often end when people leave school. Why does this happen? Is it true for Luke?
14. You could say this story plays out karma for Rankin and his men. What do you think about karma? Is it real or just a way for people to explain life?
15. You don't need to like or understand football to be swept along by this story. How does the backdrop of football shape the narrative?
16. The setting of an Australian country town is quintessentially Australian. Do you think that this story would resonate with other cultures? Do the themes and characters feel like they could be related to by Americans or other countries? If yes, would you say that the story deals with important human issues?
17. Luke has a crush on Amanda. Do you think that their relationship is natural and relatable? How does it impact the choices that both of them make about their future?
18. Luke grows from having very little idea about his goals to creating real ambitions. If you were his age, can you imagine how these changes might impact his life and future?
19. Luke and his family have strong bonds. Do you think this is important to him? How does family impact the way we see the world?
20. Did Luke's commitment to footy have an effect on his teammates and community? If so, what kind of effect?
21. Who was the most supportive of Luke's ambition? What plans did he put in place to pursue his dreams?
22. How did Luke's relationship with his dad develop?
23. Who was your favourite character and why? If this story was made into a movie, who would you cast as the main characters?
24. What did you think of the ending? Was it satisfying, or how did you expect it to end?
25. What do you think happened to Luke and Amanda after they left Ulah?

Love reading?

Do you love being taken away into the world of the story? Are you the sort of reader who looks up from their book only to find that hours have flown by? Or do you plan to read a little bit before bed, always saying to yourself, *Just one more chapter*, and next thing you know it's the early morning hours?

ECG Press is a boutique micropublisher whose interest is compelling storytelling.

We want to bring you stories you'll lose yourself in.

Happy reading!

www.ingramcontent.com/pod-product-compliance
Lightning Source LLC
Chambersburg PA
CBHW030605120726
47904CB00006B/1777